Rescued By the Scot

Rescued By the Scot

Laura A. Barnes

Laura A. Barnes

2018

First Printing: 2018

ISBN: 9781072932192

Laura A. Barnes

www.lauraabarnes.com

Cover Art by Cheeky Covers

Editor: Polgarus Studios

To: William-I love you! You are my Zane Maxwell.

Chapter One

ZANE MAXWELL DIDN'T GRASP how long he had been hanging from these chains. It felt like an eternity, but he perceived it might have only been a few days. A few hazy days at that. How he got himself in this predicament was unknown to him. He only knew he betrayed his best friends to end up here on this godforsaken hovel of a ship, chained to the walls. Zane's wrists were raw from chafing against the metal chains. His wounds were cut open, and blood soaked along his arms. His body was beaten and bruised from every angle. But it was not only his blood covering his body, his enemy's blood covered him too. The only regret consuming his thoughts was that it wasn't the blood of death. He learned Shears still lived, long enough to keep him prisoner on this poor excuse of a ship.

Zane lifted his head to look around the hold. The pit of the ship was as disgusting as the rest of everything else Shears owned. Rats were crawling around, biting at his ankles, wanting something to fill their bellies. He kicked out at them. He watched as they scurried to the pile of rubbish in the corner. The walls were lined with mildew from where the water seeped in through the bow of the ship. To think that his dear friend, Ivy survived being held captive on this ship. He would never understand how she endured such suffering. While they threw her overboard and left her for dead, it was the best thing that happened to her. When he had found out what Shears had done to her, he remembered attacking him, only for Shears to laugh at him.

During this whole time, everybody had been pawns in Shears's game of hell.

Leaning his head against the wall, he thought of how he could escape. Maxwell laughed to himself as he realized he had gotten himself in way over his head. All for what? Praise? Recognition from the Crown for a job well done? Since he'd attacked Shears, intending to kill him, he gathered he couldn't talk his way out of it this time. Every other time he had fooled Shears into believing he was a double agent. At least he killed Gold Tooth, Shears's largest man. With him gone, he might be able to fight his way off this ship.

He heard footsteps coming down to the ship's hold. He hung his head, pretending to be unconscious. He listened to what sounded like four sets of feet. One had a lighter tread than the others, but he couldn't afford to peek without blowing his cover. He had to wait for them to show themselves.

"Madam, you cannot come below deck," a deckhand explained as he chased her down the stairs.

"Why not? What are ye hiding? Since ye say ye do not have my shipment, ye must carry cargo ah might be interested in buying."

"Nothing is for sale here. Now you must leave. Captain Shears will contact you in a few days."

"I think not. I have already been waiting for two full days already. Ah noticed yer ship docked here fur for longer."

"The captain will be in touch soon."

"What of my shipment? What is yer excuse this time? I'm thinking yer captain has proven false on his claims to provide me with the firearms fur our cause."

"We have them, ma'am."

"Tsk, Tsk, Tsk, how ah hate when I am addressed as ma'am. It makes me sound so old. Am I old, Gregor?"

"No, Mac, yer definitely nae old."

She laughed, a soft husky laugh at that. Something in her voice touched Zane from across the hold. He wanted to catch a glimpse of her. Her wit and sarcasm were lost on Shears's man, but not on him.

"Ower 'ere, Mac, looks lik' thay git themselves a prisoner." Another voice beckoned for her to come over.

He heard her walk across the planks toward him. Maxwell could sense her eyes piercing his soul as she looked him over from his hanging head to his rat-bitten ankles. He could imagine her touch, as if she were caressing every part of his body. He didn't need to raise his head to sense her perusal. Who was this mystery woman? When she touched him, it took everything he had not to react to the power of her touch. The only thing she did was trace her fingers softly across the raw openings of his wrist. It should have stung, but it soothed. Maxwell let out a moan at her gentle touch, hoping she didn't hear. But she did. She put a finger under his chin and lifted, raising his head. He met her eyes as his head rose. The darkest green eyes he had ever seen gazed back at him. They appeared to read his mind, as well as his soul. They searched for the answers she already knew, but wanted him to admit to. He shuttered his gaze, rocked to his very soul by her awareness. He didn't have all the answers, and those he did weren't for her to discover.

But it wasn't only her touch and the gaze in her eyes that took his breath away. Her hair was a deep shade of red that hung to her waist. It was unusual for a woman to wear her hair loose and flowing, unless in the privacy of her own bedchamber. But she was no lady, and she was beyond bold. She was Scottish, and her speech held an accent that slipped out every now and again. There was no gown that hugged her body, but trousers molded to her legs, begging for somebody to strip them off her. They shaped and hugged her derriere. But it was the blouse she wore, white cotton that teased open to display her breasts, that drew his attention. They gleamed under the dim light the lanterns provided. Who was this sensuous creature?

"Who do we have here? I take it Shears doesn't care for this bloke much, does he?"

"No, I do not madam," said a voice from behind them. "It doesn't matter because he won't be around for much longer to even matter."

"Ah, Captain Shears, ye finally grace us with your presence. Ye know how I detest to be kept waiting."

Zane was so distracted by the goddess before him that he hadn't hear the clomp of Shears's footfall as he entered the hold. Maxwell watched as the overweight captain limped over to the intruder on his ship. The man's greasy hair hung in his face. He swept it from his face so he could view the lady. Shears held his hand to his side in pain as his eyes devoured her in lust. The captain's eyes took in how her clothes molded her body leaving nothing to the imagination. Maxwell could see that Shears was distracted by her charms, but not enough for rage filled Shears's eyes too. When Maxwell's eyes moved to her, he noticed she had been aware of Shears's presence the entire time. She raised her damn eyebrow at Maxwell and gave her head a small shake, showing her disappointment in him for not being aware of his surroundings. He cursed himself for his mistakes and blocked her beauty from his mind. He needed to focus if he was going to get off this ship alive.

Captain Shears bowed before her. "Please accept my apology."

"I won't. Not until ah see the delivery of my goods."

"We ran into a problem with your shipment. You see, the gentleman before you destroyed my merchandise."

The green eyes raked over him in disdain and flashed with anger. "How?"

"He," he said, pointing to Maxwell, "and his friends work for the Crown, and they destroyed every one of my loads the last few weeks. I stand before you to beg for a loan to replenish my supply. There is a seller arriving in one month's time. When he has arrived, I will provide you with the weapons you need to carry out your plan."

"I already gave ye a hefty sum and received nothing in return. Now ye have the audacity to ask for more money?" she questioned in anger.

As she spoke, her two henchmen flanked both sides of her. Their size only dwarfed her but didn't take away her sense of control. If anything, they seemed to enhance her power. As her anger grew, her brogue disappeared and her English became more direct. She was a professional, and Maxwell was intrigued by her.

"As I said, one month and I will double your arms. Then we can destroy England."

"Rumor has it that you are near destruction. That your whole operation is blown asunder." She laughed her sarcastic laugh that Zane was beginning to admire .

Shears scowled at her humor. He puffed up his chest and advanced toward her, trying to threaten her. But she only stood there, her eyebrow raised at his advancement. Her men tightened themselves around her for protection. She held up her hand, halting them, and they backed away from her—not too far, but far enough to show Shears he did not intimidate her.

"What are you implying? That I cannot destroy England?"

"The only one you are destroying is yourself. You ruined the destruction set in play to achieve your own agenda. For petty revenge against a French girl and her lover, from what I hear."

Shears whipped his arm toward Maxwell. "His friends, madam. They set out to destroy us from the beginning. Even Maxwell here betrayed us. He was on our side, but his love for Ivy Thornhill brought on the wrath of her husband and brother. He double-crossed us for a pair of thighs that will never part for him."

She turned toward him, scrutinizing him for a reaction. To see if he would defend his friends. He spoke not a word.

"He ruined you for a lady married to another bloke. That must be true love. Was it worth it?" she inquired.

No answer uttered from his lips. He wouldn't be a pawn in their game. While she was a means of escape for him, he wouldn't give her any ammunition in this fight.

"Mmm, a question for another time. I would love to hear the backstory on this, but I must leave. The docks are being patrolled, and I won't have the guards catch me."

As she continued observing him, Shears had come up behind her. He brushed the hair back from her face. She stood still regarding Zane. If Zane wasn't watching her, he would have missed the repulsion that flashed in her eyes. It was gone in an instant, replaced by humor. When she turned, her lips twisted into a smile at Shears, shaking her head.

"You know the rules, Shears. You can look, but not touch. Now remove your hands from me if you want me to continue to grace you with my presence in the future."

Shears dropped his hands as her men pressed closer. One of them sent a hard elbow into his side. Shears gasped for air as it connected with his wound. Blood seeped through his shirt, soaking it to a darker red.

Her eyes viewed the wound then landed back on him. She tilted her head in question. Zane tilted his head in return. *Of course. Who else?* She nodded back her approval. Why that gave him justification, he didn't know. Who cared if she approved that he tried to kill Shears. She was working alongside Shears for the same revenge against England that he was fighting against to stop.

"Well since we appear to be at an impasse, I will take your prisoner here as collateral."

"His Lordship is not for trade." Shears scowled.

"But he is, you see. You owe me money and weapons. You can provide neither. I will take him until you do. At that time, I will return him to you. If not, I will add him to my collection."

Shears observed the two men flanking her side. Zane finally regarded them too. They weren't any ordinary henchmen. The brutes almost looked too handsome. They were tall, with wide shoulders with muscles stretching the material of their clothes. Their long hair was pulled back and showed off chiseled cheekbones. As he looked closer at their hands, Zane saw the sheer brute of her guards. Their hands were those of warriors, rough and calloused and displayed signs of demanding work and defense. Defending her. He could tell their loyalty by how protective they were.

"Why don't we continue this discussion in my cabin? I am sure we can figure out an agreement."

Her husky laughter filled the air again. "Now Shears, you understand I do not mix business with pleasure."

"You mix it with your own guards."

When she walked around her henchmen, she ran her hand along their muscles, squeezing them. Her fingers trailed against their chests. They never moved or reacted to her touch, only standing as silent statues. Zane ached for her to caress him again. How could they not react? Her presence was making him hard as stone. From her long red hair to her husky laugh, he felt an attraction to her. He shook his head, struggling to get his thoughts under control. He shouldn't be desiring a lady who was in cahoots with Shears. They must have knocked him on the head harder than he thought.

"My relationship with my guards is different, Shears. You know the guidelines on doing business with me. Now, is your crew releasing my prisoner, or do my men need to take the chains off him?"

"As I told you before, he is not for sale. I have my own plans for him, and they involve a long, slow death with one act in particular I will enjoy watching my men perform on him."

"Now Shears, do not make me press my issue here. Either your men pull him down now, or I will give the signal for the rest of my men to join me."

"You have no other guards here, madam." Shears smirked.

"Do you think I came onto your ship without an army of protection? Never take me for a fool, Shears. That will be your first mistake. Your second mistake will be for me to repeat myself." She arched her stunning eyebrows at him.

Shears scowled as he motioned for his men to cut him loose. His men unlocked the chains around his wrists, and they dropped to the hardwood planks with a *thud*. The chains rattled when they settled on the floor of the ship. They weren't finished with him though, as each of Shears's men made sure they landed a blow to his sides as he became free.

Zane grunted as he fell to the floor. His legs gave out from underneath him, weak from hanging for days. His numb fingers rubbed at his sore wrists, pressing the raw flesh back into place. A hand lowered to help him to his feet. A soft delicate hand slid into his palm, beckoning him to rise. He slid his rough palm into hers, feeling the comfort of home. He let her help him rise to his feet. She slid her arm around his waist and took his weight against her own. She was no lightweight miss. He could feel her strength as she guided him from Shears's ship. Her arms squeezed him lightly as she bantered with Shears. "Yes, I think he will be a nice addition to my harem." She laughed to herself as they climbed the stairs.

Shears followed them to the top of the deck. His men gathered around as they watched them disembark the ship. Her men circled around them as they made their way along the dock. Shears noted she was too protected to execute his revenge. He would find her when she was alone and vulnerable, and then she would be his. When he captured her away from her henchmen, he would bring her back and set sail for the unknown. He missed out on that sweet Ivy Thornhill, but he would own MacKinnon, even if he had to tie her to his bed to make her his. Her sassy mouth wouldn't protect her then.

Shears watched as Maxwell made his escape. He wasn't finished with him either. He would kill him before this month was out. His backup was coming, and he would destroy them. The only thing he took pleasure in was that she held the key to Maxwell's search for the treasure, and Maxwell didn't even know it. That was a bit of sweet revenge.

"Have the boy bring a bottle of whiskey to my cabin. Follow them. I want them watched until they make their return. And for god's sake, do not get caught. Report back to me in the morning."

Shears staggered back to his chamber and sprawled out on a chair. His cabin boy raced in after him, carrying the bottle. He was a small lad, no older than six. His clothes hung on him, torn to rags. Not one spot on his body was clean. He was covered in the same grime that decorated the ship.

"Here you go, Captain." The lad rushed to his side to please him.

Shears grabbed the bottle and swatted him across the face, taking out his anger on the boy. He swigged back a drink as he kicked the young lad.

"Get the hell out of here, you gutter swine."

The young boy ran out of the cabin as fast as he could, for fear that the captain would harm him. When the captain was angry, it was always best not to be in his line of sight.

Shears leaned back in his chair, drinking from the bottle. He lowered his hand to his side, wincing from the pain. When he raised his hand, it was coated in blood. He snarled as he watched the blood dripping from his fingers and swore his revenge on Maxwell. The earl had double-crossed him for the last time. His snarl quickly turned to a smile as he began to plan his revenge on the spy and the ravishing redhead he escaped with. Neither one of them would survive what he had in store for them.

Chapter Two

HER MEN GATHERED AROUND them, providing a protective barrier against Shears. Maxwell limped alongside them, the movement coming back gradually to various parts of his body. Sharp tingling sensations were ricocheting along his arms and legs. He got dizzy as they hurried along the dock.

"Can you ride?" she asked.

He nodded. He was afraid that if he talked, he'd spill his stomach at her feet. It was awful enough to be an invalid around this lady. He didn't want to disgrace himself too. He was nauseated from the sudden movement.

There were a group of horses waiting for them on the outskirts of town. Her men helped him on top of a black steed. She gave a signal, and they took off into the countryside. She set a brisk pace, trying to get them as far away from Shears as possible.

They rode for miles in circles once they realized they were being followed. After a while, she slowed the horses to a trot after her man reported they had lost their tail. She rode toward the front, helping lead their escape to the hideout. Now and then, she would glance to see if their prisoner still rode with them. *He didn't ride off on his own? How odd.* She shook her head as she continued to ride in the darkness surrounding them.

"Mac, we better tak' a break," Gregor shouted.

Mac pulled her horse to a stop and she faced her men. What she saw, caught her by surprise. Her captive was slung across the front of his mount, passed out. She had only glanced at him moments ago, and he had stared at her as she rode in front of him. His dark gaze made her turn around and keep trudging along to their destination. It made her uncomfortable. He still had not spoken, even though they had been traveling for hours.

She grabbed the reins when his horse tried to pass her. When she shook his shoulder, his only response was a moan. When she realized he was unconscious, she needed to alter their plans. They couldn't risk being in the open for too long. It was only a matter of time before Shears's men caught up with them. They were also in her enemy's territory. The only decision Mac could make was to keep moving. They would arrive at their site in an hour.

"Tie him on so he doesn't fall off. Ion and Gregor, you ride ahead to prepare a room for him, and bring in Agatha. He will need care. The rest of us will follow at a much slower pace. Those at the end, keep doubling our tracks to throw them off our path. If they catch up to us, you know how to get rid of them. Any man who works for Shears is as low as scum as he is and deserves whatever comes to him. Now, let's go."

The clansmen did her bidding, as they would for any leader, only with more respect than they showed any man. The MacKinnon held the highest of their respect for whoever served under her, not shown out of fear but from love and gratitude. She had earned it through the trials their clan had been through over the years. There was no one stronger or more deserving than her.

MacKinnon started off along the trail again, taking a shortcut through the open glen. It would be dangerous during the night but worth the risk if her prisoner received the care he needed. She raised her hand and gave them the signal. They took off through the glen at a fast pace. Her men held the reins to Maxwell's horse, making sure he wouldn't fall. Their horses galloped faster as they made their way home. When they came upon a creek, the horses, slathered with sweat, cooled their hooves as they crossed. Once they crossed, the pack slowed their pace. They had passed without harm coming to any of them.

A loud birdsong pierced the air, and the group answered the call. A young boy dressed in the clan's plaid rushed up to Mac. She laughed and slid off her horse. Mac let out a warrior's cry as she pulled the young lad up for a hug and kiss. She ruffled his hair and set him back on the ground. More men followed the boy, relieving them of their horses and patting each other on the back, welcoming them home.

Mac gave out new instructions. Maxwell was to be moved inside for Agatha to tend him. They carried him inside and lay him upon the bed prepared for his stay. Mac wanted to follow. She was concerned for him, but she didn't want to show her clan how he affected her. Which was weird, she hadn't even spoken to him, but she felt connected to him. It was the look in his eyes on Shears's ship that had captivated her. His gaze was haunted with deep sorrow that only she could understand. When a warm, small hand slid into her palm, she looked below and smiled at the love of her life. She swung her arm out and back again, making the child laugh. They continued this game as they walked inside the castle. Mac smiled as wives and families greeted the men who rode with her to Edinburgh. She gazed in envy at the concern the women showed their men. Why she experienced a sense of loss this time, she didn't understand. Any other time, she chuckled in good cheer, teasing them.

She didn't like feeling lost in her own home, so she decided to check on the patient. She stood in the doorway as she watched Agatha care for him. He was conscious and let the old lady tend to his wounds. Still, not one word passed between his lips. He finally sensed her presence and glanced her way. She crossed her arms over her chest as she waited for Agatha to finish with him. The old healer rattled on, trying to draw Maxwell out in conversation, but nothing but silence met her attempt. She gathered her supplies, making her way to Mac.

"Nae a talker, is he?" the old lady shouted.

Mac laughed when Maxwell rolled his eyes. She laced her arms through Agatha's and helped her walk out of the room. As they walked along the hallway, she listened to the diagnosis of his wounds.

"Dehydrated he is, and starving too. His wounds ur minor. I've patched him up th' best o' mah skills. Th' rest is on him. Needs nourishment is all."

"Shears had him for over a week. Perhaps he was hoping to starve him to death."

"What 're ye planning wi' him?"

"Hold him for a month myself."

"Then?"

"Trade him back to Shears for the weapons."

"Humph," Agatha grunted.

"What?"

"Dinna think ah dinna notice what happened in that bedroom, lassie."

"I don't know what you are referring to."

"Now ah remember, it wasn't so much seeing but feeling."

"He is a means to an end."

"Ye can lie tae yourself if you want, lassie, but I've raised ye since ye wur a wee bairn."

"Humph," Mac replied.

The old healer cackled as she walked into the hall. The castle was ancient and needed much repair, and few rooms were habitable. They used the old banquet hall as a kitchen and eating space. The noise grew louder as they celebrated making it home. Mac would let them have their fun for the evening. Tomorrow they would make their plans to bring this to an end the next time they confront Shears. She turned and returned to the patient.

He tried to sit up but struggled. She came to his side, sliding her hands underneath him, propping him against the pillows. His body was burning hot to her touch. She let her hands linger longer than she should have. His body was hard and firm, despite being sick and living in deplorable conditions. When she pulled back, his hand gripped her arm. He tightened his hold. She tried pulling back, but he only held her tighter. When she realized he wouldn't let her go, she plopped next to him. Still, he didn't release or speak to her.

"How are you feeling? Agatha will bring you a bowl of broth."

Silence.

"I trust you will remain within the walls during your stay here. We won't keep you shackled as Shears did, unless you try to escape."

"Why would I ever dream of escaping this wonderful paradise?"

"Oh, he speaks."

"Mmm, I can do much more than speak," he responded as his hand slid up her arm.

This time Mac freed herself from his grasp. His touch unsettled her. She moved to the farthest corner of the room and leaned up against the wall. He smiled at her. His touch heated her in ways she never imagined. How was he able to control that power over her?

"I am aware you are capable of more, but it will be nothing that interests me."

"Don't be so sure of that, Mac," he said, emphasizing her name. "So, what is your real name, honey?"

"Well, Sassenach, it sure isn't honey."

He growled at the name she called him.

She took pity on him. "MacKinnon."

"I realize that. I listened to what Shears called you. Your Christian name?"

"No need for you to know, my lord. You can call me Mac."

"Tell me your name. It is the least you can do since you are holding me prisoner."

"Well, see, that's the thing. I am the one in charge, not you. I command you, and you have no authority over me."

"My humblest apologies, miss. I meant to say that someone as lovely as you must have a more poetic name than Mac."

"Ah, your charms won't work on me, Earl Zane Maxwell."

He raised that damn eyebrow again at the usage of his name.

"Oh yes, I know of your charm. I do wonder if the rumors are true."

"What rumors might those be?"

"The ones, where you speak in your dark voice, whispering promises of seduction, while you charm your way into the young maids' beds."

"I don't visit young maids' beds."

"Oh, that is correct, you charm the young maidens, then bed the married ones."

"Those rumors are also false, ma'am."

"Now, now. I am sure you heard me tell Shears's man that I hate when somebody calls me ma'am."

"Ma'am it shall be. Unless you wish to give me your name, I am at a disadvantage. I only wish to find out the name of my captor—or should I say my rescuer?"

"As I said, Mac will do."

"We shall see."

He lay his head back against the headboard and sighed, frustrated that he was getting nowhere with this woman. He would need to change his tactics to invade her thoughts. She appeared to be the leader here, as the men followed her directions, which was strange for a lady in this part of Scotland to have that kind of control. He shrugged. Who was he to question their ways? He realized now that she was the one to sneak around in his escape. If he could convince her to let him go, then he could be free. There seemed to be only one way. He would have to charm her. Zane saw how his touch affected her as much as her touch affected him. What made her send him into flames? He noticed she was interested when her touch lingered on him as she helped him into a sitting position. Zane would take his time and go slow with her. He heard they were keeping him hostage for a month before they returned him to Shears. He would leave this castle before the end of the month. But before then, he would earn her trust, then make her his. Then, when he was ready to leave, she would let him walk out of here. She was skittish, and he could use that to his advantage. He hadn't charmed the ladies around London for nothing. By the end of the week, she would join him in this bed, begging for more.

She glared at him, smiling smugly. His eyes weren't open, but she knew his mind thought of ways to escape. She thought he would plan to use her attraction to him as a weapon. For the first time in her life, she doubted herself. Any other man she encountered before left her indifferent to their touch, but this man was different. She must keep away from him. Agatha and the men could tend to him and keep him from escaping. She had work to do.

When she pushed away from the wall, she made for the door. Her leaving him was the best choice to do for now. She hadn't gotten very far when he moved and winced loudly. Mac cringed at his pain and rushed to his side.

"Leaving so soon, Mac?"

She growled at him as she turned and left the bedroom. He was playing with her. She had to be stronger or she would fall to his charms. When she marched into the banquet hall, she ordered Ion and Gregor to keep watch over him. They were to guard in shifts, and Maxwell was to be left alone for no reason. Mac slid in next to Agatha to eat her dinner, hoping for a peaceful meal, but it was not to be.

"A fine specimen o' a gentleman, if ah say so myself."

"Ah did not ask."

"Ah know. Ah wis only pointing out the obvious tae ye."

"Ye need not point it to me either."

"No, ye dinna need me to." Agatha cackled.

"Out with it, old woman. I see your dying to enlighten me on what humors ye."

"Ah sense it, honey, 'n' afore long, everybody in this hall will tae. So, if ye do not want that attraction tae bloom, ye best keep yer distance from that one. He is a charmer. Dinna say one word, but old Aggie here kin tell one from a mile away."

Mac listened to her advice but didn't respond. While she stayed in the room for the brief time she was with him, the attraction vibrated around them. She'd decided to stay away before she departed the bedroom, not that she would share any of that with the healer. Agatha wasn't only the healer to the clan, but she was the next best thing to a mother. She raised her after the Sinclair clan murdered her mother. Aggie noticed every one of her moods, even this one. Mac wore her emotion's like a sleeve, it was the one trait about herself she wished she could change. Anybody could tell what mood she was in by her expression. The women would see what she felt for Maxwell, for that was the expression they wore themselves whenever their men were near.

She finished her dinner and went to the nursery. Young Lachlan was settled in his bed, awaiting his bedtime story. He made her heart melt. He was small and had a huge future ahead of him. She made sure his life was simple by carrying the burdens of their clan on her own. Mac would carry the struggles now, for him to have an easy life to live and love. Mac sat next to him, bringing the blanket up around him and tucking it underneath his small form. After she tucked him in, she leaned over to rub her nose across his, smiling into his young eyes.

"Are you ready, Lac?"

"Tell me about the prisoner, Mac."

"What is it you wish to know?"

"Is he dangerous? Did he kill anyone? Are ye going to kill him?"

Mac laughed at his questions; he had such an imagination. He would lead this clan to prosperity after Mac left. And leave she would do—soon. It was time to start her life once this mission ended. She devoted the last year to this clan, and it was time their leader—the one meant to guide this clan—returned. She only had to deliver Maxwell in one month, then she could hand over the reins. But to do that, she had to destroy Shears. Maxwell was the key to her achieving that goal, only he had no idea. She was aware he had his own agenda for destroying Shears, and she had no problem with any action he took on that matter. But before Shears died, she needed information from him to make this clan thrive.

"No, he is not dangerous. And I am not aware if he has killed anyone. As for me killing him …"

"That is enough, Mac. I don't want him to listen to this horror. It is dangerous enough when you let him wander around after you."

Mac paused in her description of Maxwell when the boy's mother entered. Isobel waddled inside the bedroom and took a seat on the rocking chair.

"I'm only explaining that we will let Lord Maxwell live." Mac laughed.

"So you say. Lachlan, it is time for you to sleep. You can follow your aunt around tomorrow and watch her as she controls the new prisoner."

"But Mama, I'm not tired. I need to hear the details now. I am the man of the family," he argued.

"I know ye are dear, while your father is away. Ye father recognized when it was time to sleep, and now it is time for ye to close your eyes."

Isobel tried to rise from the chair but struggled. Mac jumped off the bed and pulled her to her feet. Isobel was nearing her time, and every movement was a struggle. Putting her son to bed brought her such joy, and she never missed it. It further helped to ease the ache of missing his father and worrying after him.

Mac helped her as Isobel leaned over to give her son a kiss goodnight. Isobel stroked her fingers through his hair and whispered her love for him. Mac always teared up as she regarded their sweet moments. It was the love of a mother for her child, who loved her in sweet return.

"Goodnight, lad. We will play tomorrow," Mac called out from the door.

"Night, Aunt Mac, dinna kill him till the morning."

"I promise." She laughed as she hooked her arm through Isobel's, walking with her into the bedroom across the hall.

Mac helped Isobel undress and lay next to her in the bed. Isobel moaned and turned on her side, studying Mac as Mac stared at the ceiling. Mac was afraid to tell Isobel how Maxwell made her body come alive from his touch. Isobel had the patience of a saint though and would lie there throughout the evening, waiting for her to talk. That was the bad thing about your best friend marrying your brother. There were no secrets in their family. At least her brother wasn't here to see this. He would tease her over her dilemma.

"Is it that obvious?"

"Only to me, but the others will notice soon enough."

"I will stay away from him."

"But will ye be able to?"

"I must."

"I dinna think ye will, even though I believe ye will try."

"Is it this way with Logan?"

"Yes."

"I am sorry, Isobel."

"It is not your fault, Mac. He took th' mission for the Crown. I understand ye are trying everything to get him back."

"It was stupid of him to leave, with young Lachlan and you with child. What was my idiot brother thinking?"

"Do not be so harsh. Ye realize he took the mission to save our clan. He shall return, and everything will be well. I trust in ye."

Mac rolled over, lacing her fingers through her friend's hand. When Logan courted Isobel, Mac was furious with him for stealing her friend away. Once they married, she saw the love they shared and realized she was gaining a sister, not losing a friend.

"I will bring him back. Give me one month, and he will be home."

"Ye will enlist his help, won't ye?"

"Who?

"Ye know who. Lord Maxwell."

"No, he is only a pawn in my game."

"He can help ye destroy Shears. Why not work together?"

"I told you. I want to keep my distance."

"Why?"

Mac rolled back over and watched the candlelight dance across the ceiling. The flames jumped around in a jig, drawing out the shadows.

"He makes me feel emotions I've never felt before."

"Is that awful?"

"They are feelings I don't want to experience."

"Why not, Mac? Love can be a wonderful affection."

Mac's laugh held a bitter edge. "Men like Maxwell do not love. They lust, they get what they want, and then leave you."

"Maybe ye are the one to change him."

"I don't imagine I can. Look at me, Isobel. I am not one to entice attraction in a man as sophisticated as him."

"Ye are a goddess, and ye know it. Why do ye reason every man in this clan jumps at yer every command?"

"Because they respect me and realize I am only filling in for Logan until he returns."

Isobel laughed. "They are in love with ye, even the married ones. The only reason their wives don't attack is because ye charm them as well. Ye have a spell wrapped around everybody in this clan since the day ye were born. Why wouldn't Maxwell fall for it too?"

"Well, I won't give him the opportunity."

"I never knew ye to run away from what scares ye," Isobel baited her.

Mac didn't take to the bait. She rolled on her other side and stared at the wall. Isobel let out a chuckle, which soon turned to light snores. Mac wasn't so much as scared but cautious. She wasn't used to being so vulnerable, and she didn't care for this emotion. As she drifted off to sleep, she remembered how his touch made her feel and the promises his eyes held.

Chapter Three

SHE AVOIDED HIM FOR a week, not that it had been easy. She rose before dawn to help in the stables, and throughout the day she rode guard duty. Then when she wasn't making herself scarce, she helped the women finish their chores. Late at night, she crawled in bed exhausted. He asked for her during the day, but still she avoided him.

Mac rode with Gregor the next morning, deciding on how to proceed, when Ion rode up alongside them. Gregor was her brother's next in command and her protector.

"I thought you were on duty," she snapped at Ion.

Both men stopped their mounts, surprised at her sharp tone. She had never spoken to them in anger. Her mood was testy from not sleeping. During the night, she kept picturing him sitting on her bed wearing nothing but a smile. She finally rose before dawn, deciding to ride out her frustration. That was where Gregor had found her.

"Ewan is guarding th' prisoner, but he is demanding tae see ye. He is up 'n' out of bed wandering th' castle, asking everybody where ye are. He is bothering everybody. Said if ye don't show, ye leave him na choice but tae leave. Ah warned him, bit he said nae tae worry mah brawny self over his actions."

Mac scowled her frustration at this news. Who did he think he was? They didn't behave this way in Scotland. Just because he was an earl didn't make her bow to him. This wasn't his land to make demands on.

"Leave him to me. Ride back and warn the men of his threat. Say nothing to him. I will discuss his capture with him in my own time. Let him try to leave, and he will wish he remained in the castle."

"Ah think yer playing a dangerous game wi' that one Mac," Gregor warned.

"I think the earl needs to learn who is in charge. And what better way than letting him escape? Besides, you know what we do when prisoners escape."

"Logan wid nae approve o' this behavior o' ye."

"Well Logan is not here, is he?"

"Aggie says you're smitten wi' him."

Mac glared at him. "The ol' hag is going senile."

Gregor let out a rough laugh. "Ah think ye protest too much."

Mac turned her steed around, setting off at a fast pace, putting as much distance from her and the castle as she could get. She heard Gregor following her at a distance. He stayed far enough away that she might exercise out her demons, but close enough to protect her if he must.

Why was everybody trying to throw her in the path of that dandy? Didn't they see he was only a means to an end? And that end resulted in getting Logan rescued. Who cared if he tried to escape? It would only make for a miserable week for him. She wouldn't feel sorry for him either.

She pulled on the reins and brought Lady to a trot. As she circled back, she gradually made her way to the castle grounds. As she passed Gregor, she noticed he wore a big grin at her discomfort. She gave him a scowl as she rode toward the stables, which only made him laugh at her expense as he followed her. When she reached the stables, she slid off her horse. Mac whispered her gratitude for the exercise in Lady's ear while she patted her mane. Mac then continued to the castle.

She slipped inside and snuck up to her bedchamber. Inside, she peeled away her clothes, dropping them behind her as she walked to the bathtub. The tub was waiting for her, filled with hot water. The scent of heather perfumed the air. As she slipped into the bath, she slid down and let the warm water relax the tension from her body. She moaned at the wonderful enjoyment of the water soothing her body, and she closed her eyes to soak—which only brought more images of him. This time she imagined him helping wash away her aches. The only way to ease those aches was for his hands to caress her body.

"Do you need help, Skye?" His dark voice invaded her thoughts.

She sat up quickly and water splashed on the floor in waves. Then she swiftly slipped under the water until only her face was above it. She grabbed the towel from the stool and covered her body with it. The rotten luck with that was that it was the only thing to cover herself with when she planned to exit the bath, and now it was wet. And exit she must, to clothe herself against him. He had made himself comfortable in her favorite chair tucked in the corner next to the window. The same place where she liked to relax and read as she gazed out across her land.

"How did you get in here?" she demanded.

"Now, Skye, I can get in anywhere I want. That is a warning to you. You won't keep me from anywhere I want to go," he explained as he emphasized her God-given name.

He sounded so proud of himself that he learned her name. She wondered which one squealed first, Agatha or Isobel. Traitors the whole lot; she would handle them later. Why was everybody in her clan trying to play matchmaker with this man? Did they not see that he was a scoundrel of the highest order? He oozed his charm on the women of her clan. Well, he wouldn't charm any information out of her.

"Leave this room right this instant. Have you no shame? You, sir, are no gentleman."

"I never said I was."

"Scoundrel."

"Tyrant."

"Rogue."

"Temptress," he whispered to himself, but not quietly enough, for she overheard the words which passed through his lips.

Skye blushed a dark shade of red over her complete body. Her body heated at his words. Not only from his words but from his stare. He lounged there, sprawled out in her chair, slowly perusing her.

"Please, I will see you when I am finished. I promise."

Maxwell pushed himself to his feet, strolling over to her. He stopped at the foot of the tub and gazed at her body. Her wet, naked body she tried to cover with a towel. The towel hid nothing from his sight, only enticing him to want to view more. He tried to be immune to her, but his inner self kept drawing her to him. She was a beacon of light to his dark soul. The water danced in waves as she squirmed to hide herself from him.

He kneeled, dipping his hand into the warm water. His fingers found her ankle and wrapped around the base. He gently stroked his thumb along the padding of her foot, kneading the arch. His fingers trailed up her leg, and he listened to her gasp right before she moaned. Then he dipped his other hand into the water, wrapping his hands at the bottom of her legs and yanked on them. As he pulled her toward him, her body slid under the water, dunking her whole face. When he let go of her legs, he stood and walked to the dresser, pulling out her robe. The best action for him was for her to dress before they had their conversation. She was too much of a temptation.

Skye rose out of the water, sputtering her anger at him, calling him a variety of names that no lady should even speak, let alone know. But Skye MacKinnon was no lady. Oh, she was a goddess, of that Maxwell had no doubt. He stared as she stripped her way to the tub and regarded every delectable inch of her. She had made him so hard as he caught her undressing. It wasn't until she had dipped under the water that he was able to bring himself under control, but even then he struggled. He still fought the temptation, but at least he could talk with her now. He could handle her fury, just not her moaning and lying naked in the bathtub.

As he returned to the tub, he held the robe out for her. He turned his back and laid the robe over his shoulder. She grabbed it from him, giving him a shove as she slid out of the tub. He listened to her muttering to herself as she wrapped the garment around her wet body. When he didn't sense her behind him, he turned around. She had moved across the room, opening the door.

Zane moved to her side, sliding his palm against the door and slamming it shut. The last thing he needed was her leaving the room or calling for protection. He had to act fast to acquire his answers. Her sister-in-law calmed him earlier and explained this enigma of a woman. She was amazing and frustrating at the same time. Never had a woman crawled under his skin like her. One minute he wanted to bait her, the next he wanted to take her feisty mouth under his and savor her energy. She was all sass, but she also had a vulnerability he wanted to protect. As he observed her with her clan, he noticed what they saw, but more. When she thought no one looked, her guard lowered. Isobel explained why Skye was in power and that she would be a good ally if he could align himself with her.

He pulled her into his arms and felt her stiffen. God, she felt like heaven. If this were any other moment in his life, he would act on the opportunity, but he realized he couldn't afford to. He was running out of time. To save this mission, he must convince her into letting him help her. They could work together to destroy Shears. He realized she wasn't involved in destroying England. She wanted him to believe she was, but he had a sixth sense about people, and he knew he wasn't wrong about her.

She tried to remove herself from under his arms, but they were bands of steel. For a man starved for a week, he had an uncontrollable strength. She must get out of his arms before she did something stupid, like throwing herself at him like a hussy. The longer he held her, the more her control slipped. She tried to resist, hoping it would make him want to let her go. But it had the opposite effect. Before she understood what was happening, he pulled her tighter up against his body. When she looked up, her gaze got caught in his smoldering stare. His dark eyes grew darker, pulling her into his spell. She felt her nipples tighten under her light robe as they pressed into his chest. She noticed the effect she had on him as he pressed into her body. His hardness dug into her hip.

He tried to resist, but it was nigh on impossible to resist such a sweet package. Her robe clung to her wet body, the damp cloth outlining her against the sun shining through the window. Her nipples pressed through the robe, making him groan inwardly at their display. She melted in his arms. It was easier when she fought him to get away, but when she stood still and relaxed against him, Maxwell lost his mind.

"Ah, hell, just one taste," he muttered to himself. Or to her. He wasn't sure anymore.

Zane lowered his head and took her lips in a swooping kiss. He caught them both unaware. He drank from them like a starving man. Starving for a drink. Starving for a taste. Starving for her. She was his oasis in this lost paradise. Only a drink of her fulfilled his quench. Skye was the only one that could pacify his hunger and need.

Their lips tangled in sweet bliss, both drawing the kiss from the other. Where one started and ended, another began. There was not one taste. There were many. Their tongues slid across one another, licking, sucking, nipping off the dew from each other's lips.

"Just one touch," he muttered between kisses.

Zane's hands dove into Skye's hair pulling her closer as his lips devoured her. He held her to him as she wrapped her arms around his neck, pulling him closer. They couldn't pull themselves any tighter, but they tried. Kisses became moans, which became bolder touches. Their lips started a firestorm that couldn't be extinguished. Before long, his hands caressed her entire body, stroking her to a higher level of passion.

Skye, lost in the passion of his kiss, realized she should put a stop to this but was unable to draw away. She had experienced nothing close to this in her life and was consumed with desire. She didn't want him to stop. When he muttered just one touch, she wanted to shout, "No! Give me more than one, please more than one." She wanted his hands to caress her; her body ached for his touch.

When he pulled her robe apart and grazed her nipple, she wanted to jump out of her skin. He teased the bud back and forth, and she let out a moan between his lips. When his hand caressed her breast and squeezed lightly, Skye's legs went out from underneath her. He caught her as he drew out their kiss to a single trace of his tongue across her lips, followed by a gentle kiss.

With a deep sigh, he pulled her robe closed and separated them. He stared as she tightened the belt on her robe. Also, he watched her distance herself from him and what they'd just shared. Which was probably for the best, as neither one of them wanted this. Whatever this attraction held floated in the air around them.

Skye moved across the room to the dressing screen, dropping her robe and changing into a clean pair of trousers and a red blouse. She wrapped a stole around her shoulders, her clan's tartan colors around her as a barrier of protection from his all-knowing gaze. She knew he stood on the opposite side. Waiting. When she walked out, she located where she had thrown off her boots and sat in her chair. As she tugged them on, she watched as he settled his back against the door, blocking her from leaving. Skye leaned back when she realized she was going nowhere anytime soon.

"Say your piece, Maxwell. Then leave my room and do not darken my path until I take you back to Shears."

"Tsk, tsk is that how you treat the man your lips just devoured?"

Skye raised her eyes at his smugness.

"If I recall correctly, it was you who devoured my lips."

"Yes, you are correct. Although, from where I stood, you were more than a willing participant."

"Enough. We are discussing what you want."

"I want you. We both recognize it can lead to nothing but trouble. As difficult as it will be to resist you, I hope you will also try."

Skye let out a laugh. He was trouble—every tall, delectable inch of him.

"In the rumors I overheard about you, it's funny that nobody ever mentioned your humor."

He waggled his eyebrows at her.

"Out with it. What are your demands?"

"What are your plans with Shears?"

"I will exchange you for my weapons in three weeks."

"No, you will not."

Skye ignored him. "Then I will use those weapons to bring England to her knees."

"No, you won't."

This made Skye furious, and she came out of her chair toward him.

"Who do you think you are, coming in to my castle—let alone my bedroom—telling me what you think I will do?"

"I am a man who sees past your disguise. I see the lady you are. The woman you are meant to be. You will not use those weapons against England."

"Yes, I will," she said, walking away to stare out the window at her beloved land. She saw the heather blooming on the mountains in the distance. The purple blooms against the sun was nothing short of magnificent.

"Skye …"

"Do not call me that. My name is MacKinnon."

"Mac, let me help. I spoke to Isobel, and she told me the mission your brother Logan was working on for the Crown. Let me help you."

She turned around to glare at him. How dare he bring up Logan to her? Isobel spoke too much and trusted too easily.

"From what I hear, you are the last person to trust. Traitor is what they call you. Traitor to your friends. Traitor to the Crown," she taunted him.

Maxwell frowned at her words. How did she have so much knowledge on him and he so little on her? While she tried to portray herself as a Scottish ruffian, she was too refined. It was his job to notice people's traits that they might not even realize themselves. It was what made him an excellent spy. Her every action betrayed her to him. She had the grace of a lady but the spirit of a warrior. From what information Isobel gave him, her pride stopped her from asking for help, especially when she needed it the most. Also, she cared too much. She felt it was her duty to protect everybody.

Skye had never graced London. He couldn't have resisted her if she had. He would've remembered her. There would have been talk, and she would have turned London on its axis and spun it around. No, she had never been there. So how did she know about him? It was a mystery to solve later. Now he needed to convince her to work together. He had nobody else, which was his own fault. He realized that now. He made it impossible for anyone who knew him to trust him again. He had to learn to live with his consequences. But for now, the only person he needed to trust him was this lady sitting across the bedchamber.

"You have heard correctly," he said as he bowed to her. "Earl Zane Maxwell, double agent for the Crown at your service."

"With those words, you expect me to trust you?"

"No. I only hope you will."

"Why should I?"

"Because I can help you bring your brother home and destroy Shears. He is the one you want to destroy, not England."

Skye didn't answer him. She observed him quietly as she listened to him. His voice drew her to him like a moth to a flame. His words were soft and soothing, coaxing her to trust him. To believe in him. She felt herself responding to his promises. His voice and soulful eyes caused a reaction in her. She had observed him on the ship and saw how they shuttered when they discussed him, as if he didn't exist. They were hard and full of hatred. Now, as they pulled her in deeper, she saw the agony he suffered. When she flung the word "traitor" at him and mentioned his friends, she noticed how he flinched and how the sadness crept into his eyes. Was he trustworthy? Were his actions of one of a greater strength? What did he hide? Was it a cover-up to ensure Shears's victory? For her to trust him, she needed answers.

"Answer this for me, and I will consider working alongside you."

Zane nodded. He knew that to earn her trust he must give her his trust in return. With that trust came honesty. Honesty that might risk his cover, but not from her doing. He had faith he could trust her, as she had too much at stake to risk.

"Did you betray Thornhill and Mallory for the fortune Shears promised you?"

"How do you have knowledge of Thornhill and Mallory?"

"That isn't the agreement, Maxwell. Answer my question."

"They believe so, yes."

"I didn't ask what they believed. I asked about you."

Zane sighed and slid to the ground. He leaned his head against the door, closing his eyes. When he opened his eyes, he gazed into hers.

"No."

"Explain yourself."

"It is a long story, Mac, one we can discuss at another time. Now we need to figure out our plan for Shears."

"No, Maxwell. You either explain what happened in London, or this conversation will go no further. I will send out my signal, then my men will take you and chain you in the dungeon until we return you to Shears. I couldn't care less what he does with you. And I will execute my revenge on the man when he is least expecting it."

Maxwell sent her a glare that would make any other man or woman cringe. But it only seemed to light her fire. She settled back in her big armchair, sliding her legs underneath her, and waited for him to explain.

When he realized he needed to go into detail about what made him go deep undercover, he figured he might as well make himself comfortable too. He trusted her not to run. She wanted to learn his story too badly. Zane rose and stretched his body along her bed. He sighed as he sank into the soft, feathered mattress. It was more comfortable than the hard slab she had him sleep on the last few nights. Far be it for him to complain too much. At least he had a bed. The previous week it was nothing but chains.

"What do you want to know?"

Skye stared as he made himself comfortable on her bed. She saw the weariness he tried to cover. He sighed as he settled into the spot she slept in at night. His head nestled into her pillow, his breathing deepening, and she wondered if he drifted off to sleep. How would she sleep in her bed now? He had not only wreaked havoc on her life, but now she could never have a peaceful moment in her bedchamber ever again without remembering him. Here. In her space. He filled it completely, as if he were meant to be there. Lost in her thoughts, she was unaware he hadn't fallen asleep.

He gazed at her from under his lashes. "Skye?"

Startled, she raised her eyes to his, and he smiled his smug smile of satisfaction, knowing he was untangling her. She rubbed her hands up and down her arms.

"First, I want to know why you helped Shears escape in Margate."

"Mallory's cover was blown. We still needed the whole network behind Shears, and I realized if it looked like I was betraying my friends and my country, Shears would trust me more."

"Did you fool him? Because from how I discovered you, it didn't appear that way to me," Skye spoke with sarcasm.

Maxwell rolled on his side, propping his head on his hand. He smiled at her, seeming to enjoy her wry humor.

"You are very witty, my dear," he told her.

"I am not your dear."

"It is just a term of endearment one uses toward, say, a friend or an ally."

"Well since I am neither of those at this moment, so please refer to me as Mac."

Maxwell rolled back over, groaning as he realized she was harder to charm than he'd originally thought. She was immune to his charms. Still, it was early yet.

"Yes, for a while. I fed him enough information to give the impression I had switched sides."

"How about when Charles Mallory was ambushed in the woods and beaten by Shears's thugs?"

"No, not that time. I was unaware I was being followed. I confronted Mallory on the trail to convince him to pull out. His life and his family's lives were in extreme danger. I had information on Shears's plot to murder Mallory and the Thornhills, but the fool didn't listen. He was too busy chasing a skirt throughout the whole affair," Maxwell spoke in disgust.

"Mmm, yes. Love should not exist during war."

"He was a fool. A fool in love."

"What of your plan to kill Charles Mallory and Raina LeClair in Dover?"

"Nothing but a loose end. With them dead, I would have gained the information I needed from Shears."

"Did this information help bring the end to his operation? Or your own personal agenda that has been your goal throughout your entire mission. The personal agenda of the lost rubies."

"What is your knowledge of the lost rubies?"

"I know they are what you search for. Did you mean to kill them?"

"No, I only needed for it to appear like I did."

"Yes, but when Shears found out you didn't, your cover was blown. So, you decided to blow up the ball of the season with Prinny himself in attendance. Because then you could redeem yourself in Shears's eyes."

"That was where it went wrong."

"Explain why you threatened your friends for this swine."

"It was the only solution to keep them safe. I had an escape route. I came close to bringing Shears and the whole treason operation to justice."

"What went wrong?"

"Shears noticed me speaking with Thornhill and Mallory. I warned them to take their ladies and leave. Instead, they remained at the ball to bring the treason to an end. Stupid fools."

"So how did Shears convince you to carry out his plans?"

"He held Raina LeClair captive."

"So why save her? She was nothing to you."

"She was my friend's love, and at one time my trusted ally. I know how Shears treats women, and he meant to inflict the worst harm to her. He meant for her to suffer for what she'd accomplished in the prior months. I couldn't let that happen to her. She deserved none of it."

"But you're forgetting another in your story."

Zane knew she referred to Ivy, but his friend wasn't up for discussion. It was his fault Ivy arrived at the ball. If he hadn't gone to their townhome with rumors of Thorn's demise, she would have never been in danger. He would never forgive himself for his actions. Zane only prayed no harm came to her or the child she carried. He ignored her comment as he continued.

"So, I helped Mallory in her escape, who, with the help of Thornhill, stopped the attack. While I helped the escape, Shears arrived. For them to escape to safety, I battled Shears. He was as sure as dead until his reinforcements arrived. They helped him escape and took me as a prisoner. We set sail that night. A few days later, you entered the scene. At the time, I didn't appreciate my good fortune, but now I do."

"How so?"

"Because we can help each other. I will kill Shears and help you get your brother back."

"I haven't agreed to work with you."

After he pulled his arms from behind his head, Maxwell closed his eyes, sinking deeper into the bed.

"Oh, but you will," he mumbled.

Skye sat there, contemplating what she heard from him. While it sounded as if he worked deep undercover with Shears, it still didn't explain his own private mission. She mentioned the rubies as bait, and he didn't respond. And the rubies weren't the only topic he avoided. Ivy Thornhill. Who was she to him? Was she the love who Shears had used to bait him? He avoided explaining his involvement with her. She needed to know the depth of his mission because it would lead her to Logan. She already knew he was innocent in his actions toward Mallory and the Thornhills; her sources told her that much. But what did those lost jewels mean to him? They belonged to the Crown, but they also were the key to the personal side to his mission.

She heard the story behind them. They were meant for the King's bastard. The lost red rubies were sent with the nurse to be given to the King's illegitimate child to secure his future. His future held the shame of being a bastard. He would never hold a title, never receive the respect of the aristocracy, and never be paraded in front of the proud mamas of the ton. No prosperous future, but one of shame. The rubies needed to pave his way, to buy his status. The child would grow into a gentleman, and the only title he would hold was bastard.

But the nurse betrayed the King; she sold the rubies for her own personal gain and abandoned the child at an orphanage. The crazy nurse was captured, she didn't tell where she'd left the baby. She was still being held at Newgate in a special confinement cell, which only made the old nurse crazier—so crazy she forgotten where she abandoned the child. The only clue the Crown had was that the child possessed one ruby. So they checked every orphanage, but none held the child with the missing ruby. Aside from the missing jewel, the only identifying trait the child had was a birthmark identifying the claim of a bastard child to the King.

That was how Logan became involved. A man was hiding from the Sinclair clan on their property. He held a small bag on his person that contained a red ruby. Not any red ruby, but the missing jewel. Despite the severity of his injuries, he told Logan the story of the missing heir. Logan sent the information to the Crown. As the man recovered on their land, he confided more to Logan on the location of the child. He explained how the nurse left the child with him and his wife to raise. The man agreed because his wife was unable to have any children. They raised the child for years, and then his wife passed away from a lengthy illness. He brought his wife's body back to her family—the Sinclair clan. While there, he encountered Shears. Shears discovered the story of the missing child and the red ruby, so he convinced Sinclair to kill the old man, and he kidnapped the child. Logan set sail after Shears and was soon ambushed. Shears now held Logan prisoner too. Shears uprooted lives and left destruction in his wake wherever he traveled.

"Maxwell?"

He didn't answer her.

"Zane?"

The only response she received were snores from the man on her bed. She let out a moan of frustration. She had a decision to make. To trust him to help her save her brother or to give him back to Shears and walk away. While he didn't betray his friends, he had put their lives in danger for his own means. Could she trust him not to deceive her?

She stayed curled up in her chair and watched him sleep. He looked peaceful while he rested. Less overwhelming. When he was awake, he threw her senses into overdrive. His dark, soulful eyes always searched out her secrets—secrets she didn't want him to seek. Then his dark husky voice melted her insides, smoky with desire when he spoke her name. All the while, his smile held the humor of the sarcasm in his words.

Skye curled her legs up under her and rested her chin on her knees. She closed her eyes for a few moments. She would rise soon and see to Isobel and Lachlan. She'd been avoiding them as well over the last few days. It was time to quit running and make plans. But she would allow herself a few moments of rest first.

Chapter Four

WHEN ZANE AWOKE A few hours later, he found her with a curtain of dark red hair around her body as she slept. She looked more vulnerable than she realized. This was a side of her he was sure she didn't show to anybody. He saw the purple smudges of weariness and overwork under her eyes. She was too young and enchanting to carry the burdens of her clan. If she would only trust him, he could help lighten the load. Zane didn't mean to fall asleep on her; he was still trying to make a full recovery. He hated this sensation of utter weakness. Mallory must have felt worse pain than this. He'd endured more pain than any of them. Well, at least he was out of danger; all his friends were. They may hate him, but he could live with that if he knew they were safe. Safe and in love, it appeared. That was not a life for him. He was fine living the life of a confirmed bachelor. No lady existed to tempt him to retire from the exhilaration of being a spy. He didn't care if he produced an heir and a spare. The best thing was for his line to die with him. He lived with his parents' shame for years and carried their secret with him, which had led him to this time in his life.

He didn't want any child of his to carry their disgrace. Shame was the only legacy he had to give. No, it was best he remained alone. Hopefully, his friends would forgive him for his deceit one day. If not, it didn't matter. For he needed no one. It wasn't as if his bed was ever empty; he found sport wherever he desired. His needs were not confined to one lady, even the one sleeping before his eyes.

She tasted like heaven when their lips met. Her body was a fine silk beneath his fingers; she was all fire. Her magnificent glory of hair reflected her personality. All fire and brimstone. Fire that could burn him alive if he allowed her too close. No, he must keep it light and personal with her. He would charm her enough for her help, but not enough to experience her singe.

He slid off the bed and scooped her into his arms. She snuggled into him trustingly as her hand settled against his chest. Zane felt the scorch burn through his cotton shirt. He stopped and gazed at her sleeping, curled in his arms. Her lips parted, begging for his kiss. He lowered his head to brush his lips across hers when she muttered in her sleep.

"Maxwell."

Zane pulled back, thinking she had awakened. When he saw she slept on, he realized the effect she held over him. Lowering her to the bed, he pulled the quilt over her body and backed away. He ran his hand through his hair as he walked to the window. How was it possible for a woman he'd only just met to have this power over him? He tried to convince himself she was only another lady. A means to an end. But all he had to do was carry her in his arms and look at her lips and he wanted to ravish them. Kiss her into submission. Make her his.

Even her speaking his name in her sleep unsettled him. He watched as the sun started its descent into darkness. The bright orange rays bled into the earth, bouncing off the mountaintops, with the gray light settling in for a night of danger. Every minute was dangerous as long as Shears ran loose. He turned back around to watch her sleep. He would bring Shears to justice. The only justice Shears deserved was death, and it was the only ending he deserved. After all the injustices Shears implemented, death was too nice for the devil.

Zane departed the bedroom and searched for Isobel. She was his ally, and with her help they would convince Skye to work alongside him. When he entered the main hall, he noticed Isobel struggling with her coat. Zane went to her side and helped her to remove the heavy garment. She gave him her thanks, and he offered his arm, where he escorted her to the fire. He helped her settle in a chair and took the one opposite from her. As he gazed at the fire, he sensed Isobel watching him. When he looked up, she offered him a smile of encouragement.

"Any luck?" she asked.

Zane shrugged his shoulders in doubt.

"Give her time. She is as stubborn as her brother. In the end she will see what is right."

"We have little time."

"She will come around. She doesn't hold out for very long, only enough to make you suffer. Then she will concoct a plan that will make it look like it was her idea all along."

Zane sat with Isobel while she sewed, sharing stories of growing up with Skye and the trouble she'd got herself into. Young Lachlan joined them for a spell, telling them of his hijinks for the day. Still Skye slept on. He knew she was exhausted from avoiding him the last few days.

"How long has Logan been missing?" Zane asked out of curiosity. He wondered about the timeline of Shears's exploits and how they intertwined with each other. Logan was the missing piece.

"A few short months," answered a voice behind them.

Zane turned in his chair, and the woman who was never far from his thoughts joined them near the fire. Her tousled hair rode in waves that billowed around her face. Her sleepy eyes took him in, and he saw the desire in them. He wondered if she'd dreamed of him after uttering his name and after he'd held her. Because he had thought of her the whole time he sat waiting for her to rise from her nap.

He rose and offered her his seat. She settled in the chair and rocked as she shot Isobel a glare for consorting with the enemy, but Isobel only offered her a smile of innocence.

"Around the same time Ivy was kidnapped," he replied.

"Thorn's wife?"

"Do you know Thornhill? Only his friends call him Thorn."

"We are acquainted."

"How?"

"It does not pertain to you, Maxwell."

Zane stewed in frustration at her secrecy. He would undo her secrets before this mission ended. And when he did, she would surrender to him. Not only her secrets, but her body too, he decided. He wanted her, and he would have her. She was made for his desires, he realized. Plus, if he enjoyed her body, then he could eventually remove her from his thoughts.

"He might have kept them captive on his ship during the same time. Ivy never mentioned another prisoner, but young Tommy might know. I need to get word to Thorn. Do you have a guard I can trust with a missive?"

"You will send no missive. I don't need you to plan your escape. You need to understand, my lord, that I am the one in charge here, not you. Let me make this clear. You're only a pawn to be traded at the end of the month. I will trade you to Shears for weapons."

"I will not allow you to use those weapons to destroy England. I have stopped many before you, and I will stop you too. I'm not sure how yet, but don't make the mistake to cross or underestimate me."

"I will use whatever necessary to get what I want. And if I need weapons to bring Logan home, then those weapons are what I will use."

"Never."

By this time Skye came to her feet and stood toe-to-toe with Maxwell, each glaring at each other as the tension built in the hall. Her men overheard her anger and were behind Maxwell, their hands resting on their weapons as they waited for her to give her word to defend her.

"Skye, sit. Ye are making the men nervous. Lord Maxwell, please pull up a seat, so we can discuss our strategy as the dignified adults we are. You two are acting like savages I know ye are not," Isobel ordered.

Skye sat down in a humph. Maxwell pulled up a chair and folded his arms over his chest, holding his anger in check. His fingers drummed against his forearms. Forearms that were bulging from his shirt, molding the fabric as it pulled against his body. He was no lightweight dandy that she suspected he portrayed to the ton. Oh, he was dark and mysterious to every lady, but to the men, no one ever took him seriously because he always chased the skirts. Or he used to until the last few years when he only courted one lady. The woman he mentioned. The one who married Thornhill. He spoke her name in a tender way, which offset her emotions. Skye's jealousy over a lady she never met who was married to another man confused her. Did Maxwell still love Ivy Thornhill?

"Now, this is how we will proceed. Skye, you will let Lord Maxwell write a missive, in where you will approve what he inquiries in his letter. Then you will send Ewan to deliver the message and wait for a reply. In the meantime, you two will work out a plan on how to bring my Logan home to me and this child. Your differences will be set aside, and you will go in as a united front when you confront Shears."

They both continued to glare at each other as they listened to Isobel's words. Neither one of them wanted to give in before the other.

"Do we have an agreement? Skye? Maxwell?"

"Yes," the earl responded first.

"I will only agree to this for you, Isobel. For this plan is against my better judgment," Skye responded.

"All right, now this argument is settled. Let us adjourn to dinner. I must feed this babe. She is kicking up a storm."

Skye rose from her seat and went to Isobel. She lowered herself, setting her palm against the roundness of Isobel's stomach. She whispered her apologies to the other woman. Isobel covered Skye's hand and gently squeezed, whispering her forgiveness. They sat there sharing unspoken words to each other as they enjoyed the baby kicking against their hands.

Zane turned away to keep from lurking on their private moment. He saw the love these two women shared. It was one of sisterhood and a deep friendship. He envied them, for he had lost the bonds of friendship. He'd even destroyed his relationship with Ivy. She begged him to stop, but he wouldn't heed her advice. His quest for revenge was more important than the friendship she bestowed on him these last few years. He didn't begrudge her marriage to Thorn, for he knew of her deep love for him. Still, he felt abandoned when he could no longer share his thoughts and secrets with her. For she held the darkest secret of his life and never held it against him. She offered her love and support to him, and what did he do? He tried to seduce her on the eve of her wedding, and then he risked her life and that of her unborn baby for the ruby. He didn't know if Thorn would answer his cry for help, but it was his only option.

He also realized it was time for Skye to trust him. He would have to tell her about the red ruby and his connection to the lost jewel, which now rested in his pocket. The one every man searched for, which he held in his possession throughout the last year. For he had found the missing jewels and the red ruby, but he still hadn't located the child. Shears knew where to find the missing heir. He was close to having Shears take him to the child before he had attempted to kill the captain. The jewels were safe from Shears and the evilness behind the Crown. The Crown was not innocent in this treason plot. There were leaders in high ranks behind the Crown that were trying to sabotage the King. It was the reason he was sent on this mission, and even his friends were not privy to the information.

He needed to place his trust in this spitfire of a lady. After dinner, he would tell her the truth. The truth of the missing heir, the red rubies, and his role in the sequence of events. Also, he would confess how these clues tied back to his family. The one person who held knowledge of the truth was lost to him. Ivy didn't judge him, and she wouldn't betray him to Thornhill and Mallory. While he lost the trust of one woman, he now hoped to gain the trust of another.

After dinner, Skye wandered off with Isobel and Lachlan to the lad's bedroom. As he walked by, he listened to their private family moments as he continued to his room. When he walked into the bedroom, the old lady Agatha sat next to his bed.

"I am well. I am no longer in need of your care. I thank you for your help."

"That isn't why I'm 'ere, laddie. Ye'll need mah help more than anybody," she cackled.

"How so?"

"Ye'll need mah help wi' the lassie. A stubborn one she is, but she has a heart o' gold."

"I think I can handle her fine on my own."

"Nae from where ah sat today, laddie. Ye git her in too fine of a temper. Ne'er seen anybody do that afore."

"I find that hard to believe."

"Nope, usually laughs at everybody. Has a warped sense o' humor, she does. Confuses people wi' her sarcasm. But not ye; ye understand her. So, she cannot use her words against ye. Ye twist her up inside. Ah ne'er imagined this day tae happen. Ye two wull make fine bairns."

"You are crazy, old lady. I have no intention of ever being wedded, let alone to that hell-bent woman. Bed her yes, but never wed her."

"Och, ye wull bed her, likely afore th' night is finished. But ye mark mah wurds, ye'll wed her too."

Zane didn't answer the healer's words. She was crazy. No way would he tie himself to that lady for eternity. Now he liked the old lady's words on bedding Skye this evening. Then he could shake her from his senses and concentrate on what he needed to accomplish. Maybe it wouldn't hurt to listen to the advice of the mad woman.

"What is your offer of help?"

The old lady laughed as she explained to him how Skye worked and how to manipulate her to his bidding. Zane listened with half an ear, anything to get this healer out of his room. She rambled on how to break through Skye's barriers. Barriers that were a fortress.

Finally, the old lady left, and Zane settled on the bed and pulled the ruby from his pocket. He rubbed the smooth stone between his fingers. Tonight, he would present the jewel to her and earn her trust. As he lay there, he pictured her lying next to him. When he closed his eyes, he remembered the kiss they shared earlier. Her kiss was one of an innocent, but underneath he knew passion brimmed in her soul.

Chapter Five

ZANE HEARD HER IN the hallway leaving Lachlan's room and talking quietly with Isobel. Her footsteps took her closer to him. They paused outside his door; he waited. She didn't knock, nor did she enter, but he sensed her outside his room. He rose from the bed and moved to the door, waiting. Then he heard her footsteps move away toward her bedroom.

He opened the door and stepped into the hallway. She paused when she heard the door open but didn't turn. Zane strolled up behind her and stood silently at her back. He saw her tighten her hands into fists at her side, and then she unraveled her fingers and wiped them against her legs. Zane thought she might be angry, but she wasn't; she was nervous. Did he possess the same power over her that she did on him? She took off again, moving swiftly. He followed. She entered her bedchamber, trying to close the door on him. He stuck his foot inside, blocking her from shutting the panel in his face. She tried to push the door closed on his foot. Zane pushed the door wider, sending her behind it. He peeled her fingers away as he entered the room. When he shut the door behind him, he locked it and slid the key into his pocket.

He wouldn't leave this room tonight until he acquired what he came for. He came prepared to spend the entire evening in her chambers until she succumbed to him. There would be only the truth between them before this evening ended. They each held secrets to the answers that needed to be spoken.

She pulled her fingers from his grasp and made her way to the screen in the corner. He stared as she disrobed. What game did she play? Who was seducing whom? Because he realized from talking to the old lady that seduction was the key to his success with Skye MacKinnon. From where he stood, she was doing all the seducing. Her trousers came off, and she slid them over the screen. Next came her red blouse. Now she only stood in a chemise, which did nothing to hide the curves gracing her gorgeous body. His body grew hard all over. Hard and achy. Before he could act upon his seduction, she pulled on a nightgown and walked around the screen. It was a nightgown meant for a nun. What the hell? Did she really think that monstrosity would stop him? It was long, white, and buttoned to her throat and beyond. Could she still breathe in something fastened so high?

As he looked at her closer, he noticed the red blotches on her face. It wasn't the blush of a rose, but from being smothered in heat. Little beads of moisture budded on her temple. Zane laughed to himself. The crazy minx. This would be exciting. He sat in the chair by the fire. He lounged back, crossing his leg over his knee, and settled in to relax. She glared at him and wandered to the window. Skye leaned her head against the pane of the glass and let out a soft sigh. She then alternately pressed her cheeks against the window. Zane rose from the chair and grabbed the robe lying across her bed and made his way over to her. He set it upon her shoulders.

"You looked chilled. You'd better wrap yourself before you catch an illness, my lady."

Skye shook off the robe and pushed the window open. A burst of bitter air leaped into the room. The wind blew the flames out on the candles by the bedside. Soon the room became awash in darkness, the only light coming from the flames dancing in the fire. The orange color danced in shadows against the wall.

"You fool, you know I am burning up in this nightgown."

Zane laughed. "Fool? I am not the fool, madam. You are the only fool in this bedroom. You arc the one who dressed yourself for the nunnery." He fingered the high collar of her nightwear. "Do you think this will stop me from taking what I desire?"

Skye backed up nervously, her legs hitting the back of the chair. She grasped the handles. "I think it would be for the best if you leave my room, Lord Maxwell. It is not proper for you to be in my bedchamber alone. There could be consequences that neither of us want to happen. I don't aspire to be stuck with a stuffy earl as a husband."

Zane laughed. "And you think I want a Scottish hoyden as a wife?"

Skye's spirit deflated at the insult he threw her way. Was she that undesirable? Would no man ever want her?

"Then why do you persist to stay in my bedchamber?"

"I only want a moment of your time. Nobody knows I am in here with you."

"You could be caught."

Zane moved in closer, his fingers trailing along the buttons of her gown. "I won't, my dear. Trust me."

His head lowered as he placed a kiss along her cheek. Skye closed her eyes at his gentle kiss. His kiss slid lower as his fingers worked to undo the buttons along her neck. His warm mouth burned a path against her neck. When his fingers unbuttoned more, uncovering her chest, Skye gathered the cloth between her hands and pulled away from him. His kiss distracted her from what they needed to discuss. The sooner they talked, the sooner he could retire from her room.

Kneeling, she picked up the robe and wrapped it around her body, tying it at her waist. She walked around the room, straightening items that needed no attention, but it distracted her from him.

"What is it you wish to discuss with me, Maxwell?"

Zane brushed his hand through his hair at his frustration with himself. He said one thing but did the opposite where she was concerned. She was correct about him leaving her alone. They could discuss this on the morrow when there were others around to chaperone them. He played with fire kissing her. She was just so darn desirable.

"You are correct. We can discuss this in the morning. Perhaps you can have Isobel join us for tea. I wish to discuss a sensitive matter with you, but as I cannot be trusted to be alone with you, it will be in our best interests to have company. I believe you hold Isobel in the highest esteem, and you trust her to hold my secrets as her own. Am I correct in this assumption?"

Skye nodded. "Yes, Isobel can be trusted not to betray your secrets."

Maxwell bowed. "Then I bid you sweet dreams, my dear. I shall retire myself for the night. Please forgive me for my unwanted advances. I will keep my hands to myself in the future."

Skye listened to his sincere apology and suffered a keen sense of loss. Did she want him to keep his hands to himself? Quite the opposite, in fact. She wanted them touching her body. Should she let him leave, or should she take a chance on him? She realized they had no future, but no man had ever made her burn like him. Just the brush of his fingers at her cheek sent her aflame.

When she didn't reply to him, he turned to exit the room. Before Skye realized what she was doing, she followed him to the door. She moved so quietly he didn't hear her approach. When he reached for the handle, she laid her hand upon his shoulder. Lightly. Just the brush of her fingers. His hand stilled on the knob, his fingers tightening their grip as her hand moved down his back. Her fingers drew the path of fire on him.

Neither one of them spoke as her fingers caressed him. Zane fought his inner demons. As a gentleman, he understood she was an innocent to the ways of men. He should respect her and remove himself from this room at once. But the man inside him who desired her was fighting not to turn around, wrap her in his arms, and show her how their passion could burn.

"Skye?"

She didn't respond to him. Her fingers slid his shirt out from his trousers and touched his back, caressing his skin, light as a feather, teasing him into a hard position. When her fingers circled around to his front and brushed across his stomach, he hung his head against the door, moaning.

"If you don't want me to turn around and carry you to your bed, it will be in your best interest to remove your fingers from my body."

"And what if that is what I wish, Lord Maxwell?"

"Zane."

"What?"

Zane turned around slowly, pulling her to his chest. "My name is Zane. Say it."

"Zane," her husky voice whispered before he took her lips in a kiss built from the promise of her touch on him.

Their kiss erupted in a passion that took their breath away, passion that led him to pull her into his arms and carry her to the bed. As he lay her on the mattress, his lips never left hers. His tongue slid across her lips, guiding them open so he could fuel the fire which burned. She didn't deny him the taste; her tongue met his and dueled. His need for her was stronger than anything he had ever experienced before. He must have her now.

"We don't need this anymore, do we, minx?" he asked. Zane didn't wait for her to reply as he gripped her nightgown by the buttons and ripped it to pieces. Buttons flew across the bed, rolling to the floor and settling where they may.

She blushed as he ripped her gown from her body, but one look at the need in his eyes left her no room for embarrassment. His desire flooded her senses with everything in him. His dark, smoky eyes raked her body, taking in her imperfections. The only thing she saw in his gaze was that she was perfect for him. His hands trailed a blaze after his eyes, and there was no part of her body he did not touch or gaze upon. When his fingers finished touching, his lips burned a trail of fire, heating her to distraction. Skye ached and moaned for more.

She wanted to touch him too and needed his body pressed into hers. Skye slid her hands under his shirt and struggled to remove it from him. When he sensed her struggle, he removed his shirt. She stared as he threw it on the floor and moved his hands to his trousers. He stopped at the buttons, glancing to see if she changed her mind.

Zane paused as he started to undo his pants. He had to take this slower. He should stop now. His cock ruled his brain at this moment. Now was not the time. His life was a chaotic mess, and he didn't need this distraction. But he could no more stop making love to her now than he could quit breathing. When he looked at her lying vulnerable and naked on her bed, it took everything in his power to not plow into her. She deserved better than this, but he was a selfish bastard and would have her this evening. His need was too strong to stop, but if she wanted him to, he would stop.

She watched him pause. Was he changing his mind? Or was he giving her the choice of changing it for him? She didn't want him to halt. Skye rose to her knees and crawled over to him. When she reached his side, she brushed his hands away. She slid the buttons undone and peeled back the placket of his trousers. She saw his need strain against his pants. He wanted her, of that she was positive. Her fingers peeled open his trousers further, lightly brushing against his hardness. She heard him gasp. Skye looked up to see that he held onto his control by a thin thread. She wondered what his reaction would be if she slid her hand inside to make her attempt. Her hand slid in deeper, and he reached lower and clamped her hand in his wrist.

He rubbed the inside of her wrist with his thumb, tightening his hold. He didn't want to scare her with his grip, but he was barely holding onto what control he had. When she attempted to touch him, he almost spent himself right then and there. He needed to move slower; this woman was driving him mad with desire. His touch against her wrist became gentler. Slow, sensuous circles against the rapid beat of her pulse.

He whispered in her ear, "While I would love the touch of your hands on me, we need to take this slower or it will end before we even begin."

She looked up in confusion.

"I am mad with a need for you, my dear. I am barely keeping it together. You may explore another time, but for now, I need control if I am to please you."

"What if I don't want you to have control?"

"I do not want to hurt you, my goddess."

"I do not hurt that easily, my lord."

He growled. "Zane."

She smiled as she lay back on the bed, stretching her body out, her long limbs sprawled out for him to view. Her arm slid up her side, then casually through her hair. Both arms reached above her head as she stretched, raising her breasts higher. Her tight nipples beckoned his lips for a taste. His cock grew harder at the sight of her teasing him with her need.

"Well, Lord Maxwell, are you going to join me or not?" she asked as her eyes moved to his trousers. She raised her eyebrow in a question of their removal.

He growled as he stripped them from his body. He crawled on the bed toward her, grabbing her ankles and pulling her toward him. When he had her where he wanted her, he ran his hand up her legs, lingering on her thighs. His fingers trailed higher, sliding into her curls. Curls as dark as her hair. His fingers stilled near her wetness. She squirmed under his touch, wanting him to caress her, her eyes begging for his touch. Still he waited, making her ache.

"Touch me," she begged.

He waited for her to say his name.

"Now, Maxwell," she demanded.

His thumb lightly brushed her wetness, just enough to tease her of what she could experience. However, her wetness was a tease to his own self-control. While he was holding out from giving her what she desired, he only ended up punishing himself.

She raised her hips, wanting him to touch her. She knew what he wanted, but this game was building their desire to a level that would soon be out of both their control. She didn't want him to have control with her. Skye didn't want him to hold back. She was no china doll or innocent debutante. She was a woman who needed him and what he could give her.

"Please, Lord Maxwell, one little touch."

"Like this?" he asked as his finger slid deep inside her, her wetness coating him. Slowly he pulled out, bringing his fingers back to her thighs.

She moaned at his touch. She wanted more. Skye didn't want him to stop.

"Or like this?" he questioned as he slid two fingers inside her, spreading her tightness to accommodate himself. His fingers slid in and out this time, building a rhythm that sent her higher, making her want him more.

Her thighs spread wider apart for him as she sank into the mattress. Then as quickly as he built up the flames, he pulled his fingers away, digging into her thighs, and waited. Waited for her to give him what he wanted. Her body, needing the release only he could give her, gave in to him.

"Zane," she moaned.

He growled and lowered his head, replacing his fingers with his mouth, stoking a new flame to the fire. Zane's mouth drove the flames as high as they could burn. His tongue slid into her wetness, tasting the sweetness that was only Skye. He noticed her body growing taut in his arms as his mouth explored her. Zane found what made her moan, what made her sigh, what made her beg for more. When she said his name over and over, he devoured her, making her beg for more. Each time she begged, she said his name, which made him hungry for more.

When she exploded underneath him, he caught her. Zane slid up her body keeping up the worship, kissing a trail to her breasts. He gently sucked on her nipples, making them into tight buds between his lips. While he worshiped them, he slid his hand below and kept her fire burning with his fingers. He slid them in and out as he built her passion for him again. As he made his way to her lips, he devoured them.

He undid her, still making her ache for more. More of him, more of his desire. His lips had trailed a blaze of longing against her body. But it wasn't enough; she needed more. His hardness pressed across her stomach.

Lowering her hand, she circled his cock. He was hard as a rod. A hard steel rod that pulsed in her hand. She stroked her hand up the steel, and he pulled back from their kiss and gasped at her touch. He lowered his head to hers, breathing deeply as she stroked him faster.

"You need to slow down, MacKinnon."

"Skye."

He didn't answer her, his breathing becoming erratic as her strokes became faster. Her warm palm slid up and down on his hard cock. When she wrapped her hand around him and gently squeezed, he grew harder at her touch. Her thumb rubbed across the tip, softly stroking him into a flame.

"Mac," he moaned.

"Skye," she whispered.

He gripped her thighs wider apart, pulling his cock out of her hand. Zane grabbed her hips and slid himself inside her quickly. His mind left his body at her touch, and he only reacted from his senses and the need to fill her with himself. When he entered her and pushed past her barrier, he halted. His rush to be inside her prevented him from taking her tenderly. She was pure heaven to his pure hell. He paused, waiting for her to stop him.

She gasped as he invaded her wetness. It stung as he settled himself inside her deeper. He stilled as he waited for her body to accept him. As he filled her, her body responded by wrapping herself tighter around him. She wrapped her legs around his waist as she raised her hips to him. Skye wanted him inside her deeper, so she pressed herself against him.

He answered with a growl and pressed in deeper. When that still wasn't enough for her, she sank her fingers into the curve of his buttocks and pulled him closer. His hardness slid deeper into her wetness, filling her ache with a driving need for more.

"Skye," he moaned.

Skye smiled her satisfaction from hearing her name moaned from his lips. She slid her lips along his neck, taking soft love bites along the way, tasting the essence of Zane. She understood his need to protect her from himself, and he was fighting a battle on causing her pain. But she only experienced the pleasure of him now, pleasure she wanted more of. So, she pressed her hips against his, begging for more.

She was driving him mad. He tried to hold back, but his need for her was too strong. Slowly sliding out of her, he hovered at her entrance, and he heard her moan of displeasure. He slid inside her fast and hard, sinking into her wetness. It felt so damn good. His body only wanted more.

She tightened around him in response. His body was hungry for everything she would give. He couldn't hold on, and she pulled him in deeper. His body had a mind of its own. He slaved his hunger for her with long hard strokes. And her body answered, receiving him with an openness that was only Skye.

He pulled her to him and kissed her deeply as their bodies flew over the edge, each of them lost in the feelings of their kisses consumed each other, each hungry for more. Zane pulled Skye closer to him as his lips continued to devour her after their bodies sank into the bed together.

He still hungered for her. His body ached as if he had never made love to her. He knew he had to pull back, but damn if she wasn't so delicious tasting. Zane pulled back, rolling on his back, and brought her across his chest. Her hair fanned out everywhere, and he slid his fingers through the long strands, spreading the tresses across their bodies.

He could feel her racing heart slow down against his. Her soft breath blew across his chest. They didn't speak in fear of breaking the fragile spell wrapped around them. He felt content. There wasn't any place he would rather be. They didn't need empty words, so they welcomed the silence. How he needed to proceed was beyond him. How did one leave a bedroom of a miss? She was unlike his usual conquests, and this was definitely not his usual scene. How did one escape a maiden's room while one was held prisoner by said maiden? Did he even want to leave?

Her fingers curled upon his chest as her body relaxed in sleep. He brushed the hair from her face and gazed upon her as she slept against him, her face relaxing as if she had no troubles. She held too many problems upon her small shoulders. When she awoke, they would discuss why he came to her room. As he shut his eyes, he wrapped his hand around her small fist and threaded his fingers with hers, drifting off to sleep.

Chapter Six

AS HE STRODE AROUND her bedchamber, he located his clothing and dressed in a rush. The day was breaking, and he awoke in her empty bed. The last place he needed to be discovered was in her bedchamber. While he was sliding on his trousers and buttoning his shirt, he overheard her in the courtyard. He went to the open window and observed her arguing with Gregor, her second in command. She shook her head at the man, jumped on her horse, and took off for the unknown. Gregor called after her, then rushed into the stables. Within a few minutes, he watched as the guard followed in her wake.

She was running from him again, but this time he would catch her. They would have their discussion this morning. Zane decided to give her space, then follow along shortly. He strolled to the door and opened it a crack. When he noticed the hallway empty, he swiftly left the room and returned to his bedchamber.

He splashed cold water on his face at the wash bin in the corner. When he glanced over at the bed, he noticed it was in disarray. Somebody had entered his room to make it appear as if he'd spent the night there. She worked to great lengths to deny the previous evening. He rolled his eyes as he changed his clothes. Isobel was kind by lending him her husband's clothing. After he changed, he wanted to eat breakfast. He worked up an appetite and perceived he would need all the strength he could get if he was to deal with Skye MacKinnon today.

The hall was empty this early in the morning; he wandered into the kitchens to sweet-talk the cook into putting together a light snack for a ride. Then he continued to the stables to saddle a horse. He then set off toward Skye. He saw the hoofprints in the dew, which led him to her. Gregor waited in the distance, and when he saw him approach, he nodded his head and returned to the castle. While Maxwell may have been their prisoner, he garnered the respect of her clan over the last few days.

Skye was unaware he rode into the clearing. She on the bank of a creek, throwing pebbles out into the water, lost in thought. It appeared she left as quick as she could this morning. She threw on her usual attire—trousers and a cotton shirt that must have hung past her knees, for she had tied the material off to her side. What he wouldn't do to see her in a ball gown, decked out in jewels, with her hair swept on top of her head, curls hanging loose. A green ball gown that would hug her curves and float around her legs. Dark green that brought out the spark in her eyes and set her hair aflame. That would be the first thing he bought her when he escorted her to London.

Zane stopped in his tracks. He shook his head to clear out his thoughts. What was he thinking? He wasn't bringing her to London. Was he? He'd walked himself into a fine mess this time.

He strolled to her side and sat next to her. Zane continued to watch her. The breeze coming off the stream blew her hair around her face. She reached up to gather her hair back, twisting it around her hand. She turned to stare at him, waiting as if she expected him to speak. When he didn't, she sighed and turned back to throwing pebbles.

What did she expect him to say? Was he to offer her marriage for taking her maidenhood? Doubtful. From her expression, all he could expect was a refusal. So, sat there they did, each lost in their own thoughts. Each one questioning what they allowed to happen the night before. Both wondering where to go from here. This complicated everything.

"I guess this is the part where I need to offer you my hand in marriage," Zane offered with no enthusiasm.

"Oh, do not sound so sincere with your offer. You make a girl's heart go all aflutter," Skye responded with sarcasm.

"Ah hell," Zane growled as he rose and paced to the stream. He stood on unknown ground with this woman. She didn't follow the rules the other women in his life followed, but then, he'd never met another lady like her before. The others were all simpering fools who stroked his ego to earn a spot in his bed. This woman would never stroke his ego, nor did she care if she had a spot. Oh, they had made love the previous evening, but from where he stood, he didn't think it affected her the way it affected him. He would have to take a different approach with her.

As he watched her, he only imagined her stretched out on her back among the heather, making love to her in the open glen. He sensed if he tried, her men would surround him to run their swords through him. He needed to focus on getting himself free from the bonds keeping him in this godforsaken place.

Did he think I expected an offer of marriage, to him of all men? He was a traitor to his friends and country. Why she felt a strong attraction to him was beyond her. He was the last gentleman she wanted to be tied to. She learned everything about him from her connections in London. He was the ultimate ladies' man who seduced a different woman into his bed each evening. While his taste usually ran to the widows of the ton, there was the occasional bride who wanted to cuckold her husband, but he never touched the innocent debutantes. Their mamas always chased him, but he always ran the opposite way. He avoided the marriage trap like the plague. Why would she want to shackle herself to a man opposed to the marriage union? She never expected to marry anyway. If she did, she wanted the same union she witnessed between Logan and Isobel. She wanted their kind of love. And Earl Zane Maxwell was incapable of love, at least with her anyway. She recognized his love for another woman, even though that woman passed him over for his friend. Well she wouldn't tie herself to a man who held unrequited love for another.

"Take it easy, Maxwell. Last night was nice, but not nice enough to marry over."

Nice? What they shared was nice? It was earth shattering for him. Did she not experience what he felt? He watched her as she spoke those meaningless words. She wouldn't meet his eyes. She lied. What she felt was more than nice, and he would prove it to her.

"The offer is on the table nonetheless."

"Well, you may remove it. It will not be necessary. I have no wish to marry, and from where you stand, it's not an offer you should make to any lady."

"And why not?"

"Because you shall be returned to Shears soon. And the only thing he is planning is your death."

"I thought we agreed to work together."

"That was before."

"Before what?"

"Before I received a message this morning."

"What message would that be?"

"It is of no concern of yours."

"If it pertains to me, then it is most definitely my concern."

"You are not to be trusted, my lord."

Skye walked over to the creek's edge, bent over, and ran her fingers through the stream. The water cleaned off the dust from the pebbles. She rose to make her way back to her horse. She was finished here.

Before she realized what happened, Zane pulled her arm, swinging her around to him. He was frustrated with her cryptic comments coming the morning after they'd spent the night in each other's arms. He wanted to prove her wrong on everything, from their lovemaking being just nice to not being able to trust him. He had laid himself bare to her, and this was how he was treated in return. He felt like a jilted lover.

Before he realized what he was doing, he crushed his lips upon hers. The kiss took them both unaware. He slid his fingers into her long red hair that blew between them, bringing her head in closer to his. His lips devoured her. She tried to fight him, but when he slid his tongue in her mouth, stroking hers, she melted into him. Their passion built as his kiss grew stronger at her response. She kissed him back, wrapping her hands behind his neck and bringing him tighter against her. Before the kiss became uncontrollable, he dragged his lips from hers. His body instantly became disappointed. From the moan that passed between her lips, she felt the same.

"Nice, huh?" he whispered before pulling away. He unwrapped her arms from his neck and stepped back.

She growled and stomped over to her horse. But he only pulled her around again and held her prisoner with his hands on her arms, keeping her in one spot.

"No. You aren't running from me again. We will discuss my imprisonment right here, right now."

She raised her eyebrow at him again. Where did he get off, giving her demands? He was her damn prisoner. A demanding one at that. He caught her unaware with his kiss. Oh, why did his kisses have to be so earth-shattering? The touch of his lips upon her made her mind go blank with nothing but longing. She longed for his arms to wrap around her and hold her close. She longed for his lips to create their magic upon her body. She might as well as admit her desire to him and let it run its course. Because it would surely die out, she realized. She couldn't hold the interest of this man for very long.

"Well, maybe a little more than nice. I didn't know you needed your ego stroked, Maxwell. Are you feeling insecure?" She laughed.

"Woman, you are the most exasperating lady I have ever known."

"And from what I understand, you have known many."

"How do you seem to have so much knowledge about me and yet I have never heard of you?"

"I must be better at my profession than you."

"And what profession would that be?"

"Another piece of information not for your knowledge."

He tightened his hold on her arms, frustrated at her cryptic comments. How did she gather so much intelligence on him? Who did she ultimately work for? The information she held on him was what he had built for years as his cover. His friends knew he wasn't who he portrayed himself to be, but he didn't want her to think that was who he was. She only had information on the man he wasn't. He had to convince her of who he really was.

She winced as his grip tightened. Skye saw his mind working behind his dark eyes as they held hers captive. He wondered who she was and how she knew about him. She recognized he was the ultimate traitor. One who was now her prisoner. She would hand him over to the Crown when they returned to Edinburgh. He assumed she would return him to Shears, but the plan was already in action to bring him and Shears to trial.

She didn't care what happened after that because if the plan worked, Logan would return home. Then she could return to her life. A life where she knew the path she wished to take, and it didn't involve the dangers of espionage, treason, life, and death.

He loosened his grip on her and rubbed his hands up and down her arms to comfort the pain he might have caused. She made him so frustrated, and his emotions spun out of control. He needed to reason with her.

"Can we start again? I apologize for my rude manners where you are concerned. I have followed you here so we can discuss what you perceive to be my treason. I'd like you to listen to my side of the story and have all the information before you make your decision about me. After we return to the castle, I can write my letter to Thornhill and Mallory, if you agree."

"That seems fair enough. If I am not convinced of your story, then there won't be a letter to write. You keep forgetting who the prisoner is here."

"Well since you remind me at every opportunity, it makes a man hard-pressed to forget," he replied with sarcasm.

Skye shook herself from his touch and sat upon the rock propped against the shade tree. She picked at the heather surrounding her to give her hands something to do, otherwise she would throw herself in his arms. While she wasn't frightened from his grip earlier, it did give her doubt about his character. While the evidence she had portrayed him as a villain, his desperation to tell her his story left her confused. Thrown together with his kisses, and her mind was in a muddle.

"Well, let's hear this tall tale so I can get to my other duties. I have been away long enough."

"Can we please start anew?"

"I am confused on what you are asking."

"Can we both dispense with the innuendos and sarcasm? I wish to speak to you as a gentleman to a lady who I would lay my trust with. It will be hard for me to speak if you continue with this manner."

Skye laid her palms out to him in a show of peace, not trusting herself to speak. He did that to her, put her on the defense. She would listen to the lies he'd concoct. Then she would lead him to believe they were fighting for the same side. She only needed to pacify him until they returned him to his rightful place. After that, she didn't care what became of him. It would be out of her hands, therefore out of her control.

"I am not the villain I am portraying myself to be. It is a cover to trick the wrong people into accepting that I am one of them. That I'm after the same goal they are."

"And that would be?"

"To bring treason to British soil. That I am in cahoots with Shears and the men in high positions in the English aristocracy who want to destroy what we hold dear."

"So how have you been able to accomplish this deceit?"

"I portray to the ton that I am in a dangerous allegiance that can make their dreams come true. I seduce the ladies into betraying their husbands. Then I befriend these gentlemen and make the connections with Shears. All the while I am gathering intelligence for the Crown."

"Well I have heard about the seduction."

"Do not trust everything you hear, Skye. There is more than one way to seduce these women besides bedding them."

She raised her damn eyebrow in disbelief at his statement.

"These ladies only wanted attention they were not receiving from their husbands. A few spins around the ballroom floors, private walks in the gardens, secret meetings in alcoves at parties. While I admit I have tasted many favors from these ladies, not all have been sexual."

"So why even bother with them?"

"Because these ladies are furious at their husbands—for mistresses, gambling, but most of all for not paying them any attention. This was their way to enact their revenge. So, they would tell me of private meetings and of overheard conversations. And in return, I made them feel special; that was all they longed for."

"Why even seduce them?"

"They gave me the connections with their spouses. They would invite me to dinner parties and balls only meant for people in their private society. It allowed me to discover enough intelligence to bring my mission to an end."

"Do you have enough information?"

"I did until Shears caught me. Everything went wrong at the Pennington Ball. Our plan was to bring Shears and his connections to the Crown for justice."

"What happened?"

"Shears kidnapped two ladies and were holding them hostage. He wanted to blow up the ball and everybody in attendance, but we discovered the dynamite on the balcony. We cleared the guests before Shears caused any more deaths. He managed to grab the ladies and hold them captive in the garden."

"Who were these two ladies?"

"Ivy Thornhill and Raina LeClair."

Zane watched her reaction at the mention of these two women's names. Two ladies who should mean nothing to her, yet she appeared hurt when he mentioned Ivy's name. It was as if she knew what Ivy meant to him, which was nonsense because they were nothing but close friends.

"Who were these women to you?"

"They are the women my two best friends love."

"And you? Do you love one of these ladies too?"

Zane didn't answer her. It was a loaded question he would have a tough time explaining. He decided his silence was enough of an answer for her. It was a question that he understood now. Ivy and he were close before Thorn returned. He even believed he could pledge his love and loyalty to her, to stop her from the pain of missing and loving Thorn. But all they ever would be were friends. She was a friend he grew to love but had never fully explored what level of love he held for her. There were never any sparks, only friendship. Friendship he destroyed by his secrets. Hopefully one day he could earn back her trust, but for now, he must live with his consequences.

Skye took his silence to mean only one thing—that he still loved her. Even though he lost her to one of his friends, the lady still carried a special place in his heart. She wanted to have a man love her the way he held love for Ivy Thornhill, even if it was an unrequited love.

"So, what happened?"

"I tried to convince Shears to let the ladies go and that I would take their place."

"Was that how you became his captive?"

Zane laughed. "Not entirely. He wouldn't let the women go. He wanted Ivy Thornhill for his own pleasures, and he wanted to destroy Raina LeClair."

"Why?"

"Raina thwarted him at turns. She destroyed countless numbers of Shears's shipments and hideouts over the last year. He wanted her dead and to make it as painful as possible."

"Would he really cause harm to a lady?"

"Shears will treat a lady who crosses him no different from a gentleman who does the same."

"What would he do to her?"

"Beat her, let his men rape her, break her mentally to where she begged for her death, and then start all over again. He wouldn't be the one to kill her; he would drive her to the edge of taking her own life."

Skye shuddered at the thought. She realized she was playing a dangerous game with Shears. After listening to Zane's story, she understood what the consequences could be when Shears realized she'd duped him. She would have to make sure her plan was solid when she arrived in Edinburgh, and she would bring in reinforcements. It was time to trade in her markers and Logan's too.

"Were you able to free them?"

"Raina caused a distraction, which made Shears release Ivy. Soon Mallory and I battled with Shears. When we had him defeated, I convinced Mallory and Thornhill to leave with their ladies. I stabbed Shears and stood back to watch him die. His men outnumbered me and captured me as they made their escape. They took me to his ship, chained me, and set sail. I must have injured him badly enough because I didn't see him again until you boarded the ship."

"Why did he sail to Edinburgh?"

"It was the only location he could flee to until he could regroup. Every one of his connections was uncovered and taken into custody in London. In France, men who are more dangerous than he is want him for not paying for weapons they provided for the cause. So, he couldn't return there. He hoped to find supporters for his cause in Scotland. He assumed he could find followers who wanted revenge against the English. Also, he was injured and out of supplies. He couldn't travel far."

"He will find no supporters here. We don't take kindly to strangers, and many won't conspire against the Crown. We have lost too much and have little left to lose."

"But he found a supporter. Did he not?"

"If you are referring to me, he is nothing but a pawn."

"Skye, you cannot align yourself with him."

"Why not? Don't stick your nose into something that doesn't concern you."

"How does it not concern me? I am your prisoner, only to be exchanged for weapons."

"What was your mission Maxwell? Why are you betraying your country for this man?"

"I have told only one other person the truth in what I seek. I want to trust you with the same information."

"Who?"

"Who I told does not pertain to you." He threw her comment back at her to hide his own secrets.

"Was it Ivy Thornhill? Is she the one who keeps the secrets you hold dear?"

How did she guess who he told? Was he that transparent? He nodded. If he was not mistaken, he saw jealousy flash across her eyes. Why was she jealous of Ivy? Unless Skye denied what she felt for him.

"Out with your secrets, Maxwell. You are dragging this story on longer than it needs to be. Get to the point so we may proceed."

Maxwell sighed at her impatience but realized she was correct. He was trying to convince her of his innocence. He wanted her trust more than anything else.

"I am searching for the King's missing heir. He had an illegitimate child a few years ago. The nurse traded the baby and the jewels meant for the child when the baby grew. The child carries a red ruby marked with the King's special stamp. The child's whereabouts came to our attention through our connection with Shears. He holds the answer to the child and the missing red rubies."

Zane pulled the red ruby from his pocket and held the jewel toward Skye. She grabbed the stone from his hand and held it in her palm. It shone brightly against her pale skin. Her fingers lightly traced the smoothness, turning it over she traced the mark of the Crown. When she looked toward him, she now understood what weighed on his shoulders. The King who doesn't want war on his lands would want to know the whereabouts of his sire. Illegitimate or not, he only wanted safety and security for the child. But understanding his struggles only made her fear for Logan increase. For this was the same stone Logan left with in his search. Logan returned the stone to the Crown and was ordered to find the missing heir. How did Maxwell acquire the jewel? For her to ask him, she would have to offer him her full trust. Something she wasn't ready for—yet.

"So, you have betrayed all for the King and Crown?"

"That is what my mission is about. It doesn't matter what anybody thinks of me. The only thing that matters is returning the child to the King."

"Do you know where the child is?"

"No, but Shears does. He holds the key to this mystery. I finally earned his trust, and he was taking me to the child. Then I betrayed him. Now he only seeks my death. You can change that for me."

"How did you betray him?"

"He ordered me to kill Raina LeClair. Charles Mallory too, if I had the chance."

"But you didn't."

"No, but we made it appear as if I did. Then while at the Pennington Ball, he saw for himself they still lived and sought his revenge."

"How can I change any of this mess for you?"

"We can join forces with a plan to capture Shears and find the missing child."

"The only way I shall handle Shears will be on my own terms."

"Why do you want to bring destruction to yourself and your clan?"

"You have no clue on what I plan with those weapons?"

"I know whoever Shears provides arms to means to destroy England."

Skye stayed silent. While she understood his cover for the Crown, it didn't mean she trusted him with her plans. While she might feel this attraction toward him, she still thought he held something back. There was more to his double agent agenda than what he was telling her. He still held onto his secrets tightly. Therefore, she would hold on to her secrets as well.

He didn't know what thoughts went through her head. If she insisted on this act of destruction, then he would make sure she didn't succeed. He knew she was thinking with her heart and not her head. He concluded that her behavior was spurred to actions by the return of her brother. Shears was the key to that. He held people as his weapons to achieve his goals. Zane planned to destroy Shears if it was the last thing he did. He would back off and let her believe he supported her decisions, but he would make sure she was protected.

"It appears we are at an impasse. May I write my letter?"

"You may. And if I approve of what you write, you may send it. I can have Ewan ride for London tonight."

Zane bowed to Skye, "Thank you Skye. May I accompany you on the ride back?"

"Like I would leave my prisoner out alone on unguarded land." Skye allowed the lie to slip from her mouth and tried to look guilty. A test to see if he would try to make an escape.

Zane heard the slip. He helped her onto her horse, and they set back to the stables. As he rode, his eyes took in the landscape. He associated the landmarks in his head if he needed to make an escape. He understood there were only a small number of folks on her land. There weren't enough men to guard every direction he could leave by. He hoped he didn't have to betray her trust and leave on his own. If he couldn't convince her to work together in the next few days, there would be no other choice.

Chapter Seven

WHEN THEY ARRIVED BACK at the castle, she left him to give instructions to her men. Zane strolled inside to ask Isobel for writing material. He needed to think of how to word his letter. He would have to rely on their special code they contrived when they were young boys at Eton. They were the only ones who could help him with the mess he'd created. He wanted them to answer the call of brotherhood. Zane hoped that while he betrayed their trust, he didn't lose the remainder of their friendship.

He sat at the table, pondering the words to write when she came into the room. Her clan surrounded her with questions. She smiled at those in her care and answered their questions with patience. Then she joined Lachlan near the fire to play. She lay on the rug on her belly and propped her hands under her chin. Skye looked young and carefree as she talked animatedly with the young lad. She played with the toy soldiers with enthusiasm. He wished she would bestow the love on him she shared with the other souls. *Whoa. Where did those thoughts come from?* What he felt for her was lust. Plain and simple. There was no chance for love in his lifetime. Ever. He looked away from her as he concentrated on the letter he needed to write, a letter he hoped would save his life and hers. Because whether she believed it or not, she was walking into a trap. A trap set up by her own stubborn plans. Well, he would be her savior without her knowledge.

Skye observed him out of the corner of her eye. She sensed his eyes on her. Why was he staring at her and not writing his damn letter? Did he think the letter could save him? For being a spy, he wasn't particularly bright. Did he believe she would send the letter? Oh, she would make him believe his letter was sent. Instead, she would send Ewan to guard the clearing she Maxwell believe was unwatched. Then she would destroy the letter the first chance she got.

She noticed he began to write. He took his time putting his words to paper. Probably writing in a special code only they understood. Well, he could write in code all he wanted, for it would never land in their grasp. She was going to throw the letter in the fireplace. Her eyes followed his hand gliding across the paper with each stroke of the quill. Skye's thoughts turned to the evening before. How his hand glided over her flesh, stroking her body into flames. She felt her face growing warmer.

"Why are ye turning red, Auntie Skye?"

Skye was embarrassed to be caught fantasizing about the enemy while playing alongside her nephew. Her eyes met his, and she saw the smirk of a smile on Maxwell's face as he caught her gazing at him. He knew her thoughts. He knew what she desired. Maxwell bent his head, laughing to himself as he continued writing. The smug, irritating man.

"I must be hot from the fire, love," Skye answered.

"But the fire is out," Lachlan continued, adding to her embarrassment.

Skye stuttered out another response out when the infuriating man at the table let out a huge bellow of laughter at her discomfort. After turning redder, she stood and told Lachlan she needed to meet with Gregor and left the hall.

"She wull not take kindly to ye laughing at her," Isobel rebuked him.

Zane wiped his eyes from his laughter. "You must admit the lad's words were priceless."

"Aye, but she is unused to these emotions 'n' doesn't understand how to handle how ye make her feel. Yer laughter only embarrassed her."

"I will apologize to her."

"See that ye do. Now, how is your missive coming along?"

"You mean the letter she will destroy and not send?"

Isobel glanced at him with surprise, and then with respect. "So ye know?"

"Yes. I would do the same myself."

"So, ye are writing two letters then? One for her to destroy, and another to make it to yer friends?"

Zane smiled at Isobel. "You will betray her to help me?"

"I will betray her to save her and to bring Logan home. So, hurry and write; she won't stay gone for long."

Zane worked on his letters. He wrote the one that would make it to Thorn and Mallory first, so Isobel could take it before Skye returned to the hall. He finished and addressed it to Thornhill, slipping the letter under the table to Isobel as Skye entered the room. She slid across the table from them and looked at the letter he was writing. She watched as he continued to finish it. When he completed the missive, he started to slide it into an envelope, when she reached out to read it. After her satisfaction with what he wrote, she passed it back for him to write where to send the note. She took the letter and rose from the table, turning to leave. He grasped her wrist and halted her.

"I apologize madam for laughing at you earlier."

"I appear to be the object of your humor on a regular basis."

He rubbed the inside of her wrist in small circles. "You're an object of more than my humor, my lady."

She tried pulling her wrist free, but he only continued his caress.

"I am not a lady, nor do I want to be an object of anything concerning you."

"Don't you?" he questioned her.

"No," she denied.

"Your body tells me differently, my dear. Your pulse beats faster under my touch. The color of your eyes grows darker with desire. Do you need for me to continue with my observations?"

He was correct on everything. Her whole body throbbed from his touch. She knew her eyes deceived her; they always did. She was too transparent with her emotions. It remained her greatest downfall. Her mind didn't want to desire him, but her body did. His fingers drifted along her arm, making her hotter. To be alone with him was her greatest desire. She wanted the touch of his lips on hers again.

"Now can you send my letter out for me tonight?"

She was such a fool. He played on her attraction to distract her, and she'd fallen for it. She grabbed the letter from his hand and left to find Gregor. She whispered her instructions to the guard, and he looked up to glare at Maxwell as he left to do her bidding. Oh, they were fooling nobody. He knew where the letter would go. In the fire pit, most likely. But he had an ally in Isobel. She appeared to be the only sensible person in this clan.

He continued to sit and dine at the table where he wrote his letter. There was nothing to do but wait. Wait for when they returned to Edinburgh. In the meantime, he would learn everything he needed to know about Skye MacKinnon by watching her. It was the only way to understand your nemesis. Only she wasn't his nemesis. She was a lady in over her head, and Maxwell decided he would be her rescuer. She didn't realize she needed rescued yet, but she would.

~~~~~

Skye went to bed alone. She tried to relax in her bed, thinking of the last week and the changes that had occurred in her life. Her emotions lay scattered around her in piles. She needed to pull herself together and decide on a plan. The man down the hall from her wreaked havoc on her. She had two options. She could give into these emotions and spend time with him to remove him from her mind. Or she could avoid him until she returned him to Shears. She wanted to avoid him, but she had realized over the last few days that she couldn't. Oh, she could keep herself busy, but he always remained in her thoughts. So, the only choice she had was to pass the time with him and rid herself of her desires.

She threw the covers off and strayed to the window to gaze at the stars dancing alongside the moon. Only they weren't dancing tonight. They were as still as her, deciding if the dance was worth it. To spend time in his company would be her most logical choice. This way she could keep an eye on him and make sure he didn't escape. If she left him to his own devices, he might plan a getaway. Yes, the best thing to do was to stay near him. When she looked to the stars again, she saw one wiggle closer to the moon like it was drawn to the mystery.

As she made her way along the hallway, she realized she was that star and he was the moon. He drew her to him. She opened his door to find him asleep on the bed. The covers were kicked away from his body. He slept naked, bare on the sheets for her to desire. His black hair was mussed, and the dark whiskers on his face only made him appear more dangerous. Dangerous to her and all who gazed upon him. He continued to sleep, unaware that she watched him. She slid the door closed and moved to the bed. Skye slid off her nightgown, standing naked in the moonlight gliding in through the window. Still no movement from the bed. She stood silently as she stared at his form. The bruises were fading from his body. Throughout his captivity, his body stayed hard and lean. She wanted to run her fingers across the muscles on his chest and lower. Where her eyes devoured, she wanted her fingers to follow. Where her fingers followed, she wanted her lips to savor.

She didn't notice when he rolled over and gazed at her. When she did notice his eyes upon her, she waited for a smart quip to pass from his lips, but he surprised her. He held out his hand for her to join him on the bed. She slid her palm inside his. He gently tugged her to him, pulling her alongside him on the mattress. No words needed to be spoken. Their bodies understood what their minds did not. He placed a gentle kiss on the edge of her lips. She sighed. His lips placed light kisses along her jaw, making their way to her neck. Her neck arched for his lips to have better access. He made his way along her neck down to her chest.

"Oh, Skye," he whispered as he took her breasts into his hands. Skye watched him as his fingers played upon them. His long fingers brushing across her nipples, making them tighten into firm buds. It was when he placed his lips upon them that she shivered from the desire coursing through her body. He slid his tongue in circles around the tight buds, bringing them between his lips to suck lightly.

Skye arched her breasts into his mouth, running her fingers through his hair. She tugged his head tighter as her body arched into him, wanting him to ease the ache consuming her. He seemed to realize what she needed as his hands found her wetness. When his finger slid inside her, she let out a moan as her body opened for him. Her grip on him tightened as he sucked her harder, his finger gliding in and out of her, building her climax to the heights she desired—only to pull back as he sensed her near the edge. She moaned her displeasure.

He rose and kissed her lips. Drinking the sweetness, she showed him her desire. Their kiss became more passionate, building to a higher climax—only for Zane to pull back again. His fingers trailed over her body, touching, tempting as he saw her need for him build in her eyes. He wanted more from her. She arched and moaned to his touch, and yet it still wasn't enough for him. He wanted more. He needed more. When he saw her draw her lips between her teeth and moan as he slid his fingers inside her, he was done for. It made him harder for her. He wanted to ease the ache, realizing this was much more than passion they were playing with tonight. This was about trust. When she arched her body to his touch, he growled and bent over, lighting her body alive with kisses. Zane trailed a path down to his fingers. He wanted to taste her. He needed to taste her.

His mouth replaced his fingers at her wetness. He felt her body shudder under his kiss. His tongue stroked her core, tasting all that was Skye. Wanting more, he slid his tongue inside her. When she dug her heels in the bed and rose her core to his mouth, he devoured her. His tongue glided in and out, drawing out her wetness to his lips. It wasn't enough; he craved more. His fingers found her clit and stroked faster as his tongue drove her to new heights in pleasure. He brought her to the climax her body begged to release under his attention.

He savored her release as her body melted into his kiss. When she sank back onto the mattress, he slid his way up her body. His kisses kept her melting under his touch. He arrived at her lips to sink into them, lost in their passion. While she exploded under his lips, she left him shaken to the core. Her passion for him made him lose himself in her. His kisses were soft and sweet, drawing her soul into him. He drank from her lips in long, slow, mind-drugging kisses, thirsty for more. She fulfilled his quench of thirst for her with her lips drinking from his. Her little whimpers begged for more.

He entered her slowly. She gasped between his lips and then sighed as her body molded around him. He gently slid in and out of her, drawing their passions higher. Each moment slower than the last as their emotions surrounded each other. Where one of them started, and the other ended, and neither of them knew or cared. He slid in deep inside her and pulled back from their kiss. He waited. Waited for her. He pressed in tighter as her center clenched around him. Still, he waited. He gave her the control.

Her fingers tightened around his hips. He was torturing her. She needed him to slide deeper, but he wouldn't move. She could see the amount of control it took for him to wait. Skye arched into him, and he moaned but still didn't move.

She wrapped her legs around his hips and arched her body into his. He moaned and grabbed her legs, rolling them. She rose above him, and he lay there, waiting for her.

She lowered herself and drew his lips between her own and kissed him deeply as her body moved against him. Her tongue slid across his lips as she rotated her body in small circles. She felt him harden inside her, pulsing from his need. Need he gave her control over. Skye understood what he was giving up for her, and it empowered her. She set the rhythm of their bodies. Long slow strokes that built their passion higher. Skye sensed her body exploding around them as she sank around him. Zane let out a growl as their bodies became one.

He pulled her to him for a soul-searching kiss as their bodies joined and melted together. He drew back, breathing heavily. Zane guided her to his chest and held her as their passion subsided. He didn't understand why she came to him this evening, and he didn't care. The only thing that mattered was the barrier she let down between them. He felt the trust build from their lovemaking. He only hoped he wasn't wrong for allowing her past his own barriers.

Skye glanced outside to witness the stars dancing around the moon. They twinkled down around them. When she gazed into Zane's eyes, she realized it wasn't only the stars twinkling but his eyes too. Like the stars had succumbed to the moon, she succumbed to the mystery of Zane Maxwell.

Chapter Eight

FOR TWO WEEKS SKYE watched Maxwell work his charms among her clan. He worked alongside the men during the days. While they were weary and on guard around him, she noted the respect growing in their eyes. The women were swept away by him. There wasn't a woman young or old he didn't charm. He helped them with small chores, always smiling at them and treating them as if they were grand ladies.

But they were not the only ones charmed by him. She was too, against her resistance. Each night they came together to explore the passion that continued to build every day. She would fight against it, but when the moon rose and the stars begged to dance, she found herself in his arms. Her mind was consumed by him. While she should make sure everything was going as smooth as planned, she found herself making googly eyes at him and daydreaming of when they could be together again.

Maxwell didn't even discuss his return to Shears. He acted as if he trusted her to do the right thing. Would she? She still had no clue. Her emotions only grew stronger the more time she spent with him. She thought their desire would wane by now. Skye needed to focus; she had to quit mooning over him and work on bringing Logan home. Her brother needed to be her main agenda.

She caught his eye from across the room as he was helping Aggie to the table for dinner. He paused in helping the woman into a chair, smiling at Skye with his undeniable charm. Zane winked at her as he spoke to the healer without taking his eyes away from her. After he had the old woman settled, he made his way toward her.

This has to stop. One glance from him and I want to throw myself at him. Then have him kiss me in front of the entire clan. As he advanced toward her, Skye rose from the table and turned to make her way outside. She had to put distance between them; she was becoming too attached.

Zane saw the longing in Skye's eyes from across the hall. He knew she felt as strongly for him as he did her. She uttered no words to tell him of her emotions during the time they spent together. However, Zane knew what she felt by the expression in her eyes and the touch of her hands. When he caught her regarding him from afar, he sensed it before he glanced her way. Her eyes held the look of passion and longing. As he strolled over to her, he saw her eyes shutter. When he almost reached her, she turned and walked away. Zane recognized her look and action well. How many times had he done the same action to a lady to distance himself from the fluffy thoughts they wanted to share with him? Was he as obvious with her?

He followed her from a distance, giving her the space she needed. He couldn't leave her alone. He was hungry just to spend time in her company. He would take anything she would offer to him. How pathetic had he become?

She wandered to the stables, dismissing the grooms to eat dinner. He trailed quietly behind her as she made her way to her horse and began brushing Lady's long mane. He eavesdropped on her whispering tenderly to the animal. Her hands brushed the horse with long, slow strokes. Maxwell's heart twisted with jealousy at the attention she paid to a damn animal and not to him.

Maxwell leaned his arms over the stall. He noticed her body tensed at his nearness. Neither of them spoke. Maxwell opened the stall door and entered behind her. He settled his hand over hers as she brushed the horse. Their long strokes comforted the animal. He brought her body up tight against his, molding her backside to him. Her buttocks settled into his hardened cock. He slid his lips to her neck, brushing soft kisses along the length of her exposed skin. He listened to her moan as her body melted into his; she didn't even try to fight the attraction.

Zane removed his hands from the brush and slid them up inside her shirt. He cupped her breasts as he continued the assault on her senses. His fingers found her tight nipples and squeezed them gently. He heard the brush hit the ground and the snicker of the horse at the invasion in her home.

He turned Skye in his arms to devour her lips. Zane drank from her lips like a man starved for her taste alone. Lifting her in his arms, he wrapped her legs around his hips and backed her against the wall of the stall. Their kiss turning hungrily into the passion pouring from their souls.

They were so caught up in each other that they didn't hear the throat clearing behind them. Although, they did hear the stall door swinging open. Skye immediately dropped her legs from around Maxwell's waist, straightening her shirt. Maxwell pulled Skye behind him, blocking her from prying eyes. Gregor stood at the stall door with the rage of thunder upon his face. His face was beet red, with veins popping out of his neck. His fingers rolled into tight fists, ready to pull Maxwell from the stall to pound him to a bloody pulp.

Maxwell gulped and realized he crossed a line where Skye was concerned. He wouldn't blame the guard for taking out his anger on him. He let his desire and need for Skye overrule his rational thinking. When he looked behind his shoulder, he noticed Skye had pulled her clothes back into place. Maxwell held up his hands as he stepped away from her, showing the bodyguard she was fine.

"Ye wull mak' right by th' lass Maxwell," Gregor growled.

"Yes, I will."

"Whin Logan returns, ye wull ask fur her hand in marriage, since ye have ruined her fur any other man."

"You are correct. I erred in my treatment of the lady, and I shall not dishonor her or her family."

"Ah gave her brother mah vow on protecting her in his leave 'n' ah hae failed."

Skye let out a humph. Men. Did she have no rights? Did they really think she would marry herself to this excuse of a reprobate? She had a say whether or not they realized it. She knew if Gregor told Logan of this scene, her brother would either kill Maxwell or make them speak the vows at once.

"There will be no wedding. You owe me Gregor, and you won't breathe a word of this to Logan. How many maidens have you dishonored in your life? I see no parson's noose around your neck."

She made the big brute blush, but Maxwell knew there was no amount of embarrassment to make him dishonor his vow to the MacKinnon. Zane stayed silent while she spoke her words with the man. In time, she would understand the reason for their union. If not, he knew her brother would demand marriage of her and him for that matter.

While at one time he cringed of ever walking down the aisle, the last two weeks with Skye made him change his mind. What man wouldn't desire to have earth-shattering sex every evening with a sexual goddess? His nights would be filled with passion while his days could continue at their normal pace. He would even allow her to follow her desires during the day, whatever they may be. Just so long as her nights were devoted to him. He smiled at his plans for their future.

Skye glanced over at Maxwell, wondering what the fool smiled about. Didn't he understand what could happen to them? They would be stuck with one another forever. Wouldn't she put a crimp in his bachelor's lifestyle? He appeared awfully content about Gregor's threats. Was he contemplating them getting married? Fool. Well, those thoughts were for another time. There must be a reason for Gregor to seek her out. He must have word on Logan. She needed to get rid of Maxwell.

"Maxwell, if you would excuse me, my man and I have a few details we need to discuss."

"Well if those details include me, then I'm not going anywhere," he said as he leaned back against the stall, crossing his legs in front of him.

"Maxwell, you seem to keep forgetting you are the prisoner," explained Skye.

"Well, my dear, I forget because you keep giving me mixed signals on my status during my stay at your fine castle."

She growled at his words. All he did was provide Gregor with more information to pass along to Logan.

"If ah believe yer saying whit ah think yer saying, ah wull fetch the preacher now."

"No, that wasn't what he was saying, was it Maxwell?" she stressed.

"Well …"

She was cornered, if she didn't let him remain, he would spill to Gregor about their time together. If she let him stay, he would learn of their plans for Shears. Then he would become angry at her for going back on her word to him. She promised him she wouldn't return him to Shears, but she had to, it was the only way to ensure Logan's return. Skye must sacrifice one for the other. She couldn't have both. Skye sent a quick look to Gregor to not disclose the details of their plan. He sent her a nod so small there was no way Maxwell could have seen.

Maxwell did though. He saw the silent message that passed between the two. She was holding out on him. She had plans he wasn't privy to. Did she mean to double-cross him? After everything they shared, she would betray him? What a fool he had been. He was a spy, the king of double crosses. He had been so smitten with her, he didn't recognize what was right in front of his eyes. He was a means to an end with her, and he hadn't even realized it. Maxwell put his feelings aside at once because emotions had no place in war. Had he not spoke those same words to Mallory? He dished out the advice but didn't heed it for himself. He closed off his sentiments at that moment and shuttered his expression from her.

Skye felt the chill that came over him. He knew. Well that was too bad. She never made promises to save him. She was relieved he put distance between them. Now she could focus. There wasn't any room for feelings during this ordeal.

"What did you discover, Gregor?"

"Shears has returned to Edinburgh."

"Does he carry the shipment?"

"Aye."

"Take the men to scout out the shipyard and oversee his movements. We'll prepare to meet Shears in three days' time and put the plan into action. I want you to get a man on his ship to supply us with details of his crew and cargo. Do we have a clansman who is able to blend in with Shears's crew?"

"Ah have just th' man."

Skye gave him her nod of acknowledgment. Gregor turned and left the stables. She waited for Maxwell to voice his anger at her betrayal. She was disappointed, for all he did was follow Gregor out of the stables. Skye let out the breath she held and slid to the stable floor. Resting her forehead on her bent knees, she let the tears fall.

The pressure from the last few months of her missing brother to the emotions Maxwell made her experience, took over her senses. She felt so lost and alone trying to keep it together. When he entered her life, it appeared she had help for the first time. She suffered his rejection deeply when she betrayed him. He left without even a glimpse in her direction. She made a fine mess this time. Her horse nudged her and whickered. Skye looked up and brushed her hand between the horse's eyes.

"I made a mess of things."

Lady seemed to understand her because she nodded under Skye's touch. Skye rose and patted the horse.

"There was no other way," she explained.

When the horse settled to sleep, Skye wandered away into the courtyard. It had grown dark since she first entered the stables. The night was silent around her. As she walked inside the castle, she looked behind her. When she searched into the distance, she detected nothing out of place, just an eerie silence. The back of her neck prickled, sensing she was being watched. But there was nothing out of the ordinary. She shook her head at her fear and turned to go inside. It was only her plight coupled with her guilty conscience playing tricks on her mind.

But it wasn't the tricks of her mind. She was being watched. For this was what he did best—watching other people. It was what made him most successful. Maxwell guarded the people he trusted most to ensure their safety and observed his enemies to find their habits. He wasn't sure what category she fell into. He fooled himself into believing she was different, and so he'd never studied her in depth. Her actions this evening changed everything. Now over the next few days he would observe her. He had let his desire for her rule his heart and emotions. Since he removed her from his heart, he would let his eyes see what his heart did not.

Chapter Nine

A FEW DAYS LATER, they rose early for their ride to Edinburgh. Skye rode at the front of the pack as they took the back trails to stay out of sight. Zane rode toward the back, flanked by her guards. The very same men he had worked alongside during the last few weeks. Now they were back to acting as if he were a prisoner. While she had kept the chains off, he could still feel them as if they were shackled around his wrists.

They had spoken no words since the stable. Not that there was anything to discuss. From what he gathered, they were returning him to Shears for the weapons. The original plan was put back into play. She never trusted him or even tried to. While he laid himself bare to her, she had no intention of doing the same. As he reflected on their time spent together, she had never opened herself to him. She kept a part of herself closed off from his eyes. He was a fool to believe trust existed between them. Well he had on his part, but obviously she had not on hers. He only hoped his missive to Thornhill and Mallory arrived in time. They were his only hope to escape.

When they arrived at the outskirts of town, their horses stopped at an abandoned warehouse. To Zane's surprise, it was a headquarters of some kind. There were offices lining the back wall and a flurry of activity in the center. Weapons were being distributed to men, with instructions for their assignments. He searched for her, only to see her swamped by her men, shooting off questions rapidly only to have her answer just as rapidly in return. Her attention was no longer focused on him, but something much more daunting. He turned in a circle to take in his surroundings. What was this place? It was more elaborate than any operation he set his eyes on before. He took in the number of weapons in store and the manpower scurrying to get ready for battle. More importantly what were they preparing for? Did this have anything to do with Shears? Maxwell also wondered why Skye was in the center of the chaos. What role did she play?

When he saw Gregor's familiar face striding toward him, he meant to question the man, only to be grabbed and taken into a room. The guard turned and left the room without saying a word to him. Zane moved to the door to discover himself locked inside. He pounded on the door, shouting for his release. After a few minutes when his shouts went unanswered, he took in his surroundings. They delivered him into a room that resembled a parlor. There were chairs set around a tea table. The table was laid out with tea, cakes, and small sandwiches, awaiting a visitor. A couch with lace draped on top of the cushions sat along a back wall. Positioned in the corner was a desk with papers scattered across the top.

He walked to the desk to look through the papers, hoping to help identify his location. The papers were only scribblings of drawings. As an artist himself, he was drawn to the detail of the illustrations. They were real life, capturing your attention to the scenes. He searched the desk for more clues, only to come up empty. Where was he? He decided they brought him here to keep him out of her way. Zane decided to settle in for the long haul, waiting until she gave him her undivided attention. Because Skye would come for him before she betrayed him for the final time.

Zane relaxed his body on the couch, poured himself a cup of tea, and ate the small spread that could only have been meant for him. He was never one to pass on food. With his stomach full, he stretched out on the sofa. He lay there with his arms folded behind his head and began to piece together what Skye's role might be in this operation. When his thoughts became jumbled and his eyes unfocused, he tried to rise off the couch, only to feel a sense of dizziness. Damn her. The last time he'd felt this way he ended up tied up in the back of a cart with Charles Mallory and Raina LeClair. The goddess drugged him. So, this was how they were going to return him to Shears. He could summon no anger toward her, only a sense of disappointment that she couldn't be honest with him about his demise. If he was going to be angry with anyone, it would be at himself. He let down his guard for what, lust? It was his fault that he didn't stay focused on his mission, not hers. He lay back against the cushions and closed his eyes. He knew there was no use fighting the drug. Maybe he could sleep it off before they came for him. As he drifted off to sleep, his last thoughts were of her.

Slowly waking, he sat up shaking the sleep from his head. He sensed her before he saw her. She sat before him in a chair watching him as he rested. Usually he heard everything in his sleep, but he was unaware of her entering the room. She talked to him softly, but he was unable to make out what she said. Her lips looked to be saying she was sorry. Sorry for what? Then he remembered that she'd drugged him.

"What?" he muttered.

"My apologies, Maxwell, but it is the only way."

"Only way for what?"

"Your return to Shears. Believe me when I say that if there was any other way, I would make it happen. But there isn't."

Maxwell was too disoriented to fully understand what she told him. He only wished to shut his eyes and escape this madness. After he closed his lids, he finally understood what she said. She was returning him to Shears. He opened his eyes and tried to force his body to move toward her, but he was wrenched from behind before he reached her. His wrists were shackled behind his back, and he was thrown over Gregor's shoulders. His body jostled against the guard as they dragged him out of the warehouse. They threw him into the back of a cart and he listened to her in the distance shouting out instructions. From what his mind understood, she meant to ride to Shears's ship and exchange merchandise. The merchandise being him. He struggled to his feet, trying to make his way to the back. He meant to jump off and make his escape.

"Ah, hell man," Gregor muttered before the guard slammed his fist into Maxwell's face.

The force of the hit and the drugs running through his body passed him out against the hay, cushioning his ride in the cart. It was the last thing he remembered.

Skye watched as Gregor slammed his fist into Zane. She wanted to rush to help him. She'd only drugged him for his best interest. The less he was involved in this transaction the better. She bore his silence the last three days as her guilt weighed heavily on her mind. She never meant to betray him. With the help of her organization, she developed a plan to rescue Logan and secure Maxwell's safety from Shears. To achieve his protection, Maxwell needed to be kept in the dark. For this to work, Zane needed to believe she had betrayed him. The less he interfered, the less her plan would get screwed up. When his friends arrived unexpectedly this afternoon, she had Zane taken into her private sanctuary, so he wouldn't note their presence. If he saw them, her plans to rescue Logan tonight would be ruined. With their help, Shears's demise would go as planned. It hadn't been her idea to drug him. It was Mallory's wife's idea; she swore by it, much to Mallory's expense. The young woman laughed as she explained to Skye what the effects were. Raina Mallory implied she had done the same to her husband and Maxwell with much success. Charles Mallory must have forgiven his wife by the affection they bestowed on one another.

"We have him from here, MacKinnon." Thornhill reached out to shake her hand.

"He will be angry when he awakens," she muttered as she regarded him sleeping.

"It couldn't have happened to a better chap," laughed Mallory.

"He will hate me for this."

"After we explain the reason why, he will understand," Raina said, trying to comfort her.

As much as the woman's kind words meant, they still didn't take away the guilt. He would be furious when he realized she'd tricked him with the help of his friends. Maxwell wouldn't get the opportunity to destroy Shears, she would, and with no help from him. He would experience the ultimate betrayal when he realized she didn't share who she was with him. He trusted her with his information, although she didn't do the same. It was as she had told him before, it was in his best interests.

"Are you sure you can handle Shears on your own?" Thornhill questioned.

Skye waved her arms around her. Her guards fell into place, ready to destroy Shears. Nothing would go wrong today. Everybody and everything was in place. Shears's reign of terror would be over tonight.

"As you can see, my men and I have everything in order. We should put an end to him tonight. Then we can all live in peace."

Charles drew Raina into his arms and rested his chin upon the top of her head as he watched Skye's men move into action. Skye could sense Thornhill's eyes upon her. She'd worked closely with him over the years. Their inner actions had been top secret government business. His wife didn't join him on this journey. She had given birth to their first child, a girl. Thornhill beamed like the proud papa he was. Skye was happy these men found love in this war of madness. She wanted to meet Thorn's wife, the lady who held Zane's heart. While Skye recognized Ivy Thornhill's complete devotion to Thorn, it didn't stop Skye from feeling jealous.

"We should leave you then; we need to get Maxwell loaded on the ship before he comes to. We need to put as much distance between him and Shears. He only wants to kill the man."

Skye nodded in agreement. They said their goodbyes as they drove the cart to Thornhill's ship. He docked his ship on the other edge of Edinburgh, away from Shears. Shears landed back into port a week ago and waited for her. There had been little activity aboard his ship. Skye's contacts reported that he held the cargo on board. After tonight, she would have her brother back, and her mission would be complete. Then she could return to living her life, which didn't involve the day-to-day danger of espionage. While being a spy was adventurous, she'd also lost sight of herself and who she had become.

The coach pulled up to her. Gregor helped her inside and sat across from her. He watched her with a wariness that set Skye's nerves on edge.

"This plan is crazy, Skye. Are ye positive ye'll want tae proceed?"

"It is the only way to bring Logan home."

"But if it goes wrong, ye wull be lost tae us."

"We must make sure everything goes as planned."

"Ye should have kept th' Sassenach bloke. Maxwell 'n' his friends would hae bin of some use."

"No, Shears would recognize them and blow our plan to smithereens," she argued.

"Thay might hae stayed in th' background. Now thay wull return tae their comfy lives 'n' leave us tae pick up th' pieces in th' aftermath."

"This ends tonight, Gregor. Then we all can return to our comfy lives."

Skye turned her head to the window and watched the passing landscape, ending their conversation. She needed to clear her head before she confronted Shears. Her emotions were all over the place as she pictured Zane passed out in the cart and then the anger he'd feel when he awakened. For he would be in a fine temperament when he came out of his drug-induced state on Thorn's ship. She only hoped he might forgive her in time. She closed her eyes, going to the quiet place in her mind, and let herself rest. As her mind cleared she became more focused on what she needed to accomplish.

The carriage stopped along the dock. She alighted from the carriage and observed as her men took their places. She took a deep breath and sniffed in the dank stench of the sea. The aroma almost bowled her over, for it carried an odor of death. The smell was raw to her senses. Death was waiting to happen tonight.

With her men flanking her side, Skye strode along the plank onto Shears's ship. They were met with an empty topside. There was no one in sight; she sensed a trap. If Skye wasn't too caught up in her pride, she would have noticed the signs before it was too late. Her arrogance put her crew in danger. While she prepared to take Shears down tonight, the old sea captain still had a few cards up his own sleeve. She was wrong, it didn't end tonight but would continue. Because everything that could go wrong, did.

~~~~~

Maxwell fought the drug that kept him from coming out of his deep sleep. He struggled to rise from sleeping, his body moving in slow motion. His mind moved even slower. Damn her. He suffered the sway of the ship as his body was thrown back and forth across the bed. Bed? He opened his eyes, taking in his surroundings. Where the hell was he now? He lay in a bed tucked in the corner of a ship's cabin. At that moment he realized he wasn't aboard Shears's ship. Shears wouldn't be so accommodating, for the last time they shackled him in chains against the wall in the ship's hold. Zane overheard the chuckle from the other side of the cabin and recognized where he landed. Damn them.

He sat up to see who he amused. Marcus Thornhill and Charles Mallory, his two best friends at one time. They sat staring as he came out of his drug-induced state. They'd probably put him in this condition. He threw his legs over the side of the bed and tried to rise, only to suffer as a wave of dizziness came over him. Maxwell sighed as he rested across the bed with his legs dangling over the edge. He threw a hand over his eyes, waiting for it to pass.

"Do you think he needs a nurse?" Mallory asked.

"He might. He appears a little weak in the knees to me," Thorn quipped.

"Just get me a damn drink," Maxwell muttered.

His two companions laughed. Maxwell heard one of them rise to pour drinks. A glass was thrust into his hands. He rose and drank it in one swallow, the whiskey burning a path to his gut. His stomach felt nauseous from the drug. He jumped from the bed and made it to the commode in time to lose what remained in his stomach. After he finished, he staggered back into the cabin and slumped in a chair.

"Where is she?" Maxwell demanded.

Neither man answered. Their laughter came to a dead silence. This was what they both had dreaded, especially since the attack hadn't gone as planned. Instead of heading home, they were now on a rescue mission.

"Shears captured her aboard his ship."

Maxwell sat up in his chair, glaring at the two men. He rose and paced inside the small cabin, which only became smaller as his fears were put into words.

"What the hell happened?"

"Things went wrong," Mallory answered.

"What kind of things?"

"Shears outmaneuvered us again," Thorn replied.

"Quit with the cryptic talk, and start at the beginning. Like why the hell was I drugged? Then explain why you two didn't help her. Most of all, enlighten me; who the hell is she?"

"She is Skye MacKinnon."

"I know her name, you fools. Who is she?"

Thorn sighed. "She works for the Crown."

"You were taken to the Edinburgh headquarters when you arrived. We received your letter and waited for you to enter the city. When Thorn's man Jake saw you ride into town with Skye and her men, he sent word to her. We confronted her with your release. Thorn had worked with her before, so she believed his story. We made a deal—your return for her men to capture Shears. Her plan was foolproof, but Shears had an inside man in her crew. Her plan was leaked to Shears, and they waited for her arrival. They took her, injuring half her men, and departed to parts unknown. Her man Gregor sent word and informed us of Shears's plan. They were left for dead. Everybody but her," Mallory explained.

Zane sank back into the chair. He had grown pale at the news. If Shears captured her, she was as good as dead. Her death would come after Shears had his way with her, which would make her dead inside. As angry as he was with her, he still ached for her. He sensed her pain, miles away.

"There is more. He delivered a message for you. We can't solve the code but was hoping you can," Thorn told him.

"Tell me the message."

"That after he tasted this jewel, he would enjoy your other jewel."

"What did he mean by that Maxwell?" Mallory asked.

"It is of no concern of yours."

"Well considering we rescued your ass, you are now aboard my ship, and we are on the way to rescue your damsel in distress, I think it most definitely is my concern," Thorn growled

"She is not my damsel."

"I beg to differ, drugging you aside. She needs our help, which I will admit we should have given her earlier. Then she wouldn't have landed in this predicament."

"Why didn't you? Why did you think she could handle Shears on her own?"

"We thought her plan would work, Maxwell. Plus, we were only sent here to bring you back home."

"For what, the hangman?"

"No, the King has given you a full pardon, much to everyone's surprise. Care to enlighten us on why?"

Maxwell shrugged his shoulders. In time, he would tell them part of his story. Each one of them held onto their secrets, and he wouldn't tell them his until he had to. Maybe he wouldn't have to divulge his secret at all. Even though Thorn's wife knew part of his story, he hoped she wouldn't betray him. He could work alongside them to free Skye and rescue the missing jewel, and then he would retire to his estate away from this mess. He had given enough of his life to his country.

"So, it all comes back to your jewels. What is Skye MacKinnon to you?" Mallory asked.

"She means nothing to me, and from where I sit, it must have been the same on her part too."

"Did you bed her?" Thorn questioned.

"That is none of your concern."

"Damn it, you did, didn't you?"

"Who I sleep with or kiss is of no business of yours."

"You seem to make a habit of kissing and bedding women who you shouldn't even touch," Thorn growled.

"Mmm, yes. I remember. She is the most delicious kisser I have ever had the chance to kiss in a closet," Maxwell taunted.

Thorn dragged him from the chair, pulled back his arm, and sent a punch into Maxwell's gut and dropped him to the floor. He picked him up to repeat the action when Mallory pulled him away. Maxwell came to his knees, laughing a dark laugh filled with no sense of shame.

"Calm down, Thorn. Maxwell is baiting you. You know the kiss meant nothing to Ivy."

"Are you a crazy man? Why are you isolating the only friends on this earth who care for you and want to help you?" Thorn asked.

"Do you care for her?" Mallory questioned.

Maxwell went to the bar and poured himself another whiskey. As he nursed the drink, he pondered the question. Could one care for a woman who betrayed him at all costs? Who drugged him? Who owned a part of his soul throughout this ordeal?

"Yes."

It was only one word, but it held the impact of a thousand. Both men understood the effect that one word had on him. They had been in his place throughout the last year. They realized how he suffered and what he still had to endure. While he might have betrayed them over the last few months, it was only out of his sense of duty.

"So, what is the plan?" Maxwell asked his friends.

"We are following on his tailwind. Our contact on his ship sent word before they departed. The fool is sailing back to England. I have sent a messenger by horse; this will end in London."

"Did he even carry the weapons for her on his ship?"

"There were no weapons," Mallory replied.

"She was insistent on getting them."

"That was how she disguised herself, as a weapons dealer. She convinced Shears she could organize clans who would attack England. Over the course of the year, she purchased weapons and then destroyed them. After a few purchases, she persuaded Shears to release her brother. She was to make the exchange the morning she saw you on the ship. When she discovered who you were, she made the quick decision to rescue you. But to do that, she couldn't get her brother. Shears backed out of the deal on returning her brother, so she took you as ransom. Shears wanted your head and was angry that she'd thwarted him. Shears concocted his own plan upon her return," Thorn explained.

"It was a trap."

"Yes, but he was furious when she didn't return with you. So, he took her to entice you to chase him."

"Where is her brother?"

"We have no information on his whereabouts. Nobody has ever seen Shears with Logan MacKinnon. He disappeared a few months ago while on a mission for the King and nobody has seen him since. We don't even know if Shears even has him. We think it is a lure to capture her. Our belief is that Shears discovered her identity and used Logan as bait. From my contacts, her brother has disappeared off the face of the earth," Mallory said.

Maxwell thought this through. Skye would be devastated if her brother was dead. So would Isobel and young Lachlan; the pain would be unbearable for them. He felt their loss deeply. He couldn't bring Logan back to them, but he would make sure Skye survived Shears.

"Shears will disappear when he hits London. There will be no way to find him if he goes underground," Maxwell told them.

"Well, my friend, that is where you are wrong. Over the last few weeks, the last of Shears's contributors have been taken into custody and now await trial. Nobody remains for him to take refuge with. Shears's demise ends when he arrives in port," Mallory explained.

"What is our plan?"

"For now, my friend, you need to rest and eat. We shall discuss this in the morning."

"No, we must discuss this now," Maxwell demanded.

"There is nothing to accomplish tonight. You are of no help to her in your state. Rest, and we will make plans on the morrow," said Thorn.

"We will rescue her," Mallory promised.

Zane leaned back in the chair and nodded his head in acceptance. He knew they were right, but he was enraged because he didn't keep her safe. He let her double-cross him and make him believe she needed his help. Obviously, she thought she didn't, but she did. He only hoped she would keep herself safe from Shears's advances.

Zane looked up to find Thorn standing over him, his hand held out in front of him. Zane shook it. He needed to offer no words of apology. The handshake spoke it all.

Chapter Ten

SKYE FOUGHT AT THE RESTRAINTS that held her captive in the pit of Shears's cabin. Trash was scattered around, and a stench worse than anything she ever smelled before permeated the room. It reeked as if somebody died in the room. She wouldn't be surprised if it were true. She spotted discarded rags covered in blood in the corner. Rats scurried across the floor, searching for scraps to eat. They had yet to notice her, which remained in her favor. It wouldn't be long before they searched her body to appease their appetites.

She closed her eyes at her predicament. How did she not recognize she was walking into a trap? All the signs were there. But her thoughts were consumed by the man being carted away by his friends. She didn't detect the covert glances some of her men passed back and forth. They were not her clansmen, were they? She had been double-crossed. They worked for Shears and had conveyed her plans to ruin him and bring Logan home. Now he held her captive, and many of her clansmen met death on that dock.

Only she was a fool. Logan wasn't on board, and Shears never captured him. Shears lied to her. He didn't even know Logan's whereabouts, even after he tried to search for him. Logan was nowhere to be found. Skye didn't believe Logan was dead; she would feel his death in her soul.

Skye understood what Shears had planned for her. He meant to rape her before he tortured her to death. She was to be his ultimate revenge toward Maxwell. She knew Maxwell would not rescue her. She betrayed him, and he owed her nothing. They may have spent time under the bedsheets, but neither one of them confessed their undying love for one another. They burned out their passion between the sheets, nothing more.

But she had felt more. Skye realized that now that it was too late. She had fallen in love with the earl. Every time she thought he portrayed somebody else, he proved to her that he wasn't that man. He was a man of strong character who cared for others before himself. In some small way, Skye believed he cared for her. She thought her need to rescue Logan and destroy Shears was stronger than her feelings for Zane. She was wrong.

Skye shut her eyes, disappointed in herself. She hoped one day he would forgive her for what she did; she only wanted him safe from Shears. Skye thought her men would protect her enough to finish the mission. She'd put her trust with the wrong men. Her trust needed to be in one man's hand, but she had refused to give him her faith.

Skye heard the commotion outside the cabin door before it was flung open. Shears himself limped into the room, holding his side, which bled profusely. It was the same wound Maxwell inflicted a month ago. The wound had opened again upon fighting Gregor. That explained how the rags in the corner of the cabin came into play. He was losing a lot of blood, more than a man needed to lose. If he didn't seek medical attention, he could bleed out. A fitting death for an evil man. Skye smiled to herself at his own demise.

"What are you smiling at, wench?"

"I am enjoying myself, watching your death."

He snarled at her, "I am not dead yet."

"Well it won't be long."

"Long enough for my plans for you," he threatened.

"And what does that entail, Shears?" Skye's arrogance empowered her.

Shears limped to her side, grabbed her hair, and yanked her head back. He ran his hand along the slope of her neck, his fingers stopping at her pulse. The touch of his fingers on her flesh made her skin crawl, and she felt her body break out in goosebumps from his eerie touch. She finally felt fear—fear of what he was capable of. Fear that this time she had no one to rescue her from the danger she landed herself in. He yanked harder on her hair. Her head aching from the roots being pulled out of her head. Shears leaned over and breathed his harsh breath on her neck, blowing heavily, and then his face was in hers. He laughed as he observed the fear take over her eyes.

"I think your pretty head realizes what I can do to you. The only question is when. When am I going to break your spirit? Will it be now?" he asked as he ripped apart the front of her shirt.

He looked and caught her shirt hugging her breasts. It was ripped open enough for him to view the globes begging for his touch. He noted how she watched the lust come into his eyes and how her body shook, then he laughed.

"Or will he wait?"

A knock banged upon the door, saving her from his assault. Shears shook his head in disgust at being interrupted.

"Well, lucky for you, MacKinnon, you are being offered a reprieve. Let me promise you, it won't be long before you are mine. When I return to this cabin, it will be to break you and make you pay for what you have caused me to lose. In case you are unclear, madam, that is a promise, not a threat."

He let go of her hair abruptly and left the cabin.

Skye stood, shaking from the revolt of his hands on her person. She realized she had a limited amount of time before he came back. She needed to bring her mind to a place where he couldn't destroy her. What he did to her body would not reach her mind. She knew he meant to rape and beat her upon his return. Her eyes searched the cabin, looking for something to aid her in her escape or to allow her to torture Shears. She roamed as far as the chain wrapped around her ankle allowed her to wander.

The deeper in the room her search permitted only brought her deeper into despair. Dark circles of grime and blood covered the filthy bed. The stench overtook her, and she brought her hand up to cover her nose. It was then she recalled her state of undress. Her mind scattered in pieces from her thoughts. She couldn't bring the ordeal into focus. She felt herself panic. She kept turning around in circles, her eyes growing wider the more she witnessed signs of Shears in the room. The more she saw, the higher her panic escalated. Her breath came in short gasps. Skye sank to the ground and cried.

Never one to succumb to this wasted emotion, Skye was unprepared for where her mind took her. They returned her to a place she hadn't been to since she was a small child. A child who lost her mother and thrust into a world that wasn't normal. Her brother tried to help ease her way into the harsh life, a life in which no little girl should have endured. But one none the less she did. Her father died the same day as her mother. Not physically, but mentally. She reminded him too much of her. So, to make her look less like her mother, he forced her to be more like him. Her mother's fragility got her killed. Therefore, there was to be nothing fragile about Skye. She must hunt and kill right along with her brother Logan. And she did.

Skye did it so well, she became an undercover spy for the Crown and ran her own agency, her own headquarters, and her own men. Now her empire was destroyed. She had become her mother anyway. Fragile. She let her emotions for a man make her vulnerable. Vulnerable to love. Vulnerable to losing her life.

When she lifted her head, Skye gathered her emotions under control. She set them in their special compartment she had trained herself to lock away over the years. Now wasn't the time to dwell on her feelings; it was time to figure a plan. She wouldn't allow Shears to break her. Before he returned, she must be ready for him. Ready to destroy him for everything he took from her. She smiled, and Skye felt like her old self again. When Captain Shears returned to his cabin, he wouldn't find a damsel in distress. He would face a warrior.

~~~~~~

The next morning, Maxwell found himself on the bow of the ship looking to the horizon for any sign of Shears. He waited at this spot since daybreak. Unable to sleep, he came topside to search for any sight of Shears's ship. Sammy spotted a dot and called out for him to look. Zane took the spyglass, adjusting the lens to scan the distance, and located a ship. Unable to tell if it was the enemy, he motioned for Sammy to steer them closer. He knew Thorn's seaman would keep them far enough in the distance not to be discovered, but close enough for Maxwell to see if it was his quarry.

After a while, Sammy didn't disappoint. It was Shears. He would recognize the swine's vessel anywhere. He searched the deck and didn't notice any sign of Skye. Shears kept her below. Oh, not below, where they held him but in someplace much worse—in Shears's private cabin, where he held every woman against their will. Maxwell understood how Shears tortured women in there. He heard the horror stories from some of those women. Only one woman had escaped those horrors. The only way she escaped was because Shears thought he had killed her. Luckily, she didn't die.

He prayed Shears hadn't broken Skye's spirit. For she would need her spirit to help get herself out of this mess. Maxwell observed Shears limping across his deck, holding his blood-soaked side. He was injured. Not a small injury at that, but one they could use to their advantage.

Maxwell called out for Thornhill and Mallory to take a look. They both observed Shears arguing with his men and came to the same conclusion as him. They could overtake the ship. Thornhill had more crew on board his ship than Shears did on his.

"Get me within distance, and I will swim and board his ship."

"That is suicide," Thorn argued.

"It's the only way for me to rescue Skye. He is hurt, which means he won't drag this out. He will destroy her at the first chance he can get. If he hasn't already."

"Let us overtake him. Then my men can board the ship with you."

"We don't have time. If it were one of your women aboard his ship, you would do the same thing. You know I am right. This is the only plan that will work. After I am aboard, I will send you a signal and you can overtake him."

Thorn understood what Maxwell felt. His Ivy had been in the same plight over a year ago. He didn't know it at the time, but after he rescued her, he learned of her ordeal. He only hoped Skye MacKinnon was as lucky as Ivy had been. Ivy escaped from Shears's clutches before any harm came upon her. He didn't imagine Skye had been as lucky. She had been held in captivity too long for Shears not to have violated her. He also realized that Maxwell cared more deeply for the lady than he showed them. He recognized the signs, he had fought them for years when it came to his feelings for Ivy.

"You have to be prepared for what she might have endured," Mallory told him.

"What are you implying?"

"He may have already ..." Mallory began.

Maxwell became wild at the thought even being spoken. To realize it might have happened was one thing, but to listen to the words spoken was something he didn't know how to handle. If it happened, he would deal with it later, but hearing the unknown made him come unhinged. He wanted to inflict the possible pain Skye suffered on anyone near him. Charles stepped to the side of his punch before he could lift his arm to throw another. Thorn grabbed him from behind and pinned his arms behind his back. Maxwell tried to shake him off, but Thorn's grasp on him was solid steel. He tightened his hold even more to bring home the point: he had pushed their friendship to the brink, and he remained here by a thin thread.

"Are you calm?" Thorn asked.

Maxwell nodded. Thorn loosened his hold but didn't release him entirely. Thorn then spoke words in command of the situation which made Zane see reason.

"Mallory is only preparing you for what scene you may walk into. We know the violence Shears is capable of. We want you to have a clear mind when you board his ship. Your only mission is to bring Skye to safety. You must leave your emotions on this deck. So, if you want to have a go around, we will stand in line for you to beat out your frustrations. When you step aboard Shears's deck, you must have the mind of a soldier, not of a gentleman seeking revenge. Do you understand?"

Maxwell shook off his hold and walked to the edge of the deck, running his hand through his hair in frustration. He heeded Thorn's words and knew he spoke the truth. His emotions didn't matter. Maybe that was part of the problem. He hadn't admitted to himself the depth of his feelings for her, but perhaps she meant more to him than he allowed himself to see. It appeared she sank deeper into his heart than he realized. The only issue he focused on was her betrayal, but she hadn't betrayed him. She had made sure of his safety. She put her life on the line so he could be free. He turned toward his friends as his enlightenment came into focus.

"She tried to save me?" he questioned.

"Yes," Mallory answered.

"Why?"

"I think you already know the answer to that, my friend," Thorn said.

Maxwell laughed at the irony of the situation. What a fool she was. For him.

"Well, let us move this plan into action. Because if I know her like I think I do, she will spite him. And when she seeks her revenge, I want to be there to rescue her."

Thorn shouted directions to his crew. The ship went into action, preparing to overtake Shears. The crew gathered their weapons and took their places. Maxwell made his way to his cabin to prepare. When he entered, he was taken back by Raina LeClair, another lady in his life he had taken advantage of for his own means. She was awaiting him in a chair, sitting with her legs crossed. They worked as allies for a time, but when it came to her safety, he had betrayed her for information. Information he didn't even obtain. He thought he would see anger in her eyes, but he only saw amusement. He wearily strode into the room and sat across from her.

He waited for her to speak, staring as she laughed at him. He glared at her. What was so amusing?

"The mighty Maxwell has fallen. What a sight to behold. Has the love bug taken a bite out of your arse?"

"Get to your point, LeClair."

"Mallory."

"I beg your pardon?"

"My name is Lady Mallory. Charles has made an honest spy out of me."

Maxwell rose and bowed to her. "May I offer you my sincerest congratulations, my lady?"

"You may, and I want to thank you."

"May I inquire for what, Lady Mallory?"

"Well, if it wasn't for you, I would have never met Charles. I must thank Shears too, for he made it possible. Our coming together, that is."

"I will pass your message along to him when I rescue MacKinnon."

Raina didn't answer, but instead she continued to scrutinize him. He grasped she perceived more than he wanted anybody to see. Her perception was what made her so successful. She could detect what others did not. He knew she saw his vulnerability.

"What do you want Raina?"

"I want to go with you."

Maxwell laughed. "No way. Mallory will kill me."

Raina laughed. "He wants to kill you regardless. Your long withstanding friendships and Ivy are the two reasons why you aren't at death's door with those two gents."

Maxwell went soft at the mention of Ivy. He owed her his life, in more ways than one. He knew he betrayed their friendship the most above all others. He also knew she would understand his reasons for his actions better than the others.

"How is Ivy?"

"She is well. Recovering, but well."

"I am glad for her happiness."

"Well now that we have the sweetness out of the way, let us discuss our plan."

"There is no us to my plan," he emphasized.

Raina smiled the secret smile that only women gave men when they would ultimately get their way. The only thing gentlemen were blind to notice were the devious expressions in their eyes. They were always too taken with the seductive smiles entrapping their senses. Maxwell stayed immune to those smiles, as they had plagued him his whole life on every lady he'd ever met. He saw it coming before they lifted their luscious lips into place. Skye never did though. She never tried to portray anything she was not. Skye had been honest from the start. He was the fool who believed her to be anything but who she presented herself to be. This wasn't the moment nor the lady to ponder on his train of thought. Raina cornered him, and he only hoped Mallory forgave him.

"I see you are concluding that I am right."

"What do you have in mind?"

"We will swim to the ship, and I will be the distraction you need to rescue MacKinnon."

"What kind of distraction?"

"One that will aid help you. That is all you need to know."

Maxwell sighed his frustration. He knew she was right. She could cause enough of a diversion for him to reach Skye. Mallory would have his head when this rescue mission was complete. If they timed this at the right moment, then Mallory and Thorn would board the ship after he had Skye in his possession. Raina could handle herself. She always could.

"You are not seeking your revenge on the man. We only rescue Skye, and then we leave the ship. Thorn and his men will capture Shears. I must have your promise on this," Maxwell demanded.

Raina rose from her seat and held out her hand. He shook on her promise.

"Let's go," she urged.

"We need to get closer."

"If we get any closer, Shears will spot us, and then this plan won't work."

"You only want to leave before Mallory gets wind of you sticking yourself where you don't belong."

"I belong here more than anybody else on this ship. He destroyed my life, so it is only fitting that I am involved in bringing his to an end."

"You promised no revenge."

She hadn't uttered those words. She'd shaken his hand but had not actually promised him anything. Damn these women in his life. Why could they not make it easy for him? They were all trouble.

"I met your Skye," Raina changed the subject.

"She is not my Skye."

"Mmm."

"What?"

"Well, she appeared genuinely concerned when you passed out in the cart. I saw the regret in her eyes. I also saw the fear for your safety."

"All you saw was guilt."

"Mmm, you may be right. You must admit it was very clever of her."

"Clever of her or of you?"

"What are you implying, Maxwell?"

"Do not think for one instant I don't realize where she got that drug. If I am not mistaken, you used the drug on Mallory and me."

"Maybe a time or two." She laughed at her own cleverness.

Maxwell walked to the door, holding the door open for her to exit. "Shall we?"

They sneaked to the opposite side of the ship where Thorn and Mallory couldn't spot them plunging into the North Sea. The water would be bitterly cold, but Shears's ship was only a few hundred yards away. For whatever reason, he'd set his anchor along the bank. This made it possible for Thorn to draw his ship in their blind spot. But Maxwell worked alongside this man for years and knew Shears always had a plan. He knew the outcome of every action he took, which was why it had been impossible to bring Shears to justice for so long. But today they would. Shears's reign of terror would end today.

Maxwell followed Raina down the rope and plunged into the icy cold sea. As their bodies adjusted to the temperature, Maxwell instructed her where to climb aboard Shears's ship. They set out, Maxwell adjusting his long fast strokes to slow down to her pace. She kept alongside him at a brisk swim. When they reached Shears's ship, Maxwell helped her climb onboard. Her chattering teeth and blue tinge to her skin made him regret bringing her along. Mallory was going to kill him for bringing Raina with him to rescue Skye. Maxwell pulled her under a beam as they heard approaching footsteps. He watched as two men came to a halt a few feet from their hiding spot. He noticed the puddle of water near where they had climbed aboard and hoped it would go unnoticed from Shears's crew.

"We need to depart; that ship was gaining on us. I tell you it is Thornhill's ship. He will kill us all."

"We need to stop for a quick repair. If not, we will sink. Then it won't matter if he kills us or not because we'll be dead anyway. Plus, the captain wants to have his fun before we set sail again."

"Is he gonna make that bitch squeal?"

The crewman laughed. "Like a pig in heat."

They laughed as they wandered off, the puddle going unnoticed.

Maxwell tensed at the words spoken, his anger consuming his body. He had to rescue her. Now. He felt a hand tighten on his arms and look down, confused. In all his anger he had forgotten Raina stood with him.

"We will rescue Skye in time," she whispered.

He gulped and nodded. They had to. He wouldn't let Shears lay a hand on her. If he did, he knew he couldn't stop until the captain was dead. It didn't matter anymore why he headed down this path with Shears for information only this man held knowledge on. The information he needed no longer meant anything to him. The only thing that meant anything to him was her.

"You need to find Skye, and I will start the demise of this vessel."

"If I don't get the chance, I thank you for this and more."

"You will get the chance. Now go rescue your damsel."

Maxwell strode toward the direction of Shears's torture chamber, his cabin. He turned to tell Raina to be careful, but she had already disappeared into thin air. When he glanced around the deck, there was no presence of her. He realized he didn't have much time before her destruction began. He ran toward the cabin.

Zane felt her scream right to his core. She let out a blood-curdling shriek. He froze, knowing she needed him now, but too afraid of what she was enduring. He only paused for a second as his emotions rushed to the front of his brain. He closed his eyes, pushing those feelings away as he focused on what he needed to do.

Raina heard the shriek too. She understood the scream only too well. It was a terror she overheard from many women while in the clutches of Shears's evil. It was the reaction that could break most women. Raina glimpsed the steel in Skye MacKinnon when she met her and recognized the scream to be one of a warrior, not of a beaten woman. Raina laughed at what Shears would receive for his torture.

Chapter Eleven

HER SEARCH FOR A weapon had come up empty. There was nothing for her to use in defense, only herself. Skye waited for him with no weapons to help her in her aide against him. The only weapon she possessed was the one that never betrayed her—her mind. He would not destroy her. She would destroy him. She must look out for herself. There would be no Maxwell coming to her rescue. She had made sure of that.

Shears entered the cabin and went to the bar. He grabbed the whiskey, drinking a long swallow of the fiery liquid. As he wiped his mouth on his sleeve, he staggered to the bed, bringing the bottle with him. He spotted MacKinnon cowering in the corner. His side burned like hell. He took another drink, hoping the alcohol would subdue the internal flame his body suffered. He realized his time was coming to an end, but before it did, he would have one more taste of a woman.

The woman who stood before him had eluded him for months. He played at her games of innocent virtue. Her guards always stood to protect her, and he could never get close enough. He made sure to get rid of her henchmen this time. Now she was alone. Alone in his room for him to taste. He leered at her as his thoughts turned to carnal images. He tried to get his lust under control before he took her. There were a few things he wanted to discuss with her before he stripped the clothes from her body and threw her on his bed, where he would then part her creamy white thighs and slide his cock into heaven. Oh, he realized she would fight him, but that was what he loved the most. The part where he captured a woman against her will. He enjoyed holding them down and plowing into them, destroying what innocence they had remaining. He licked his lips, and his cock grew harder in anticipation at bedding the red haired wench.

"Maxwell is not coming to your rescue."

Skye raised her chin, her dignity intact. "I do not need Maxwell or any other man to rescue me."

Shears laughed at her brazen words, . The wench had moxie. He admired the trait in a man, but on a lady it only made him want to take her with force. Yes, he would enjoy bringing this bitch down. She would make up for every lady he was unable to destroy.

"Do you know why Maxwell chased me?"

"You held the red ruby that leads to the King's bastard."

"I am surprised you two shared secrets between the sheets. He must have been very satisfied with you if you shared pillow talk."

"What have you done with my brother?" she asked, changing the subject. Her time with Maxwell was private, and she wouldn't discuss it with anybody, least of all Shears.

"Your brother?"

"Logan MacKinnon."

"Oh, that fool. I killed him."

Skye rushed at him with her fists flying. She couldn't reach him because of her leash. Her hands flew in the air but didn't make contact with him. She knew he lied. Didn't he? She would feel pain if Logan died.

Shears laughed at her petty defense. She still contained spirit, but not for long. Shears felt his desire for her taking over but tamped it down. He needed to build it higher, for the sweeter the victory would be for him. The angrier she became, the more his lust grew. When she was beyond grief, he would take her then—the moment his lust turned into hatred. He needed to goad her more. He needed to tell her of Maxwell's involvement with him. The secret Maxwell didn't confide to anybody. The secret he knew Maxwell didn't confess to her, which would cause her total devastation.

"You lie," she hissed.

"Do I? Do I also lie that your Earl Maxwell has been my man the last few months? He works for me. How do you think I sabotaged you and your men?"

"You continue to lie to me."

"Think about it, MacKinnon. Why did I allow you to take him so easily? I didn't put up much of an argument about his release."

"You had no choice."

Shears rose from the bed and circled her. "I always have choices, my dear."

"I am not your dear," she snarled at him.

He ran his slimy hand over her cheek. "In a matter of time you will be."

"Never," she spat at him.

"Think about it. How do you think we knew when you were coming?"

"Impossible. He was not aware of my plans."

"He didn't need to be aware of your plans. He only needed to send me a signal on your return to the city. When I learned of your return, I was prepared for you."

Skye became silent at this bit of news. Could Shears be correct? How could Maxwell send any news to Shears? She watched him the entire time, and when they arrived at her headquarters, he was never left alone.

Although, he was alone for a brief time, as nobody stayed in her office with him. No, Shears was lying to anger her. She hadn't trusted Maxwell before, and that was where she went wrong. She wouldn't make the same mistake twice.

When she didn't rise to his bait, he decided to inform her of more of Maxwell's involvement with him. *Let's see if she stays calm with this bit of news.*

"So, you know of the King's bastard child and Maxwell's search for it?"

"Yes, he told me."

"Did he also inform you I promised to take him to the child and the jewels in exchange for killing Charles Mallory and Raina LeClair?"

"You continue with more lies."

Shears laughed. "I do not. He was desperate, and he realized he was running out of time. He knew I had knowledge of their whereabouts."

"Well the last I heard, Mallory and Raina LeClair still live."

"Yes, the bastard double-crossed me," he snarled.

Skye laughed. "Your defense of Maxwell being your man is falling flat, Captain."

"Do you know why he wanted to locate the child?"

"Because it was his duty to the Crown. It was his mission to locate and put the child into protective custody."

"Duty to the Crown, was that what he led you to believe?"

"Why else?"

"He has his own personal agenda."

"How is any of it personal?"

"The child is his sister."

"I do not understand."

"Maxwell was only involved in finding the child because she was his mother's love child with the King. He needed to find the child to cover up his family's involvement in this mess. His mother was a slut and cuckold her own husband with the King. If this truth were to be known to the ton, his family would be ruined. His father held a high rank in Parliament, and his mother was a do-gooder. His family held a very prestigious position in the aristocracy. So, you see it was in Maxwell's best interest to locate this child and keep her whereabouts the ultimate secret."

"Stop with your lies," Skye shouted.

"Am I lying? You will have to ask him yourself. He will soon arrive in this cabin any minute to rescue you."

"Maxwell was on his way to London before I even boarded your ship."

"Thornhill's ship has been trailing mine for half a day now. I docked my ship on the bank so they can catch us. I know Maxwell will come for you. Or is he coming for me? The man is not thinking clearly. He isn't making decisions with his mind but with his cock. I can understand why; you are a very pretty package, especially when you are angry. Well it doesn't matter anymore. I will take great pleasure in his demise."

His lies combined with the idea of Maxwell walking into another trap caused her to lash out. She slandered him with her words and reached out to hit him. Her hand connected with his face before he pulled back fast enough. Her palm slapped him solid across the cheek, with her fingernails following in the trails and slicing down his neck.

This was exactly how he wanted her. Feisty. Angry. Ready for him to take. He grabbed the hand that had left damage on his face and crushed her fist in his hand. He heard her whimper and smiled. As he pulled her against him, she came up short, and her body jerked forward toward him. He released her instantly, and her body rebounded backward, sending her sprawling across the floor. Her body lay spread out before him, the shirt he ripped earlier coming apart from where she tied it together. Her breasts fell out, gleaming for him to touch.

He ripped the placket of his pants open, his shirt falling out over his trousers. This would be his ultimate pleasure. He pulled his sword out of the sheath and traced it down her pants. His wicked smile showed his intent.

She tried to push herself back across the floor, her palms pushing through the trash as her feet slid across the floorboards. She watched as he drew his sword out and realized his intentions. He meant to rape her and destroy what sanity she had left.

His sword swiped across, cutting her trousers to shreds, leaving her body bare to his eyes. Her hands lowered to cover herself from his view. His eyes devoured her body and filled with lust. She managed to rise to her feet, inching back from him. For every step she took backward, he advanced on her. He cornered her, and her only defense were her fists. They pummeled him but only bounced off and did no harm. When her leg kicked up and found the one spot to undo him, he roared with pain. In doing so, she only angered him more.

"You bitch," he yelled as his fist connected with her face. The force sent her head flying back to hit the wall. He wasn't finished yet. He was tired of these women thinking they held more power over him. This slut would make up for all the ladies who escaped his clutches. When her head came back up, he smacked her again. When she slumped against the wall and slid down, he picked her up and threw her over his shoulder. She never gave up though. She was feisty. Her fists punched his back, yet still she remained no match for him. As he yanked the restraint off her ankle, he strolled to the bed and threw her across. She tried to escape, but her hands became tangled in the dirty sheets. He pulled her by her ankles and slid her back to him. Shears held her still with his hands.

His hands felt like iron holds on her wrists and ankles as he held her to the bed. Skye grasped his full intention. There was no way she would let him win. She would fight him to the end. When he ripped off what remained of her chemise, she continued to cry for help. She let out a blood-curdling scream, hoping to bring somebody from the ship to help her. Maybe what he spoke was true and Maxwell was coming for her. Maybe he was aboard the ship now. When Shears only laughed at her scream, she yelled louder and bucked her body from his unwanted touches. When his filthy hands tried to part her thighs, Skye managed to come to a sitting position and ram her head into his chest, pushing him back from her. This only angered him more, and his hands gripped her thighs, spreading them wider.

"Why fight the inevitable, my dear? We were meant to do this since the beginning. I allowed you to lead me on your merry cat-and-mouse game for months. Now I will finish what you began."

"You will regret this, Shears. Now let me make myself clear. This is a promise, not a threat," Skye said, repeating the words he taunted her with hours ago.

Shears laughed as he began to slide between her thighs. Skye trembled from the fear of being taken against her will. She tried to blank her mind to this violation but was unable to find a calm place in her soul. There was nowhere peaceful for the mind to wander with Shears's act of violence. Silent tears streamed down her face, betraying her fear to this man.

Before either one of them realized what was happening, Shears was thrown off her and flew across the room. His body slammed into the wall. When Skye began to understand her release, a man advanced on Shears, pulling him off the floor to slam him back down again. This was repeated, along with kicks to his injured side. Skye saw the blood flowing out of Shears's side. It had only been seeping before. When she looked toward her savior, she saw a man she had never seen before. A man bent on murder. A man out for revenge. The worst kind of man. It was a man avenging the woman he cared for, perhaps even loved.

Maxwell.

Maxwell was crazed. He knew he should quit pummeling this asshole to death, but he couldn't remove the image from his mind of Shears between Skye's thighs, raping her. This man deserved nothing except death. Death at his hands. He would avenge Skye and every woman this slime ever touched. His fist connected with bone over and over again, but the man only laughed. He kicked him in the side, which caused a reaction out of him. Shears gasped for breath. So, Maxwell repeated the action. Then before he realized, he wrapped his fingers around Shears's neck, choking off the very breath the man was gasping for. His hold tightened, watching as the man turned purple as his hands clawed at his fists. Still, Maxwell would not let go. Small hands wrapped around his fingers, peeling them back from Shears's throat. He felt the tears splashing upon his tightened fingers.

"Stop," she whispered.

"No." His fingers tried to tighten more, but only intertwined with hers.

"Please, Zane," she croaked out between her tears.

"He deserves to die."

"He will, but not at your hands."

"How can you ask me to stop after what he did to you?"

"I am fine. Please, he has information we need."

Her fingers continued to pry his fingers loose. Her willpower was the only thing pulling him off Shears. She guided him away from the man.

He looked at her and swore at her state of undress. Maxwell ripped the shirt off over his head, pulling it over her body, and brought her into his arms. Holding her to his heart. Her tears poured along his chest as her body shook. He gathered her tighter into his arms. Maxwell swung around and watched as Shears regained his breath. His blood soaked the floor around them. The devil would bleed out. A fitting death for the captain. He rested his boot on the man's chest and pressed deeper into his lungs. Shears fought for breath, and Maxwell ground his foot more.

"The bitch is mistaken if she thinks I will give you any more information on your loved ones," Shears choked out.

"I have all the information I need," Maxwell told him with a final kick to his side.

Maxwell watched in pleasure as Captain Shears took his final breath and his eyes rolled to the back of his head. He realized Skye was too wrapped up in her own grief to know the despicable man was dead. He turned to carry her out of her terror, encountering Thornhill at the door. Thorn looked over Maxwell's shoulder and then back at him. Maxwell nodded his head at Thorn's unspoken question. The villain who terrorized them over the last year was dead. While not completely at his hands, but as a result of them.

Thorn stepped aside for Maxwell to leave the cabin. He followed them as they climbed the stairs to leave the ship. When Maxwell came topside, he saw Thorn's men rounding Shears's crew into captivity. Mallory was rushing him, with Raina pulling on his arm. He understood the man was furious for putting Raina's life in jeopardy. Right now, he didn't care. The only person who mattered was Skye. Her body shook in his arms. Her quivers turned to full body spasms as her mind replayed her terror over and over.

Maxwell shook his head at Mallory. "Later," he told him as his eyes lowered to Skye and back to Mallory.

Mallory acknowledged Maxwell by putting his hands up in the air in surrender. He viewed the devastation in Maxwell's arms. He was angry at Maxwell for allowing Raina to help him on Shears's ship. Mallory was also man enough to admit that without Raina's help, Maxwell wouldn't be holding Skye MacKinnon alive. He'd met the brave woman a few days ago, only to see her now as a mere slip of a girl. These were entirely two different women. He only hoped Shears didn't destroy her. He glanced up and saw his friend on the verge of crumbling.

Maxwell felt the tears coming to his eyes as he held the woman he loved. Her beautiful face and body were covered in fresh bruises. She earned those by fighting for her life. Her body kept trembling, and any small noise around them made her jump.

Maxwell carried her across the plank to Thornhill's ship and down to the cabins. He lay her across his bed, bringing his hand up to comfort her. His fingers slid into her long mane of hair spread across the pillow. She whimpered and pulled back from him, her green eyes widening with fear in her pale face.

"Shh, it is me, Zane," he tried to comfort her.

Her only reply was to whimper. Maxwell felt a hand on his shoulder and turned to discover that Raina followed them into the cabin. She tried pulling him from the bed, only to meet his resistance.

"Zane, leave her to me. She is reacting to you because any man is Shears. Her mind cannot tell the difference. Give her time for her mind to adjust to her surroundings. I promise you I will take good care of her."

Zane nodded his head at her words. He knew she was right, but it didn't stop him from wanting to stay with her. He wanted to be the one to heal her. Raina pulled him away from Skye and walked him out of the cabin. She called for supplies for Skye's wounds and a fresh bath. He stood outside the cabin. He would go no farther. While he couldn't be inside, he would be near, just in case she wanted him.

He stood on guard as Sammy came to the door with supplies. When Thorn's men carried buckets of water and a bathtub into the room, he followed them inside the cabin. He wanted to protect her from the fear of seeing men, only to notice Raina had already thought of the possibility. The bed shrouded with bed hangings kept Skye shielded from any prying eyes. He stepped back out in the hallway with a relieved sigh. He should have known Raina would protect her. The woman always had every detail covered. There he remained through nightfall and the following day. Supplies and food were delivered and then carried away the entire time. He never removed himself from the post outside her room, even when he heard their whispers and Skye's tears reaching through the door. He wanted to rush in and hold her in his arms. Still, he stood and guarded her from afar.

Thorn and Mallory tried to persuade him to join them for meals, but he refused their offers. He waited for any sign from her that she needed him, but none ever came. When Raina exited the room late the next day, Maxwell was at his wit's end for any news about Skye.

"She is finally resting. I gave her a sedative in her tea," Raina informed him.

"How is she?"

"Her body is recovering. She will be fine after she rests. The terrors in her mind will take longer to heal."

"I want to see her."

"Maxwell, she isn't ready to see you or any man. You need to give her time."

Maxwell raked his fingers through his disheveled hair, an act he repeated countless times throughout the night.

"You say she is resting, I only want to see with my own eyes that she is well."

Raina saw Maxwell as a man undone by the destruction of the woman he loved—a lady unable to understand love at this moment. It was a love that could only frighten her. Raina knew Skye was fast asleep and wouldn't rise for hours. She needed a small respite herself. If she allowed Maxwell to sit with Skye, it could help him with his own grief.

"You may sit with her for a couple of hours while I change and rest. If for any reason you see she is awakening, you must leave immediately. Do you promise?"

"I promise," Maxwell swore to her.

He squeezed her hands in his with undying gratitude to her for taking care of Skye. He was too choked to put his emotions into words. Raina squeezed his hands back in understanding.

Maxwell walked into the cabin. He pulled a chair next to the bed and settled to watch Skye sleep. Dark bruises covered her face. Her lips were split open, and a small crust of blood coated them. Maxwell tightened his hold on the armchair. He remained furious and wanted to kill Shears all over again. He was angry he couldn't hold her in his arms and soothe away her aches and pains.

Her hair swam around her face, framing her in the shadows. He saw in her sleep her fingers held on tightly to the quilt. He raised his hand, wanting to unwrap them from the blanket and hold them but knew it could frighten her awake. So, his hand hovered above hers, feeling the heat of her body wrap around his fingers. Feeling Skye.

He pulled the chair closer and lowered his head to lay next to her hands. He watched her as she slept, secure in the knowledge that she was safe. The tears streamed down his face as her pain seeped into his soul, soaking deep inside, drowning him in fear and heartache. His tears soaked the quilt, but he didn't notice. All he took notice of was her. *Skye*, he whispered over and over in his head. Maxwell only hoped she could hear what his heart was silently shouting to her.

Chapter Twelve

SKYE AWOKE A FEW hours later. The room was dark except for a small lantern next to the bed. The flame danced shadows on the dark wall. She became startled, unaware of where she lay. Her heart settled as her eyes wandered the room and her memories returned to her. She was aboard Thornhill's ship and Raina Mallory took care of her.

Her hand smoothed the quilt at her side. It was wet, and her fingers slid back and forth over the wetness, wondering at its appearance. When she closed her eyes, a flashback of a dream drifted into her conscious. It was of Zane resting at her side with tears coursing from his eyes. Skye wished to speak to him, but no words came out. Opening her eyes, she shook her head, wondering if it was only a dream. As her fingers continued to stroke the quilt, she knew it was no dream. He had been in her room while she slept.

Her fingers shook. Why did he not hold her? Did he not want to touch her after Shears had his hands on her? Was he disgusted with her? If so, why the tears?

Skye tried to rise from the bed, wincing at the pain her body suffered. She pulled the blanket from her body and took stock of her injuries. There was not a single spot on her body not covered in bruises or cuts. With shaking limbs, she rose and walked to the chair pulled up next to her bed. She lowered her hand to touch the warm cushion. From him. He must have only left moments ago. She knew it was him because she sensed him. He may not have embraced her, but she remembered how the touch of his arms felt embracing her.

She settled in the chair and soaked in his essence. The arms of the chair reminded her of his arms holding her. She was afraid to see him. Afraid to see any man. She overheard the men come in to fill up the bathtub and the old man who brought in nourishment for her, but Raina kept her hidden from their eyes. Just hearing a man's voice brought every memory back to her. Her body shook with fear, which was ridiculous, for the source of her fear was dead. She watched Maxwell kill him while he held her in his arms. Her mind departed from her body long before Shears's death. She only allowed Maxwell to hold her as they left the ship because she was too numb. Her mind had finally gone to the place that allowed her to escape her horror.

When the room grew chilly around her, and she realized Zane's warmth also left, and she rose to wander around the room. It was a small cabin and held few personal effects. It held startling differences from the room she previously occupied, and it comforted her. While the other room held terror, this only offered her solace. It was a neutral environment, one that reflected her.

Skye ran her fingers along the edge of the wall as she walked in circles around the small room. This movement helped to ease her aches and pains. Also, allowing the repetition to soothe her mind and bring her thoughts into focus. It was silly to fear every man, for the one man who brought terror to the forefront of her mind had only harmed her with his words and his fists. He didn't finish his final act of violation; Maxwell made sure of that. While he nearly succeeded, the only thought replaying in her mind was that he'd failed. She understood it would take her awhile to come to terms with the violence done to her mind and body, but she would recover. Even in death, he wouldn't succeed in turning her into a broken woman. She was injured, but not broken.

When a light knock sounded on the door, Skye jumped at the noise. After her heart quieted, she walked to the door, laying her ear against the panel and whispering, "Yes?"

"It is Raina. May I enter?"

Skye turned the knob and held the door open briefly for Raina to slide into the room. She backed away, turning from the woman's prying eyes.

Raina understood how Skye felt. Her sense of pride was broken, and she wanted nobody to witness the loss of strength she sustained. She hoped to ease the young woman's feelings.

"I have brought a change of clothes for you, and Sammy is bringing a bite to eat. Is there anything else you need for your comfort?"

Skye turned toward the kind woman, ashamed that her injured pride overcame her gratitude. If not for this lady, she wouldn't have survived her ordeal. She would have gone crazy from the images flashing through her mind.

"I thank you."

"No need to thank me. I am glad to be of help. How are you feeling?"

Skye breathed a long sigh. "Believe it or not, I am well."

"This is wonderful news to hear. We shall sail into port soon, and Thornhill will have a doctor examine your injuries as soon as we dock."

"There will be no need. I have no broken bones, and these cuts and bruises will heal on their own."

Raina didn't know how to bring up the delicate subject of why the doctor needed to examine her. It appeared sleep helped the girl recover from certain aspects of her ordeal. Her eyes were brighter, and she didn't appear as skittish, but looks could be deceiving. But the matter needed to be addressed, and she was the only lady on board. None of the men would be able to discuss the sensitive issue without bashing it. Raina cringed at the discussion she must have with a lady she didn't even know well, but it must be discussed.

Raina sat in the chair and patted the bed for Skye to take a seat. When Skye rested upon the bed, she reached out tenderly for Skye's hand. Her hand trembled under her own, and Raina realized this woman held a deeper strength than anybody gave her credit for.

"The doctor will examine your minor injuries. The one we are most concerned about is the injury Shears inflected upon you when he took you by force."

Skye stared at Raina in confusion until her words sank in. Skye realized that from her state of undress and cries, they thought Shears raped her. She understood how they came to the conclusion. Even how Maxwell thought the same horror. For Shears had her pinned to the bed with his pants lowered and had lain between her thighs. Before he could finish the act, Maxwell yanked him off her and pummeled him to death.

"Shears did not rape me."

Raina squeezed Skye's hand in understanding. "You are confused with the details of the events that took place yesterday, and it is understandable for what you have endured. Nobody is judging you, my dear, and only you will live with the stigma of the rape. Everybody on board has sworn to the secrecy of what we witnessed."

"No, you do not understand. Shears did not violate me," she emphasized.

Raina continued to pat her hand, which only antagonized Skye. While Shears struck her, he did not rape her. And her mind wasn't confusing the details. She rose from the bed, putting distance between the other lady and turned back around.

"Let me be clear on this. That slime did not rape me. Oh, believe me, he tried. He was almost successful too, but he failed. Maxwell yanked him from me before he completed the act. Now do you believe me when I say he didn't rape me?"

Raina sighed and leaned back in the chair as she listened to the passionate speech of denial. Skye had not been raped. She might have come close to being destroyed by Shears, but Maxwell had rescued her in time.

"He didn't succeed?" Raina asked one more time.

"No, he did not."

Raina jumped from her chair and brought the young lady into her arms, hugging her in relief at this news. The outcome just became so much better than what they feared. It would take her time to heal, as she noticed how skittish the young girl still behaved, even with her. But time was the best healer. Raina would make sure Skye received all the time she needed. She could enlist Ivy's help in the matter. Between both women, they would help Maxwell find happiness with this lady. Leave it to them, he would mess it up too much.

"What a relief."

"Is it?"

Raina confused by the question asked. "What do you mean?"

Skye laughed with sarcasm. "I am skittish at every noise and touch from another human being."

"You only need time to heal, Skye."

"Then what?"

"Then you will pick up the pieces of your life and live."

"You make it sound so easy."

"Oh, it won't be easy. But you possess a strength that few people hold. I see it in your eyes, you will persevere, and then you will live to be stronger than you are now."

"What of Maxwell?"

"What of him?"

"I cannot see him at this moment."

"He wants to visit with you."

"No. I don't know if I can ever talk with him."

"He cares for you."

Skye shook her head. "I am not ready."

"He only wants a few words with you, then he has promised to leave you alone."

"I cannot."

"If I promise to stay with you, will you at least allow him to ask after your welfare?"

Skye pondered her words. She was frightened to see Maxwell. To view the disgust in his eyes, eyes revealing the scene over and over of Shears beginning to bed her. She realized the image would be something he would never forget. She witnessed his rage. Although, his rage didn't scare her. His disgust of looking at her and only picturing that scene was what she was afraid to view in his eyes.

"Only if you stay in the room, will I allow him a few moments."

"I will leave you to dress, and then I will arrange for Maxwell to visit with you."

"Thank you, Raina, for being so kind to me."

"We are your friends. When we dock in London, you can stay with Thorn and Ivy while you recover."

"No, I will travel home. I won't be an imposition."

"You are no imposition. Also we need your help in locating your brother."

"Do you have any leads?"

"A few, but we will leave that discussion for later."

"Please allow me an hour to prepare myself, and then I will meet with Maxwell."

Raina agreed and left to tell Maxwell of Skye's conditions for visiting her. Maxwell wouldn't be happy with the arrangement, but it was for the best. They were two troubled souls after what they'd endured. Hopefully, they could move past this and share a life with one another. Obviously, the couple was meant to be together. She would enlist Ivy's help to guide them along. A smile stretched across her face as she went in search of Maxwell. It would be entertaining to watch the man suffer for love.

~~~~~~

Raina found Maxwell in Thorn's cabin. They were discussing the search for Logan MacKinnon. Only a few leads existed. Thorn's connection had spotted him with the missing heir. If they could locate him, then they could put this mission to rest.

Maxwell jumped from his chair the instant Raina walked into the cabin. She didn't discuss Skye's condition with him. Instead, she went to rest on the arm of Charles's chair. He watched the affection between the two as Mallory held her hand. They whispered quietly among themselves.

"Well?" he demanded as he stood in front of them.

The two fools looked up and smiled at him with their own sense of humor. What was so damn funny? A lady lay hurt and in pain only a few yards away. There was also missing people they needed to find. This was a moment for seriousness, not humor.

"She is doing well."

"Did she agree to my visit?"

"On one condition."

"Anything, what is it?"

"Only if I am present in the cabin when you speak with her."

"No."

"Yes, Maxwell. She lives in fear."

"Of me?" he asked in despair as he slumped back into his chair.

"Of everything and everybody."

Maxwell sulked in silence as he soaked up her words. Shears damaged her more than any of them thought. Her fear of him, it devastated him the most. All he wanted to do was to hold her in his arms and help heal her. Now, not only was he unable to embrace her, he must have a chaperone in his interactions with her. How would he be able to explain to Skye his feelings for her and offer his support with Raina present?

"She needs time, Maxwell. Speak with her to let her understand you are there for her and offer her your security. She is too fragile to listen to your feelings for her. She is trying to handle her own emotions."

Maxwell leaned his head back and closed his eyes. He thought of everything he wanted to tell her but understood it must wait. Wait? For how long, he wondered. Would he ever be able to tell her, or was she too damaged for him? He would take her any way he could have her, but would she take him?

He jumped from the chair and strode to the door, and he waited for Raina to join him. He swept his hand, indicating for them to be on their way. Still, she didn't move and kept the same damn silly grin on her face.

"What the hell has you so amused?" Zane growled.

"You."

Zane raised his eyebrow for her to elaborate. When she didn't, his gaze roamed to the two men in the room and noticed they wore the same ridiculous grins on their faces.

"What?"

"Oh, the mighty Earl Zane Maxwell has fallen," Thorn quipped.

"Yes, the debonair, charming rogue of the ton has fallen for a mere Scottish lass," Mallory joined in.

"Oh, how the ladies of the ton will cry with misery when their conquest will no longer be joining them in their boudoirs," Raina continued.

"Well at least now he will leave my wife alone," said Thorn.

"I have never touched your wife in that sense, nor will I. Ivy is my very dearest friend," Zane said, defended himself.

"Please sit, Zane. She needs a moment to prepare."

"Why does she need to prepare?"

"I sense she is afraid of your reaction to her."

"I only want her to know how I feel."

"Yes, I understand. But today isn't the day for her to hear of your love. She only needs to understand your support and that you will give her the space she needs. She needs time to heal emotionally."

"My love can help her heal."

"Shears put her through his torture. She is broken, Zane, and only time will help her."

"I don't care what Shears did to her. None of that matters. I know he violated her, but I still want her."

"Shears didn't rape her Zane. On that she was lucky, but not so lucky from the other terrors he made her suffer."

"But I saw …"

"You witnessed him beginning to rape her; you arrived in time to save her from that nightmare. However, he inflicted other scars. Just the act of him almost succeeding in raping her has her frightened."

Thorn walked to his friend and put his hand on his shoulder in support.

"Ivy will help her; we all will. Give the girl time to heal."

Zane nodded at Thorn's words of support. While he understood what they said, his inner emotions struggled with what he wanted to do. He only wished to wrap the woman he loved in his arms and protect her from her demons.

Raina rose from Charles and walked over to the open doorway. She patiently waited for him to get his feelings under control. They all waited for him. He realized what he must do. He had to give Skye a sense of security without him. It would tear him apart, but for her sake he would sacrifice his love for her. He only hoped in time she would return to him.

He followed Raina along the hall to Skye's cabin, where once again he stood out in the empty hallway, waiting for permission to enter. Raina opened the door and beckoned for him to proceed. When he entered, it was to find Skye standing in the middle of the floor, her hands twisting in front of her. Raina had provided her with a dress, which hung on her body. Raina was more voluptuous than Skye; Skye was tall and lithe. She only wore a day dress with a shawl wrapped around her as a protective barrier. A barrier against him.

That wasn't the only barrier she had. He could see it in her stance and in the look in her eyes. Eyes which held fear. Fear of him. He frightened her. He murdered a man within her sight. Even though it was a villain who abused her, it was still a death. She must understand he wasn't that man. It was seeing her destruction that had pushed him to that point, but today wasn't the time to explain. Now was the time to ease her mind and make her feel secure. He would do anything to remove her fear and replace it with the sassiness and feistiness that made Skye who she was.

Zane walked to her swiftly, which was a mistake, for she shifted to her side. He came up short and realized his error. He scared her—the very thing he was trying not to do. Seeing her standing before him scared brought out his protective instincts. All he thought of was holding her in his arms. Arms she wanted no part of.

"I am sorry. I didn't mean to frighten you," he spoke calmly to her.

She raised her chin in denial. "I am not frightened." Skye denied. His Skye still had spirit deep inside her.

Maxwell breathed a sigh of relief; Shears didn't destroy her. He now understood Raina's words and noticed for himself what Skye needed. Time to heal. He could give her that. He had plenty of that and would bide his time. If he found her brother, it could help to heal her scars. He considered a new plan he needed to carry out.

"Are you well?" he asked her, clasping his hands behind his back. He held them there so he wouldn't reach out to hold her, also to calm her of his intentions toward her.

He took a non-threatening step toward her again, and again she darted to the side. Her eyes glanced to both sides, looking for escape. She had plenty of room to walk behind her, but she didn't. Zane figured out why. If she kept retreating backward, she would run into the wall and feel trapped. Zane saw in her eyes that she already thought she was trapped. He wanted to ease her fear, so he walked backward near the door. He noted relief filled her eyes.

"As well as can be expected, considering I was used as a punching bag."

Yes, his Skye was still in there. She still possessed her wicked sense of humor. This he could work with. He had learned she used her humor as a shield, but then it was what made her Skye.

"Well, you look lovely." He smiled wistfully at her.

"Yes, dark purple and blue are my colors."

He lowered himself in a chair so as not to be so intimidating. While she spoke with her usual sarcasm, he regarded how her body shook and how she jumped at any noise or movement of the ship. He wanted her at ease, so he sprawled himself out lazily.

"We will dock soon. Raina tells me you will recover at Hillston House, Thorn's townhome."

"Yes, so it was suggested. Only for a spell, and only until I receive word of Logan's whereabouts."

"We have a couple of leads. I will help Thorn find your brother for you."

"Also, the missing heir. Correct?" she asked.

"Yes."

She wandered around the cabin, her body unable to stand still. She realized he was pretending to be nonchalant toward her, but she understood him and figured it was a front. He gave himself away the moment he walked in the cabin and advanced on her. It had frightened her. But she hadn't seen his advancement as Maxwell coming toward her, just as somebody coming at her rapidly, and everything else faded away. She couldn't discern him from somebody who wanted to hurt her. Maybe Raina was correct and she still needed time to heal.

She saw in his eyes he wanted to care for her. She couldn't allow it; her body couldn't process what her mind told her. There wasn't anything Skye wanted more than for Zane to embrace her and whisper that everything would be well. That he would stay with her throughout every step of her recovery, but he didn't. He held his hands behind him or slumped in the chair as if her feelings meant nothing to him.

Did she misunderstand what she saw? Maybe after seeing her, he only pictured Shears atop her and it disgusted him. Well if this was the case, she would make this easy on him. She would relinquish her hold on him, but his next words threw her by surprise.

"Skye, I want to offer you my hand in marriage. After you have recovered, we can marry. I am offering you my protection."

His offer of marriage surprised her. From the sound of the marriage proposal, he only offered out of a source of obligation. She understood gossip would result from her capture on Shears's ship. This was not how she pictured Maxwell offering for her hand. What did she imagine, that he would lay his undying love at her feet and whisper words of love and happily ever after? Now he only offered an escape from a scandal. What arrangement of marriage would that be? An earl disgusted with his countess, who he never bedded. She guessed it was the kind that suited him. It would allow him to continue to live his life, leisurely bedding the ladies of the ton. While she did what, waited around begging for his scraps of attention? Hoping for one day he forgot the image of what he witnessed on Shears's ship?

"I require no need of any offer of protection. Once my brother is found, I shall return to Scotland with him."

"Skye you were violated, and there will be a scandal. My offer to you is a chance to live without shame."

She raised her chin again. "I suffer no shame."

Maxwell raked his hands through his hair in frustration. This was not going as he planned. Hell, none of this was. He was awkward, playing at the simpering idiot. He wanted to speak plainly with her but couldn't because of his witness in the corner—a witness who shot glares his way at every opportunity. He even thought he heard her tsk at him. Hell, he knew he talked like a fool.

"That is not what I meant. You misunderstand my intentions."

"Oh, I think you are being very clear about your intentions."

He rose from the chair and came her way again. "Skye, let me explain."

She cried out when he advanced. Raina came to her side swiftly and held up a hand to stop him.

"That is all for now, Maxwell."

"Let me explain to her."

"You are only frightening her. Perhaps you can try later when she has had more time to deal with this."

Zane waited for Skye to object to Raina's words. When none came, he whispered how sorry he was and turned to leave the cabin. When he reached the door, he stopped with his hand on the handle, waiting for her words begging him to stay. When no words were spoken, he turned the knob.

"Why did you not trust me with the full truth on your relation to the missing heir?"

He released the handle and laid his forehead to the door in defeat. Shears must have told her his darkest secret while he held her captive. How else could she know his shame? He knew he could mention her lack of trust with him but realized the blame game would only result in more distance between them. Zane wanted to close the gap, not spread it further apart. As he turned back toward her, he did the only action he could and spoke the truth.

"I was ashamed of how you would look upon me."

"Why did this information shame you?"

"I am disgraced by my parents' involvement, and I didn't want their actions to reflect how you thought of me."

"So instead you lied and therefore didn't give me your full trust."

"I was in the wrong. A regret I will always live with."

"How am I to trust you now?"

"Of that I have no answer for. I only hope you can consider my actions from here on out and base your trust on those. I promise to be honest with you from this day forth."

Skye listened to his words, wanting to believe him but knowing there was a great deal of misplaced trust on both of their parts. She knew he could have countered with her lack of faith in him, but he didn't. For she trusted him no more than he did her. They both kept secrets from each other. Secrets that might have helped the other but only harmed them instead. Throughout her talk of trust, he never asked for hers in return. He only offered his, sacrificing what should be offered to him with the hope that she would give him hers in return.

She turned her back on him, not wanting to show him any more vulnerability. His honesty unsettled her. She wanted to trust him with all her heart, but to achieve that, she would have to give him her love. While he wasn't offering his heart, he was offering his trust and honesty. A far cry from what she desired from him. She trembled with overwrought emotions. She wanted them both to leave the room so she could cry. Her body began to shake, and tears moistened her eyes.

"Skye," he whispered.

She heard him coming toward her as Raina's arm circled her shoulders, shielding him from his touch. While she was grateful for the intervention, her heart ached. She longed to be held in his arms. For him to whisper the words to help her heal.

When she turned from him, Zane felt his heart drop to his stomach. She couldn't even stand the sight of him. He knew he botched the entire conversation. She strung his emotions all over the place. He wanted to hold her, and she had turned away from his touch. When she continued to keep her back to him and he saw her body shake, he wanted to fall to his knees to cry with her. He wanted to shed his tears with her for everything she lost.

"Please, both of you leave," she whispered between her tears.

All they could do was leave her. They owed her that much respect. He escorted Raina back to Charles, holding his emotions in check the entire way. He saw the glances Raina passed to him. Pity. He needed no pity.

Chapter Thirteen

MAXWELL WENT TO THE bar in Thorn's cabin and grabbed his best whiskey, drinking a shot straight from the bottle. He carried the bottle as he punched the wall over and over until his skin peeled away from his bloodied knuckles. Mallory and Thorn tried to stop him, but he threw them off with punches. Only when his anger waned did he slide down the wall he had beaten and got himself stinking drunk. He drank half the whiskey before he realized it was only him and Thorn in the cabin. Charles removed Raina from his drunken stupor. He would behave as a gentleman and apologize to her in the morning. For now, he would remain the scoundrel they believed him to be. The one of the rottenest core.

"Are you going to share your drink?" Thorn asked.

Maxwell raised the bottle, offering it for him. Thorn shook his head; his comment was only spoken to drive him to stop his drinking. Maxwell didn't feel the need to halt his misery. So, he drank another long swallow. He realized he was in for a lecture, and it was one he didn't want to hear. Nonetheless, he would endure, for he was on the man's ship and owed him his gratitude.

"Out with it."

"With what?" Thorn inquired.

"With your speech."

Thorn laughed. "I have nothing to say, my friend."

"Are we?"

"What?"

"Still friends?"

"Yes, Maxwell. While I have not agreed with your decisions of late, we are still friends. Or so my wife tells me I must be with you."

"She has forgiven me then?"

"Yes, though she was never mad, only disappointed in you."

"Well, I guess I have given her more to be disappointed in."

"Yes, I will agree with you."

"What am I to do?"

"First, you can inform me why you have betrayed us and what your connection is to the missing heir."

"I never meant to betray any of you. I had to make it appear as if I had switched sides for Shears to trust me. He had information I needed."

"What kind of information?"

"He knew the location of the missing heir."

"What is your relationship to this child?"

"She is my sister."

Thorn stared at Maxwell in disbelief. The expression would adorn many faces of the ton after they were made aware of the scandal. For the heir to be his sister, it would mean his mother betrayed his father with the King.

"How?"

"Why, the usual way a man would acquire a sister," Maxwell drawled in sarcasm.

"Don't be a smartass."

"The King seduced my dearly devoted mother. My parents' marriage was a sham; they were only devoted to each other in the ton's eyes. My father no longer bedded my mother after he obtained his heir. He didn't even want a spare, so he carried on with his mistresses. My mother sought her revenge and bedded the King, only to everybody's despair a small baby was born nine months later."

"From what I understand, the heir is a boy."

"That is what they led you to believe, but she is a girl. She should be fourteen now. I know because I was present the night my mother gave birth, the same night they seized the baby and disappeared. The whole ordeal was covered up, of course."

"Did you divulge this information to Skye?"

"Only the part where I searched for the missing heir. The same child her brother searched for. Shears told her the truth."

"Did Shears inform you where you could locate the heir or Logan MacKinnon?"

"No, his final words were that he would never divulge where our loved ones were. He got his ultimate revenge on us. He led me on a wild goose chase for months, only to die with his secrets."

"I have Jake and Sammy searching his ship for any clues he might have left behind."

"You will find nothing. I never could. He kept them all up here." Maxwell pointed at his head.

"Nonetheless, it doesn't hurt to search."

"So, what becomes of me when we dock? I understand I am a wanted man."

"You are no more a wanted man than I am. You received a full pardon."

"How?"

"Another reason you can pay your gratitude to Ivy."

"It appears I will forever be in the lady's debt."

"As long as that is all she remains."

"Still jealous, are you?"

"Never was to begin with."

Maxwell humphed his reply. They both recognized the lie as a line of crap, but he wouldn't bait the man who graced him with his help.

"Do you love her?" Thorn questioned Maxwell.

"Who, Ivy?"

"No, Skye."

Maxwell didn't answer him. Love? How could he describe the agony he suffered right now? He felt so helpless. Did love ache as if your heart ripped in two and the only way for it to become whole again was for your other half to love you too? He understood what Thorn was playing at.

"Well, do you?"

"Did you ever find the meaning of love with Ivy after I described it to you?"

"Yes, believe it or not. You helped me envision what Ivy meant to me and what I meant to her. It took me a while to look past the green monster, but eventually I saw reason. Do you believe it with Skye?"

"More than I ever thought possible I could with another soul."

"So, what shall you do about it?"

"What am I to do? She won't let me touch her, let alone be with her in the same room without a chaperone."

"She only needs time, Maxwell. After she has had time to recover, how will you gain her love?"

"I ache for what she is enduring. I feel her pain as if it were my own."

"Then I would say yes, you are beyond in love with her."

"As for your answer, I will leave her be. I am not good enough for her."

"Bull."

"You didn't see her reaction toward me."

"Then I will need to search for a groom to protect her honor. I think I can find her somebody worthwhile."

Maxwell came off the floor and rushed toward Thorn, but Thorn was ready for him. Thorn grabbed the bottle out of Maxwell's hand and knocked him across the cheek with his fist. Maxwell slid backward, caught unaware. His drunken stupor delayed any reaction he might have taken, for Thorn held up his hand, halting him from any advancement.

"I deem that was sufficient payback."

"What the hell did you do that for?"

"I have been waiting to punch you for a long time. Doesn't sit well, does it my friend?"

"What?"

"Knowing another man might touch your love and you have no power over stopping it."

Maxwell cringed at those words. He owed Thorn an apology for making a play at Ivy. He only acted out of jealousy at losing their close friendship and held disappointment in Thorn for upsetting Ivy. Zane realized he was wrong when he kissed her, but the temptation of giving into a desire overtook him in the moment. The feelings he held for Ivy were of friendship and nothing more. He was a fool for even crossing that line.

Maxwell walked over to Thorn and held out his hand. "My humblest apologies for attempting to seduce your betrothed."

"You are forgiven. Now let us begin again. What are your plans for Skye MacKinnon?"

"She refused my offer of marriage."

"When has rejection ever stopped you before? You need a game plan before we find her brother and he hunts for you."

"Have you met her brother?"

"Yes, he has helped me on many occasions. My allegiance with him is how I met Skye. She operated the Edinburgh War Office."

"She is a spy?"

"Yes, a very clever one at that."

"How come I wasn't made aware of her?"

"We all have levels of intelligence with the War Office that required us to identify with only who or what they wanted you to know. I am assuming with your connection to Shears, they didn't want to leak out any information on her. You might have heard of her though. She is called Fionnlagh."

Maxwell sat in silence as he acknowledged the information. Fionnlagh meant "white warrior," and her last name MacKinnon meant son of the fair born. She was clever to combine the two meanings and disguise herself as a man. From what Isobel told him about Skye, that was how her father raised her—as a man. He had heard of her, but her name never meant anything to him, so he never pondered over her. Also, he didn't know Fionnlagh was a woman. He knew she completed many missions for the War Office, so he presumed she was a man, not a lady with long red hair and generous curves. A lady he bedded only to be betrayed by.

"Yes, it seems I was kept in the dark on much-needed information."

"That is what happens when you act as a double agent. Even a double agent with instructions from the Crown."

"What is her brother like?"

"Exactly like her, but much bigger."

"Bigger, as in?"

"Bigger, as in if you don't make an honest lady out of her before his return, there will be no way for us to save you this time."

"So, I am a dead man then."

Thorn laughed. "This shall be fun to watch. I will truly enjoy watching you squirm."

"Friends, huh?"

"Yes, and I will offer you the same advice I think you were trying to offer me. I was just too pig-headed to listen to."

"Which is?"

"Show her you love her."

"Easier said than done."

"Oh, I think you will find a way," Thorn replied as he left the cabin.

Maxwell sat, staring at the spot where he left, pondering the hidden meaning behind his words. He searched for the bottle, only to discover Thorn had taken it with him. It was probably for the best. He was no longer thirsty anyway.

How do I tell her what she means to me when she doesn't even want the sight of me around her? Although, Thorn didn't say tell, he said show. Then new ideas came to Maxwell on how he could show her he cared. The first was to give her space. The rest would fall into place. He started to plan his seduction of Skye MacKinnon.

Chapter Fourteen

SKYE TRAVELED IN THE carriage through London with Raina. The men didn't join them, providing Skye the privacy she needed. They rode their horses alongside the carriage. When they docked, Thorn obtained guards to seize Shears's men into custody. They would proceed straight to Newgate, where they would hang for their crimes. Thorn and Mallory questioned them about Shears's agenda. Most of the prisoners talked, hoping to save their lives. The interrogation was to no avail though, as most of what they learned from the men they had already gathered intelligence on. So, their information was of no use to them.

Skye gazed through the window at the passing scenery. It was early yet, dawn only breaking the surface. Early morning vendors were out, yelling to sell their wares, and prostitutes were finding their way home. Occasionally, they passed a carriage of the gentry or rogues returning from their late-night card games or visits to their mistresses.

Now and then, her glance found Maxwell riding near the carriage. He looked magnificent on a horse. His gaze never left the carriage. Skye always looked away when their eyes met. His eyes held sorrow, reflecting his pain for her. She did not want his pity. He didn't speak to her when Mallory helped her and Raina board the carriage. He only stood silently, regarding her. His stare was unnerving. Skye wouldn't let him see how his presence affected her. She knew Raina also watched her. Raina understood how to be there but not to smother her. She was grateful for the woman.

Skye wondered how her host, Ivy Thornhill, would act. Skye's curiosity was piqued about meeting her, but it also left her nervous. This was the woman who truly held Maxwell's heart. How would Ivy treat her?

The carriage turned into Mayfair. Gone were the storefronts, loud vendors, and noisy streets. Large townhomes surrounded the neighborhood, welcoming the aristocracy home. Skye felt uncomfortable in this environment. She was used to large open areas where she could roam free and a welcoming castle bustling with her loved ones. Now she would be surrounded by proper lords and ladies drinking tea and gossiping on the ton's latest scandal. Which would be her. She realized it was the best choice for her to finish her recovery here and wait for word of Logan. Would she be able to endure this prim life, or would she cause more disgrace by acting as herself?

The carriage stopped in front of the largest townhome Skye had ever seen. The house was surrounded with iron fencing with the same iron decorating the balconies in splendid design. The townhome took up an entire block with its grand décor. The front lawn welcomed her with an array of beautiful flowers inviting her into their home. Skye's nerves were settled as she soaked up the comforting atmosphere. When the carriage stopped, Mallory assisted Raina out and up the stairs to the townhome. Thornhill waited patiently for Skye to exit. When Skye alighted, she saw Maxwell hang back from them at a distance. Her eyes met his, and they begged for her to ask for him, but Skye diverted her gaze to Thornhill, where he waited with a smile of patience. She tipped her head for him to lead her inside his home. When they entered, the house a flurry of activity greeted her.

A lovely woman with long, flowing blonde hair greeted Charles and Raina, wrapping each of them in hugs. A young boy rushed forward and threw himself at Thornhill, who wrapped him in his arms and lifted him above his head. The young lad let out a whelp of glee. Everybody laughed at the young child. The lady chided Thorn to putting Tommy down, which only led Thornhill to throw the lad up again.

He then carried the boy over to Ivy, sliding the lad to the floor. Tommy ran over to Charles and Raina, asking them tons of questions about their adventure. He appeared to be a much-loved child for the attention they bestowed upon him. She observed the tender exchange Thorn shared with his wife. He bent to kiss her gently on the lips, pulling her tenderly in his arms. He whispered words to her, and Ivy smiled in return.

Skye glanced over at Maxwell, who leaned against the wall taking in the scene of his friends being welcomed home by their family. She expected to see jealousy at the scene between Marcus and Ivy Thornhill, but the only expression gracing his face was a smile of amusement. When he caught her scrutinizing him, he raised his eyebrow in the silent mockery he only displayed toward her.

Skye glanced away, and her eyes met Ivy's. Ivy looked between Skye and Maxwell, viewing their interaction. She smiled secretly, as if she noticed something that neither one was aware of. When Skye looked back at Maxwell, he saw Ivy's smile too. He shrugged his shoulders at Skye as in who knows.

Ivy came forward and wrapped her arm around Skye's shoulders, leading her up the stairs. She never spoke to her, waiting for the privacy of Skye's bedchamber before she addressed her. Ivy could tell the happy greetings overwhelmed the girl. Ivy also saw Maxwell eating Skye up with his eyes. The rascal would have devoured her if there were not so many souls present. She would speak with him after she had Skye settled. For now, she needed to place the young lady at ease.

They walked into the bedchamber that was decorated in many shades of green. Skye glanced around and saw the bedroom was small but held a soothing charm. A small writing desk sat in the corner, and a divan rested against the window, overlooking the garden. A small fire was lit, warming the room in a cozy atmosphere, and fresh flowers graced the nightstand. Red roses overflowed a dark green vase. Their fragrance graced the air with a light perfume. Skye wandered deeper in the room, looking out at the garden. She stared as Thornhill chased the young boy through the maze. Ivy joined her at the window watching the two.

"I don't know which one the child is."

"Your husband acts like a different man."

"Yes, young Tommy brings out the boy in him."

"I was not aware of Thornhill having any children."

"We adopted young Tommy. He was my savior twice."

Skye looked toward Ivy in question. She wondered about Tommy's story. Ivy wandered to the chair by the fire and motioned for Skye to join her. Skye sat in the opposite chair. Ivy poured them each a cup of tea, which had been waiting for them. Skye drank the tea as Ivy described how she met Tommy and how Tommy had saved her life, not once but twice. Ivy also described her own capture by Shears and how she recovered. Skye at once felt kinship with the young lady.

Ivy reached across and held Skye's hand. "I relate to some of your fears, my dear, and I will be available to talk whenever you wish. Please take your time to recover and inform me if I can be of any help."

"I thank you and Thornhill for your generosity. I don't mean to be a nuisance. I will be leaving as soon as I am able."

"You must do whatever you believe is best for yourself. I will leave you with these parting words: we are here for you, if you allow us to be. Please join us for meals and consider this house yours."

Skye rose and bowed to Ivy. "Thank you, my lady."

"Just Ivy, please."

"Ivy." Skye smiled at her.

When Ivy left, Skye lay on the divan. She reflected on her time with Ivy. Skye felt a friendship forming with the lady, for Ivy had also been held captive by Shears and was able to escape from any harm. While she was not as forceful as Skye, she was somebody who Skye could confide in. Skye's also felt more settled toward the woman after she witnessed the love she shared with Thornhill. Feeling exhausted from the short carriage ride, she covered herself with a blanket and closed her eyes for a short rest.

~~~~~~

It was late afternoon when she awoke, and the sun was setting. She sat up to take in her unfamiliar surroundings, remembering where she was. She rose to fix her hair and smooth out her dress. It was rude of her to stay in her room. Skye wandered to the windows to calm her nerves. When she looked out, she saw Zane sitting on a bench. He looked so lost and alone. She realized she treated him badly and owed him an apology, at the very least. She owed him more than an apology, but it was the only thing she could manage at this time.

Skye decided to visit him and set off to find her way to the garden. As she traveled along the stairs, she hoped to encounter a servant to ask for directions, but she didn't find any. When she wandered through the different rooms, she found no doors that lead outside. After a time, she entered what appeared to be a study with doors out to the gardens. When she was just about exit, she noticed Zane was no longer alone. Ivy had joined him on the bench. Ivy had her hand lying atop his in a familiar fashion. Zane smiled at her lovingly. She felt like an intruder watching them. Zane's affections were on open display. He still cared deeply for Ivy Thornhill. Skye experienced a deep sense of loss. She had spoken hastily toward him, but as she regarded him now, she had been correct in letting him go. She would never have his total love while he still yearned for another. Her fingers touched the windowpane, as if she touched him one last time. With a deep sigh she rested her head on the glass.

"They are only friends," a voice from behind her defended them.

"Maybe from your wife's feelings, but Maxwell's actions tell another story."

"At one time, but now his heart is with another."

Skye didn't reply. She disagreed with Thornhill. It didn't matter anymore.

"I was called away on business and missed luncheon. Would you care to join me for tea?" he asked.

Skye was famished. She'd slept through luncheon. She nodded and let Thorn lead her near the fire, where a tea table sat with a small repast. Small sandwiches and cookies were arranged on a plate. With needing something to keep her occupied Skye poured the tea and served them refreshments. They ate in silence, each occupied with their own thoughts. Skye's thoughts couldn't move past the two talking out in the garden. Was Thornhill jealous of their exchange and thinking the same thoughts? When she glanced at him, Skye doubted he was. He appeared confident and not the least disturbed by the two.

"I have a few leads on your brother, and my men are looking into them. When I hear more news, I will inform you, and then we can proceed from there. In the meantime, I hope you will accept our generosity in aiding with your recovery. If you require anything, please let Ivy or me know."

"I need to send word to my family."

"I have already dispatched a rider to carry news of your safety to them."

"Thank you."

"It is my pleasure. I understand what you endured aboard Shears's ship was traumatic, but understand that you have friends who care for you and want to help. Do not shut yourself off from your emotions."

"I am a stranger to every one of you."

"In a way, but we share a kinship with one another. We were instructed to bring Shears to justice. The man got what he deserved. Now his reign of terror has ended, and we can return to our lives without constantly looking over our shoulders."

"Easy for you to say. Your family is safe. My brother is still missing as a result of Shears's machinations."

"We will find your brother, Skye, and when we do, it will be finished. Think of every life we have saved. Think of the safety of our countries. The man nearly succeeded in bringing the war to our shores and without the work everybody did, he almost achieved his goal."

"I realize what you are saying is true, but it doesn't wipe from my memory the terror of being held under his hands."

"Those memories need time to fade, and even then, you won't forget them. From here on out, it will only make you a stronger person than you already are."

Skye finished her tea as she absorbed his words. What he said was true, but it left her feeling a vulnerability that frightened her. She had not felt this way since her mother passed. It was a feeling she never wanted to experience again.

"Are you going to put the poor chap out of his misery?"

Skye raised her eyebrow in question. She knew who he was referring to, but she was letting him know this conversation was off the table between them.

However, Thorn was determined to have his say. "He cares deeply for you."

"There are too many lies between us. Neither of us trusts one another, and a relationship cannot flourish without trust."

"But it can be rebuilt if the level of trust is open and if honesty is spoken between the two of you."

Skye rose from her chair and Thornhill followed. Skye dipped into a curtsey, thanked him for the lovely tea, and excused herself from his company. She didn't bother to reply to his comments. Her wounds were too fresh to discuss what she herself didn't understand.

~~~~~

"You look like you can use a friend."

Maxwell rose at those words and offered his arm to Ivy. He led her back to the bench to rest beside him.

"Is it that obvious?"

"Well, you appear as if you lost your best friend, and considering I am right here, it must be more ominous."

Zane chuckled at her lighthearted words. His gloominess was much more dire. He had lost the love of his life and didn't grasp how to win her back. Maybe if he discussed his misery with Ivy, she could offer him a bit of sage advice. He wiped his hand across his face as he sighed.

"Where to begin?"

"Well, from the start is usually the best choice, but feel free to share what you will. I am only here to help."

"Before I ask you for your support and advice, please forgive all the sins I have committed against you and yours these past few months."

"Zane, you are your own worst enemy. We forgave you, and you must learn to forgive yourself. I know I betrayed our friendship, but it was in your best interests for me to tell them about the missing heir."

"I understand, and you were correct to do so."

They sat together, their apologies floating away in the wind. Their friendship was always stronger than their actions. However the other friend acted, the other always forgave. She laid her hand atop his, gently squeezing his fingers, letting him recognize she was still there for him whenever he needed her friendship.

"Will you tell me about her?"

"Skye?"

"Yes, Skye."

"What do you care to hear, Ivy dear?"

"I want to learn everything about the lady who captured your heart. First start with how you plan to win her back. Because from what I see, she is upset with you."

"There will be no winning her back. She despises me. The very sight of me causes her to cringe."

Ivy laughed. "You fool, the girl is smitten with you."

"You are the fool and seeing things, my dear, that are not present," Zane answered in a harsh laugh.

"Tell me what happened."

Zane told Ivy how he came to meet Skye and about their time together in Scotland. Of course, he left out the moments they spent alone.

Those memories were nobody's business but his own. Then he told her how Skye drugged him with Raina's help. When he told her what he witnessed as he rescued her, Ivy shook from the horror. He stopped, only to have Ivy press him to finish. He didn't want her to relive her own ordeal, but she whispered to him that she hadn't experienced half the terror Skye did. She wanted to listen, so she could understand how to handle Skye. When Zane stated how Shears practically raped Skye, silent tears flowed along Ivy's cheeks. Still, she encouraged him to finish the rest of his story. He ended with his talk with Skye and his loss on how to proceed.

He pulled out his handkerchief and handed it to Ivy. She thanked him and dried her tears. Then she wrapped her arms around him and hugged him. She rested her head on his chest, comforting him. He wrapped a friendly arm around her, thankful for the comfort she offered. Ivy had always been a good friend. Why he risked their friendship over a kiss, he had no clue, for he never thought about Ivy the way he feels toward Skye. The different emotions were worlds apart from each other.

She patted his breast pocket. "You must woo her."

Zane sat back, holding Ivy apart from him, his hands on her arms. "Woo her?"

"Yes, woo her. Sweep her off her feet." Ivy laughed.

"Did you not hear one word I have spoken to you? She wants nothing to do with me."

"That's where you are wrong, my friend. Trust me, I know different."

"How do you woo a lady who wishes for me to disappear?"

"Well for one thing, you don't begin by holding another man's wife in his garden for anybody to witness."

Zane jumped at the sound of Thorn's voice. He felt guilt as he put distance between them. Ivy only laughed, jumping from the bench and running into Thorn's arms. Thorn lowered his head to give her a kiss.

"I am sorry, it was only in—" Zane began to explain.

"I am not the one you need to apologize to."

"Do you mean …" Zane looked up to the window he was sitting under, searching for any sign of Skye. When he viewed the rustling of the curtains, he realized he'd screwed up again.

"Yes," Thorn replied before Zane was finished.

"Damn."

"It will be all right, Zane. I can explain to her," offered Ivy.

"I already tried," said Thorn.

Zane paced back and forth across the garden path. He only seemed to dig himself in deeper. If he was not digging, he was sinking. He didn't know which he preferred. Neither wasn't getting him any closer to her, but further apart.

"As for an answer to your question … before we were so rudely interrupted." Ivy winked at Thorn.

"Yes?"

"You are the master charmer of the ton. Every lady swoons when you are nearby. There hasn't been a lady I have ever encountered that you haven't charmed. So, turn your charm on her."

"She is immune to my charm."

Ivy laughed. "No woman is immune to charm, my dear man." Grabbing hold of Thorn's hand, she drew him away.

Zane remained in the garden contemplating Ivy's words. Woo. Charm. Skye. Could it be done? He stood staring at the window. He thought he saw a shadow of her, peering out. Zane smiled and bowed to her. Yes, an idea was coming to him. Woo her, he would. Charm her, he would. Seduce her, yes definitely he would. Love her, most certainly for the rest of their lives.

Chapter Fifteen

SIMS CARRIED A SALVER with invitations and mail into the parlor, proceeding to Ivy's side. Ivy smiled and thanked him, taking the correspondence. As she sat at her desk, she rifled through, sorting the mail into piles. When she came across the familiar letter they received daily for the last few weeks, she set it to the side, smiling slyly. Ivy glanced up to study the young lady in the room staring out into the garden. There was a light rain this morning that kept them indoors. She held a sadness as she gazed at the raindrops dripping upon the petals. With a deep sigh, the young lady turned, pasting a smile on her face as she noticed Ivy watching her. Skye walked over to sit on the settee, pouring a cup of tea and offering Ivy a cup. Ivy declined but grabbed the letter and joined her on the couch.

"Your admirer has written again," she said, offering the letter to Skye.

Skye blushed as she reached for the letter. The same scrawl and stamp adorned the missive as the earlier letters she'd received from him. Her fingers traced the stamp, rubbing his crest back and forth across her fingertips. She didn't open the letter. Instead, she slid the note inside her pocket.

"Are you going to remove the poor fellow from his misery and write back this time?"

"Well, he isn't actually in misery, is he?"

"You don't believe the gossip you heard during tea yesterday, do you?"

"He is making his rounds again, is he not?"

"Skye, he cares only for you. He hasn't spent time with another lady since he met you. These ladies are vicious gossip whores. They rip you apart because that is what they do well. You are a threat to them. So, if they can place doubt in your mind about Zane, they will. Talk with him. He is miserable without you."

"It would be of no use. We have no future with one another."

"Why not?"

"It is complicated."

Ivy reached for Skye's hand, and Skye didn't pull away. Over the last few weeks, they grew close. Ivy told Skye her story about being held captive on Shear's ship, and it helped for Skye to open her mind and work through her terror. Her nightmares ceased to exist, and she was no longer terrified of another person's touch.

"Nothing is too complicated to work through. You two are meant to be together. If you would only open yourself to him."

"I am not ready yet."

Ivy patted her hand in understanding and rose.

"Well, if he keeps to his timing, he should arrive any moment now. Do you want to retire to your bedchamber while I accept him in the Rose Room for tea?"

Skye knew she acted childish in refusing to receive him or write back to his letters. She was nervous to be alone with him and was insecure. The ladies of the ton who wanted him were stunning, and she felt so plain and awkward compared to them.

She nodded to Ivy and left the room. She barely made it along the hallway when she heard Maxwell in the foyer. Skye peeked her head around the corner, watching him as he gave his hat and cane to Sims. Then he followed Sims to join Ivy in the Rose Room. He paused, glancing over his shoulder like he searched for her. Skye withdrew her head and pressed herself against the wall. He almost caught her spying on him. She listened as his footsteps followed the butler. She shook her head at her silliness and continued to her bedchamber.

He held a lost look about him. When she heard him with Sims, his voice was quiet and withdrawn. Was it because of her? Should she give him another chance? When she slipped into her room, she slid his letter out of her pocket. As she turned it over in her hand, she thought she might reply to his letter. Ivy wasn't aware, but she read the letters he sent her every day. Most of them inquired about her welfare. They'd turned more personal this week, practically begging to have a word with her. Then yesterday, he expressed his feelings. Her fingers trembled opening the letter. This fear was the reason she didn't want to see him today.

It wasn't only his letters he sent. He arrived every day, hoping to call on her. On these visits, he always brought her a gift. Small things: flowers, candy, or books. Then yesterday, he sent her a drawing. He'd wrapped and rolled up the present, leaving it with Ivy as he did all the other gifts. He brought the gifts hoping to give them to her, but as always, Ivy was the one who presented them to her. The drawing was haunting. It showed two lovers being separated by a storm out of their control. Skye didn't recognize the artist. Did the painting portray them? The picture expressed her own emotions toward Zane. Did his regards follow the same path? She sat alone in her room wondering what he brought her today.

Skye's fingernail dug under the seal, and she opened the letter. She didn't read the words yet. She was too afraid. Her fingers traced his letters written upon the parchment. She wandered to the divan and lay back as she closed her eyes to calm her breathing. Opening her eyes, she began to read:

My dearest Skye,

I hope the phrase does not offend you, because you are my dearest. I hope this letter finds you well. Ivy informs me you are healing nicely. I am lighthearted at this news. Once again, I am below awaiting your presence. I know you won't join us, but that doesn't deter me, for one day I believe you will. You give me hope every day. You may ask yourself, "How do I give this fool hope, when I have never answered his letters or thanked him for his gifts?" Because, my dear, you have never sent the letters or gifts back or told Ivy to send me away. While you do not grace me with your loveliness, I can feel you nearby. If your near presence is all you can gift me, then I will accept it for now. And I mean for now because I won't lie to you anymore, Skye. While I am a patient man, I am finding I am not where you are concerned. I will come for you. When I chase you, my dear, you shall discover every desire and need I hold in my heart for you. I won't leave a doubt in your lovely head. So, enjoy the present Ivy will deliver to you today. I hope it brings a desire to see me. Take care, my love, and I wait until the day when we meet again.

Your dearest, Zane

P.S. When we do meet again, you will have no doubt for I will draw you into my arms as our bodies press close together. My fingers will trail across your skin, setting you on fire. As my eyes devour you, I will lower my head to yours, our lips but a breath apart ...

I will leave your imagination to fill in the rest, my love.

Skye brought the letter to her chest and her fingers to her lips. She sensed his lips upon hers, hovering above ready to take her lips in a passionate kiss, but it was not to be. Was she being foolish to fear their passion? She rose from the divan and pressed her hands over her dress, smoothing out her wrinkles, the letter falling unforgotten on the ground. She rushed to the door, hurrying to see him below. Her steps flew along the staircase as she made her way to the Rose Room, standing outside the door. She brought her breath under control, her fingers twisting nervously at her sides. Skye took a deep breath and pushed the doors open, ready to meet him. She needed to see him.

When she stepped in the room, she expected him to be waiting patiently for her to appear. An empty room greeted her; he left, and so had Ivy. During her time upstairs the rain had abated. Perhaps they went for a stroll through the garden. When she rushed to the windows, she saw no sign of them.

"Excuse me, my lady. I thought the room was empty," a maid apologized as she went to remove the tea tray.

"You are fine. Do you know of Lady Ivy's whereabouts?"

"She is in the nursery."

"And Lord Maxwell?"

"I am sorry, my lady, but I do not know of any visitors."

"Thank you."

The maid cleared up the tea tray and left her alone in the parlor. Skye had been too late, so she decided to visit Ivy in the nursery. For she would have news on Maxwell, and she always took delight in telling Skye of his visits. Ivy always held out hope Skye might relent and join them. The day she did, he'd left early. Maybe he was tired of waiting, even though his letter suggested otherwise. Did he realize she wasn't worth his trouble?

In the nursery, Ivy fed her newborn as she listened to Tommy tell her a story. Skye stood in the doorway and watched how natural Ivy was. She was always relaxed, making everybody secure in her love. When Tommy made her laugh, she noticed Skye in the doorway and motioned her to come inside. Skye sat next to her, and when Ivy finished with her daughter, she passed her into Skye's arms. Ivy lifted Tommy on her lap as she listened to the rest of his story.

Skye held the small baby in her arms. She slid her finger into the tiny hand, and the baby tightened her grip around her finger, making Skye smile at the simple gesture. When the baby smiled and cooed at her, Skye melted completely. She wanted this with Zane, but was it too late? Could she reach out and grab what she desired? When she glanced up, she saw that Tommy wandered off to play and Ivy was watching her again.

"Why are you always watching me?" Skye asked.

"I have been waiting."

"Waiting for what?"

"For you to come to your senses regarding Maxwell, and you finally have."

"What makes you say that?"

"Well you are out of your bedroom earlier than usual when Maxwell comes to visit. That must have been a passionate letter to draw you out of your room," Ivy teased.

Skye blushed. "Well it was for naught. He has left?"

"Yes, he saw no reason to stay since you fled to your room. While he apologized, it wasn't my company he desired. At one time, it would have hurt, but now I only find humor in it. Since he wasn't up for my laughing at his expense, he left."

Skye didn't respond to Ivy's wicked sense of humor. She turned her gaze back to the baby, whispering soft words to her. The baby kicked and cooed from her attention. Skye still sensed Ivy's gaze upon her, waiting for an explanation.

"I decided to join your tea to inform him to stop sending me gifts and letters."

"Bull."

Skye raised her eyebrows. "I beg your pardon, my lady?"

"You heard me correctly. You came downstairs today because the letter he wrote you sparked a desire to see him. A desire so strong you rushed to set your eyes upon him. Now you are defensive because he left so soon and you're disappointed he didn't linger. You decided to put your fears away. Am I correct?"

Skye sighed. "You are correct."

Ivy let out a sound of glee. The smile on the woman's face was one of utter joy, but then it turned into the smile of a woman set upon scheming. Skye must stop her in her tracks before she set any scheme into play.

"Now what we need to do is …"

"No, we will do nothing. It was foolish of me to come downstairs today. I have changed my mind; I'm not ready to meet him yet."

"But you are."

"No." Skye was firm.

"Well I will leave you with one question to answer. I don't expect an answer now, but when you are ready to give me this answer, I will be waiting to help you with Zane. Whatever is stopping you from reaching out to him, only you understand the answer. I only ask you this: Do you love him?" Ivy asked as she gathered the baby and passed her to the nanny.

Skye didn't answer, instead asking a question to help make her decision. "What gift did he bring me today?"

Ivy turned at the door and smiled sadly at her. "Nothing, my dear, I am sorry," she replied as she left the nursery.

Skye stared at the door, lost in those words. She rocked the chair back and forth, realizing she only had herself to blame. She thought over Ivy's last question. Did she love him? It was an emotion she didn't want to ponder. Whenever she thought of Zane, she froze, too afraid to open those floodgates of emotions because it made her too vulnerable. Experiencing any emotion frightened her. She lived her life in fear now. This was not her. She did not love this Skye. She wanted to be herself again. For that, she needed to face her fear—all of them.

Throughout the gloomy afternoon, she sat in the quiet nursery. Her tears fell silently as her mind wrapped itself around her fears. Her mind fought through her fears as she confronted them. Every fear, emotion, and terror she fought and conquered. Wiping the tears from her cheeks, she rose and walked to the windows. When she gazed outside, she watched the sun fighting through the dark, heavy clouds moving swiftly across the sky. The sun fought its way free and sent rays of sunshine shooting across the city's skyline. Skye sensed the clouds fading away from her mind and heart too. She knew the answer to Ivy's question but was unable to admit it aloud.

When she walked into her bedroom, she rang the bell for a maid to help her change for dinner. It was time to live again. To do that, she needed to interact with society. She knew it would only be Thorn, Ivy, and their families joining them for dinner. She remained in her room on other family meals, but she would join them tonight. She would accompany Ivy on more outings in time. First things first, small steps. Then those small steps would lead to larger steps, and those larger steps would one day return her back to Zane.

Skye moved to the divan as she searched for her letter from him; she wanted to stash it with the others. It was nowhere to be found. She dropped to her knees as her hands searched underneath the furniture, brushing across the floor, hoping her fingers encountered the scrap of paper. She came up empty. It wasn't behind the furniture either. The maid must have cleaned her bedroom. Her eyes searched the room, expecting to spot the letter. As she turned in a slow circle around the room, her spin stopped at the bed. For there lying on her bed rested her opened letter propped up against a package. He did leave her a present today. How? Was he in her room? Did he search her out? She hurried to the bed, picking up the package and holding it in her hands. Skye looked around her room as she searched for him, but he didn't linger. Her hands shook as she held the package, too afraid to open what he left her today. But she wouldn't let the fear that controlled her life the last few weeks to control her life anymore. She wanted to reach out to grab what destiny threw at her feet. Skye ripped open the wrapping with eager fingers and stood in awe of what she held in her hands.

She embraced the gift in her open palm and reveled at what he gifted her. He'd given her his heart with this gift. More tears slid down her cheeks. She was an ultimate crying pot these days, but these tears were shed from happiness. Her fears drifted into the wind, if there existed a wind to drift away to. They were all gone, replaced with determination. Determination to win him back. Skye now realized he had been wooing and charming her with the visits and small gifts. Now she would chase him, and he wouldn't even see her coming.

Skye smiled as she gazed upon the red ruby and began to make her plans. Plans which would only succeed with Ivy's help. She slid the red ruby in her pocket as she set off to find her new friend. They had scheming to do. She found Ivy in her bedchamber and knocked on the door. She didn't want to intrude on her private chambers, but she could answer Ivy's question now and knew Ivy wouldn't mind.

"Please enter."

Skye walked into the enormous suite and saw Ivy at the dressing table. Her maid was pulling her hair into curls on top of her head.

"I am sorry to intrude. I needed to speak with you right away."

"Please give me a few moments. Mabel is nearly finished." Ivy waved at Mabel to hurry.

"I will wait, my lady," Skye replied, and she wandered to the painting hanging on the wall.

The painting drew Skye's eyes to the delicate setting. The portrait portrayed Ivy. She sat on a blanket at the park, feeding the ducks. She gazed at somebody with utter devotion. Whoever she smiled upon held her heart, and obviously she held his heart too. The painting must have been drawn by her husband. She didn't know Thornhill to be a painter. She glanced in the corner and gasped in shock at the initials nestled in the corner. For they were not MT, but ZM. Zane Maxwell? If he drew this portrait, then he painted the drawing he delivered to her yesterday. Were they the two lovers separated in the storm? Obviously not, for his love for Ivy was displayed by the painting on the wall.

She turned around slowly and saw Ivy walking toward her. Mabel had left. She caught the look of concern in Ivy's eyes. Skye knew her thoughts were expressed on her face. Through her confusion she didn't understand what to think of this new dilemma.

"I know what is running through your overactive mind. It is not what you think."

"What am I thinking?"

"You are imagining Zane painting me in love with him and he in return painted his love for me. Am I correct?"

"The painting does not lie, my lady."

"You are as much of a fool as my husband was when he discovered the picture. Now he cherishes it."

Skye tried not to jump to a hundred different conclusions, but she couldn't stop herself. She kept leaping to the same assumption. She decided to listen and not allow her jealous heart to make judgments for her anymore.

"I am listening."

Ivy stood before the painting with a wistful smile on her face and told Skye of the time Maxwell and she were close friends. How Thorn asked Maxwell to keep her company while he was away fighting in the war. While during their time together they grew close, not in a sexual way, but as close friends as only a gentleman and a lady were allowed. They shared everything with each other—well, almost everything. So, during that outing, Maxwell did what any friend would do when their best friend pined for their lost love. He set out to cheer her spirits. He painted in the park and enlightened Ivy with stories of Thorn. She missed him terribly and was miserable. When Maxwell regaled her with stories of Thorn, Ivy became sappy. So, it was then that Maxwell drew her while she spoke of her love for Thorn. He captured a lady expressing her true love. Not of a lady he loved.

Skye looked at the picture in a different light. She noticed the differences from her first glance. Ivy held a faraway look in her eyes as she stared off in the distance. She didn't focus on the painter but on an image in her mind.

"Do you see?"

"Yes, I am sorry for jumping to the wrong conclusions."

Ivy laughed. "You are not alone, which is a story for another time. Now what brings you to my bedchamber? Wonderful news, I hope."

"An answer to your earlier question."

Ivy came to her tiptoes in anticipation of Skye's answer. She understood the excitement in Ivy's eyes. Skye joined in Ivy's laughter. She had not laughed for a long time. She felt a new sense of lightness in herself.

"And?"

"Yes," Skye spoke with a smile.

Ivy let out a whoop of glee and danced around Skye. The lady was much too excited. Skye shook her head at the woman's silliness.

"Finally. Now you must promise to let me help you. If it were not for Maxwell, Thorn and I would not be together. I want to help you two. It would be my greatest pleasure."

"How did he help you and Thorn?"

"Another time, another story. I will just say he made Thorn so jealous. It was such a delight."

"I don't wish to make Maxwell jealous."

"No, no, my dear, of course not. What made you change your mind?"

"He left me a present in my room."

"Oh, that man is such a romantic," Ivy sighed.

Skye didn't reply to Ivy's comment. She realized she didn't know Maxwell that well, which remained part of the problem. Their desire spun out of control, and they never took the time to learn about one another. Maybe if they had, they could have trusted each other with their secrets.

They couldn't return to fix the actions of their past. They could only move forward from here. It was time for Skye to open her heart to him.

"I would like to accept your invitation to dinner, if it is not too late."

"Oh, this is perfect. I must warn you, I invited Zane this afternoon. I can send word to him to cancel, if you wish."

"No, I was hoping he would be at dinner this evening. Can I ask you a small favor?"

"Please do."

"Can you please place him next to me?"

"Are you sure you are ready for this, Skye?"

"Yes, I believe I am."

"Perfect, now hurry. I will send Mabel to help you prepare. I think the white gown will be lovely for this evening."

"Will that not be too debutante?"

"Not with your curves. It will be a perfect mixture of innocence and minx."

"Are you sure I won't be intruding on your family dinner?"

"You are family, my dear. Now hurry. I cannot wait to witness Maxwell's expression when you join us. Also, make sure you come downstairs fashionably late."

Skye returned to her room. Mabel waited with a bath. She bathed and set at the vanity for the maid to fix her hair. She never had her hair styled before. This was a new experience for her, even having beautiful dresses to wear. Ivy's seamstress came to the house her first few days here, and with Ivy's help, they created a small wardrobe for Skye. After Mabel finished with her hair, she guided her into her dress. As she stood before the mirror it was to gaze upon an unfamiliar woman staring back at her.

"You look gorgeous, my lady. Earl Maxwell will drop to his knees. Lady Ivy is correct, as usual. Now wait here, and Lady Ivy will send word on when you are to arrive below."

"Thank you so much on making me beautiful tonight, Mabel."

"You needed no help; you just are," the maid told her as she straightened the room.

When the maid left, Skye still couldn't remove herself from the mirror. She couldn't believe the vision staring back at her. She wiped her palms down the front of her dress. Ivy was correct. She didn't look like a debutante in this dress. She looked wanton with a touch of innocence. The dress was white and hugged her curves. White pearls laced through the fabric covering her bust line. Her breasts were tucked in tightly with enough to tease a gentleman's eye. Skye picked up the dark blue shawl and draped it across her shoulders. She wasn't quite comfortable showing her assets so wantonly. She swung around in a circle and her skirts danced around her legs. Her body was graced in lace and tulle, making her feel soft and feminine. It was an experience she'd never felt before, except when Maxwell held her in his arms. It was a sensation she quite enjoyed.

A knock sounded upon the door. On the other side stood Thornhill decked out in his evening clothes. He bowed when she answered the door.

"I am here to escort you to dinner, my lady, by instructions of my wife." He winked at her.

"Thank you, my lord." She took Thornhill's elbow, and they proceeded downstairs.

He chuckled to himself, and Skye glanced at him in confusion out of the corner of her eye.

"Is there something about me that amuses you, sir?"

"No, but when you and my wife finish with Maxwell, he won't realize what hit him. And that is what amuses me and will continue to do so. I cannot wait to watch him fall."

"Fall?"

By then they had reached the library, and he escorted her into the room. He never answered her question, only squeezed her hand as they arrived. She wanted to correct him on whatever he thought about Zane when she heard a loud crash and a string of curse words that made even her blush.

Chapter Sixteen

ZANE DIDN'T UNDERSTAND WHY he tortured himself. As he glanced around the room, the Thornhills and Mallorys enjoyed themselves immensely while he hid in the corner, nursing his drink and feeling sorry for himself. His gaze caught Ivy, who was once again smirking at him. What had her so amused? His misery? Why did he come tonight? Did he really imagine she would emerge out of her cocoon? If she knew he came to dinner, she would make herself scarce like all the previous times when he came for tea. To know she remained up those stairs in her bedroom made him crazy with desire. What would they think if he climbed those stairs to her? What would she think? She would probably scream, and then they would throw him out into the street.

He'd tried to woo her for weeks now, only to have her reject him. Visits to tea, daily letters, gifts that came from his heart. Nothing in return from her. If he couldn't woo her, how could he charm her? Now here he stood, once again, hoping beyond all hope she would come to dinner. He wondered what she thought of his gift today. It was his last attempt to reach her. He slipped into her room after he inquired about her whereabouts. When the maid responded that she wasn't in her bedroom, he slipped in secretly. The room smelled of her, and he could feel her essence. He didn't linger though, but he noticed the discarded letter thrown on the floor. While he was thrilled she read his letters, he didn't know what to think about this one lying on the floor. Did the note upset her or had it made her want to see him? He grabbed the letter and laid it next to the present. On his way back to the parlor, hoping she decided to join them, he overheard her talking to Ivy in the nursery. While he wanted to eavesdrop, the presence of housemaids prevented him. So, he left Hillston House and hoped for her company tonight. As they waited for Thorn to join them, Zane realized his visit was hopeless. She wouldn't come to dinner or respond to his advances.

The door to the library opened. Finally, Thorn was joining them. Now they could get this dreaded dinner under way and he could make his excuses. Afterward, a night at the club playing cards and getting smashing drunk appealed to him as the way to end his evening. Thorn was not alone though. He escorted a vision in white through the door. The lady was gorgeous. Her white dress hugged her curves in all the right places, and her pale ivory skin glistened in the candlelight. Her breasts were on a teasing display. While not vulgar, they tantalized a man with what they might look unbound. Long red hair graced the top of her head, with stray curls sweeping along her neck. Zane searched her face, his gaze locking with hers. Her eyes spoke of her nervousness—and something else. His eyes roamed to her mouth. She bit her bottom lip, which enflamed his desire for her more. The goddess wasn't just any lady. She was his Skye.

Caught up by the sight of her, he dropped his glass. The whiskey splashed across the hardwood floor, hitting his pant legs. He swore aloud at his clumsiness and at his awkward response to her walking in the room. Zane waited to catch a glimpse of her for weeks, and what did he do? He drew attention to himself like a fool and didn't attempt to greet her. He continued to stand there like a doldrum. Ivy and Raina came to her side to greet her and tell her how elegant she looked tonight. He should compliment her, but he stood gawking at her like a lad seeing an exquisite lady for the first time. When a sound of laughter came from his side, he glanced over to see Thorn laughing at him. He rolled his eyes and let out a quiet curse at him, which only caused his friend to laugh harder.

Thorn motioned for a footman to clean the mess while he pulled Maxwell to the side. Ivy then guided Skye over to the group gathered around the settee, introducing her to Thorn's parents and her father. As Skye visited with them, her gaze kept straying toward Zane.

"Are you going to keep gawking at her like an untried lad, or are you going to greet her?"

"Um ..." He was unable to speak a single coherent word.

She was here. He only needed to go to her side and strike a conversation with her. About what? *Inquire on her health, idiot. Tell her she is a vision in white. Do anything but stand here ogling her, making her and everybody else uncomfortable.* Why did Thorn still laugh at him?

"Bugger off," he muttered to him.

"With pleasure," Thorn laughed as he went to join the small group.

Sims arrived in the doorway to announce dinner.

"Papa, please escort Lady MacKinnon into the dining room?"

"With pleasure, my dear." Duke Kempbell offered his arm to Skye.

Zane heard him compliment Skye as they walked toward the dining room. Skye thanked him and spoke of her pleasure meeting him. Still, Maxwell didn't move. Ivy walked toward him with the same smirk on her face. Now he understood the reasoning behind it. She knew Skye was coming to dinner and didn't warn him. Obviously, she no longer stood on his side. Of all the help he gave her to win over Thorn, this was how she repaid him?

"Are you coming into dinner, my lord?"

"Oh, I am my lord now? I see where your loyalties lie."

"Why they have always lay with you."

"Traitor."

"Shall we say I am an ally to both sides?"

"How so?"

"Escort me to dinner and you shall see."

Zane offered his arm to Ivy and followed the rest of the party into the dining room. Duke Kempbell placed Skye in her seat and sat across from her. Charles sat on her right with Raina seated next to the duke. Thorn presided at the head of the table with his parents surrounding him. Maxwell escorted Ivy to the other end of the table, and when he glanced, he noticed the only spot not taken was next to Skye. The seat sat open, waiting for him to slide into and rest next to her. After all this time, he was close enough to touch her and breathe in her scent. Close enough for her soft brogue to soothe his mind when she spoke. When he realized what Ivy meant about being an ally, he squeezed her shoulder in thanks. She reached up to pat his hand in response. He took a deep breath as he walked to his seat and slid his chair in next to her. As proper etiquette demanded, she turned to him and made small talk.

"Lord Maxwell, how are you this fine evening?"

"I am well. May I say how happy I am that you decided to join us for dinner?"

"You may."

"It is a pleasure to set my eyes upon you, Skye," he whispered quietly enough where only she heard him.

The servants served them dinner, and conversation between them ceased. With the rest of the meal spent in open discussion, there wouldn't be a moment for them to talk. If he wanted to tell her anything, everybody would listen. While it was damn inconvenient, it remained a blessing in disguise, because he became tongue-tied around her. There were so many things he'd wanted to tell her for weeks, but now that the opportunity presented itself, he couldn't utter a single sentence that made sense. So, he sat there at dinner, watching her when nobody was looking and listening to her as she talked. Her voice soothed his soul, though he couldn't recall a word she was saying.

Once during dinner, she surprised him. When she reached for her napkin, her fingers slid atop his. Her fingers brushing his, the touch so light he barely felt it. Then as quickly as she caressed him, her touch vanished. He would have thought he imagined it if it weren't for her brief glance at him and her fingers shaking as they pressed the napkin to her lips.

He slid his other hand under the table and touched his fingers to the hand she'd touched. Her light caress branded him. While it was only fleeting, it held a touch of hope. Hope for them. He smiled throughout the meal. He only spoke when asked a question, his thoughts wrapped up in the very essence of her.

When dinner was finished, he stood up swiftly to pull her chair back, the footman behind her chair getting an undeserved elbow in the side as he helped her from her seat. When his gaze rose, he caught Thorn laughing at him and Ivy smirking. And they called themselves friends.

"Come ladies. We can enjoy tea in the library, while the gentlemen have their port and cigars. Do not be too long, dear," Ivy directed toward Thorn.

Thorn came to Ivy's side and pressed a small kiss to her lips. "Give us a few moments, and then we will join you."

Ivy led the ladies to the library as Thorn directed Sims to pour the port. The men returned to their seats and lit their cigars. Zane was determined to join the ladies. He didn't light his cigar but drained his port.

When he pushed back his chair to rise, Thorn motioned him to return to his seat.

"I know you are eager to grace Lady MacKinnon with your company, but I have news to discuss."

Zane slumped back in his chair, discouraged that he wouldn't get to see her as soon as he wanted.

"Before we join the ladies, I have news of Logan MacKinnon. He has been located and dispatched to return from his mission. It is not known if he has succeeded or not. While we wait for him to return, I want none of this intelligence to leave this room. I know Skye is eager to learn news of her brother, but he is privy to top secret information for the Crown. Until he arrives in London, I am swearing every one of you here to secrecy. None of our wives or Skye are to be made aware of this news. If he has located the missing heir, his life will be in danger and so will Skye's until the heir is in protective custody. Are we all in agreement?"

Every man spoke of their pledge except Maxwell. He made a promise to Skye to never lie to her again. He struggled with his conscience, deciding if this was really a lie or a safety to her. The men waited patiently for his answer, knowing his decision was the hardest to make. The others were married to women who would understand their secret and forgive them. He held no such ties to Skye. His would be an outright lie to protect her. The lie he would utter may cause harm later. He decided not to agree yet. He would give these men the answer they demanded and wait to tell Skye on a need-to-know basis. He nodded to Thorn.

The gentlemen removed themselves from the dining room and joined the ladies in the library. Skye sat alone on the settee. Maxwell worked up his nerve as he made his way over to her, settling himself on the sofa. He kept the proper distance from her, so as not to draw suspicions on what he really wanted to do. She turned toward him, offering him a cup of tea. He declined, becoming frustrated with their polite conversation. He wanted to talk to her in private if he could manage it. It was not to be, for Charles and Raina stood in front of the fireplace asking for a few moments of everybody's time. They both smiled tenderly at each other, holding hands.

"Raina and I have exciting news we wish to share," Charles announced.

"We shall have a little Mallory in seven months' time," Raina finished.

The small group exclaimed their excitement. They gathered around the couple, basking them in congratulations. The couple beamed their pride and listened to the advice being offered. Zane smiled his happiness for them. They deserved it above everybody else. It also made him ache for the same, and the sense of his ache rested but a few inches from him. While they were so close, they were miles apart. He saw the winsome smile spread across her face. She rose and walked toward the doors leading to the garden and slipped out, unnoticed from her hosts. Not wanting to interrupt the family news, Zane followed her. This was the reason she departed, was it not? Did she wish for him to join her?

He followed her outside and found her wandering the pathway lit by lanterns. He continued behind her as she made her way along the gravel path. She slid on a bench and spread out her skirts, folding her hands in her lap as a proper lady should, waiting patiently for him to join her. He never expected her to behave this way. This wasn't the Skye he fell in love with. Who was this creature? Was she a part of Skye? Did he completely understand the woman he loved? She patted the seat next to him, waiting.

He sat next to her, turning to his side to admire her, for every minute she granted him with her presence he would soak into his memory.

She turned her head at him and bestowed him with a smile that would have knocked him off his toes if he had been standing. When he opened his mouth to tell her how stunning she looked, no sound came forth. She took the very words from his lips with her smile. It spoke of healing, forgiveness, and a hint of desire. Then she laughed. It was the sweetest melody he'd heard in weeks. Was everybody going to laugh at him this evening? Then he finally realized what everybody noticed in his reactions tonight, and he laughed with her. He acted as a bumbling idiot throughout the evening, and he continued to be one now. Well no longer, for a fool wasn't what he set out to become. He wasn't himself, but that would change. He would soon sweep this woman off her feet. She wouldn't be laughing at him then but sighing at his charm. Reaching for her hand, he peeled away her white gloves and raised her hand to his lips. He brushed his lips across her fingers, smiling as they trembled, and her laugh subsided.

"You are a vision in white tonight, my dear. There are not enough words to justify your loveliness," he whispered across her skin.

Then he listened to the first of her many sighs. He lowered her hand back to her lap and slid his palm inside hers. He held her hand as they sat side by side on the bench. Neither of them spoke for a while, just sitting alone in each other's company was enough for them. It was short lived, for walking along the path toward them appeared Thorn and Ivy. Damn, he'd wasted his time with her not saying anything of significance.

"A lovely night for a stroll my dear, do you not agree?" Thorn asked Ivy.

"Why yes, a most beautiful evening. I notice we are not alone with those thoughts."

Zane removed his hands from Skye's and she donned her gloves again before the couple came upon them. He helped her from the bench as they waited for Thorn and Ivy to join them. He would take his leave before his frustrations overtook him. They wouldn't leave them alone, so he saw no reason to stay any longer tonight.

"I want to thank you for a lovely evening Ivy. As always, it was superb. Good night Thornhill." As he turned to Skye, he bowed and asked her, "Would you like to join me for a ride in Hyde Park tomorrow morning, Lady MacKinnon?"

Skye bowed her head in acceptance. "I would enjoy that immensely, Lord Maxwell."

"Then until tomorrow, my lady."

As Zane took his leave, Thorn left the ladies to themselves and followed Maxwell to the door. Ivy slid her arm through Skye's, and they wandered back into the library. Skye noticed the other guests had left in her absence. She hoped they didn't consider her behavior rude when she left. She only wanted to give them time alone as a family.

"I am sorry for leaving your guests."

"Oh, posh, think nothing of it. How did it go? Did he wrap you in his arms, kiss you, and cry out his undying love for you?"

Skye laughed. "You obviously read too many romantic novels."

"Well, did he do any of that?"

Skye settled on the settee and picked up her cup of tea she had not drank. As she took a sip of the lukewarm brew, she didn't know what to presume of Zane's actions. He barely uttered any words to her all evening until right before they were interrupted. She even felt brazen enough to touch him during dinner and still nothing happened.

"Maybe I have waited too long and he has changed his mind toward me."

Ivy laughed. "Oh, he has not changed his mind."

Skye rose from the settee and paced across the rug. "How can you be so sure? He hardly spoke this evening, and he stared at me through dinner as if I had grown two heads."

"He is utterly smitten."

"Smitten?"

"Yes, do you not see? You are a beauty he didn't expect. When you appeared for dinner, he was unprepared to see you. Every day when he visits, he prepares himself to see you before he arrives. Tonight, you were a surprise he didn't understand how to handle. Believe me, it was an utter delight to watch."

"I am glad we provided humor to you and your husband this evening. Do not think for one second I didn't notice Thornhill laughing throughout dinner at Maxwell's expense. Now he will assume I am playing with him."

"No, my dear, when he comes to his senses at home, he will replay this evening in his head and realize what this evening represents. You are opening your heart to him. Oh, how I wish I could join you on your ride tomorrow. He was so much fun to watch, floundering tonight. You took away every word from his lips. I never imagined this would ever happen to him."

Skye shook her head at Ivy's humor. Did she really do that to him? Did his emotions overtake his senses like it did hers? There was so much she desired to whisper to him this evening but couldn't. When he held her hand in the garden, she wanted to tell him she was sorry and how much she missed him. The words wouldn't come out; his touch and nearness had overtaken her. She felt he knew how she felt, because even though he also didn't talk, his touch spoke his words for him. She couldn't wait for tomorrow. If tonight ended the way she imagined, he would be here first thing in the morning for their ride. She smiled as she reflected on the surprise she left for him to discover.

Chapter Seventeen

MAXWELL CLIMBED INTO HIS carriage and leaned back against the seat. Before he left, Thorn reminded him to keep silent on Logan MacKinnon. Maxwell brushed him off and left. It was only a short ride home, but his thoughts were consumed by Skye. He decided against the cards and drinking after all. He needed no reason to be late for his ride with Skye in the morning. Tomorrow they could talk, then who knows what else would await them. He closed his eyes as he replayed their time in the garden. He still felt her palm inside his, small and trusting nestled within. Maxwell felt hope in her touch.

When he arrived home, he let himself inside his rambling townhome. He kept his staff at a minimum. He had no need for them when he returned in the evenings, so he always let them have their nights off. No sooner than he closed the door, there was a knock upon it. When he opened the door, he was caught by surprise to see Thorn's footman holding out a letter for him. He took the letter, thanking the lad. Zane strode to his study and poured himself a drink. He pulled off his suit jacket, throwing it over his chair, and ripped open the letter in excitement. She'd finally written back to him. He folded the letter open and walked over to the fire for better light. Skye replied to his questions he'd asked her over the past few weeks. She told him of how she filled her days with Ivy and the children. Then she told him of her time spent healing and that her nightmares had ended. At the end of the letter, she apologized for her absence and expressed her gratitude for his gifts. She also thanked him for his patience and understanding, asking him in return for his forgiveness on her behavior. Skye acknowledged she was in the wrong where the truth was concerned. In the end, she hoped for everything he wished and was willing for him to pay attendance on her. It was the very end that shook him to his core. It gave him the hope he needed. She signed the letter with "All my love, Skye." That that wasn't what shook him though. It was the P.S. that made him moan. It read:

P.S.

Well we have met again, and I am most disappointed in your reaction to me. While I waited patiently throughout the evening for you to draw me into your arms, for the stroke of your fingers and the brush of your lips upon mine, for that is how my imagination filled in the rest. The touch of your lips on mine, devouring from my lips my need for you. But sadly, none of that occurred. So, it only led me to believe, you, Earl Zane Maxwell, are nothing but a tease. Perhaps you can redeem yourself on the morrow. It has been yet to be determined.

Maybe, I can help you along with your imagination...

When I lay in my bed tonight <u>alone,</u> I will dream of you sliding in next to me. As I pull your head to mine for a kiss, my lips will open under yours. My fingers will wander across your chest, brushing lightly down ...

Sweet dreams, my love.

She was a devilish minx. While the picture of her tonight was of a seductive innocent in the white creation, the very devil was sent to entice him. His whole body became hard at the erotic words she wrote him. Now he finally understood the whole evening. She had forgiven him and had set out to enflame him. Well two could play at that game MacKinnon. The wooing was finished; he obviously bungled the charm. However, the desire he would do tenfold, of that she would hold no doubt. He began to plan for her seduction. Seduction that would take place tomorrow.

~~~~~~

Tomorrow found him bright and early ringing the bell at Hillston House. Sims greeted him, informing him the ladies were eating breakfast and to please join them. He told the butler he could make his own way. When he entered the room, he discovered Ivy and Skye whispering with each other. Their whispers stopped when they noticed him, smiling secretly to themselves. Zane allowed them to believe they were fooling him. He knew when two women were conspiring over him when he saw it, and these two most definitely were.

As he poured himself tea, he greeted the ladies. Zane regarded Skye in a different light from the evening before. He noticed the lightness in her gaze, which no longer held a troubled look but one full of mischief. He enjoyed this side of her; it made her softer. Her body appeared relaxed in his company, so she no longer remained in fear. The riding habit was another creation that hugged her curves. It would be his pleasure to remove the attire from her body later. He nodded to their conversation, hoping his nods were at the right points in their discussion because he didn't listen to a word they spoke. All he could think of was the letter from the night before—and imagining how to remove every piece of clothing covering her body. She wore green today; he'd always imagined she'd be stunning in green. While it was not the green he fantasized about, it would do for now.

"As I was saying, he has four eyes wandering all over you," Ivy quipped.

"Yes, I noticed his extra eyes, but I am not one to object to extra eyes devouring me," Skye replied.

Who was devouring her with his eyes? Four eyes? What? Zane shook his head to clear his thoughts as he glanced between the two women who were giving into fits of laughter at his expense again. Tired of being the butt of everybody's jokes these days, he needed to get Skye to himself so he could overcome his stupidity of acting like an idiot.

"If you are ready for our ride, Lady MacKinnon, the hour grows late."

Skye rose from the table, wishing Ivy a good morning. Zane's mouth went dry as she rose, for the fabric grew tighter as she moved. Her habit molded tightly to her frame, and her skirts swirled among the boots hugging her calves. Yes, he would enjoy removing her of those too. Her skirts swooshed behind her as she moved into the hallway. When he began to follow her like a puppy, he was stopped by the sound of Ivy clearing her throat.

"Does she require a chaperone?"

"NO!" he answered more harshly than he intended.

Ivy smirked at him. "Mmm, that is the same answer I received from her."

Zane growled at her and exited the room. He found Skye in the entryway, pulling on her gloves and adjusting her hat.

"Are you ready, my dear?"

She turned toward him and gifted him with a smile, which was all the encouragement he needed. He led her from the townhome to the two horses awaiting them. She waited for him to help her instead of mounting the horse herself. As she settled onto the side saddle, Zane admired her. She was poised and elegant but still held a sense of adventure that had been present when he had first met her. When he raised his head, he watched as she arched her eyebrow at their state of stillness. He flashed her a smile and took off at a brisk walk, with Skye following him.

When they entered the park, Zane directed them to Rotten Row. Once his horse hit the beaten path, he turned his head and flashed her a quick grin, setting his horse off into a fast gallop. He had not gotten far when he heard her horse galloping rapidly behind him. It wasn't long before she caught up with him. He listened to her laughter trailing in the wind behind them; it was a lovely sound. He turned to catch her gaiety and became astounded by her charm, which caused her to pass him. He tried to catch up with her, but he was unable to. When he finally reached her, she lowered herself to the ground and guided her horse to the lake. After their horses drank, he tied them to a tree. Without speaking, he drew her hand into his and guided her to a group of trees that allowed them hidden seclusion. She didn't resist him.

Zane drew her into his arms, brushing the stray tendrils of her hair back from her face. He tilted her head back, his fingers cupping her cheeks as he slid his mouth to hover over hers. Her warm breath mingled with his. He stared into her eyes, catching them turning into dark emeralds. Her eyes were filled with desire. He held back, nervous for her reaction, but when her body softened against his and she moaned, he realized she held no fear of him.

"I have waited a lifetime for this," he breathed before he took her lips in a gentle sweet kiss. Tenderly brushing his lips across hers. When she sighed, he knew she wasn't frightened, so he deepened the kiss. Her response was all he needed.

He growled as he pulled her body closer to his. His tongue slid into her mouth sampling her sweetness. When her tongue tangled with his and her body wrapped around him, pulling him flusher against her, he lost it. His fingers unbuttoned her habit, needing to touch her. Zane forgot where they were and didn't hear the riders approaching until their voices pierced through his haze.

"I saw them ride this way, Charles."

"Well they couldn't have wandered too far; their horses are tied against the tree," he heard Charles inform Raina.

Zane pulled away from Skye and rested his forehead against hers, breathing deeply. She averted her eyes from his. He stroked his fingers across her cheek, drawing her eyes back to him and smiled. "Forgive me, my dear, the taste and the touch of you made me forget my surroundings."

He helped her straighten her clothing, and she backed away a respectable distance. His touch didn't frighten her, but his passion did. It was more powerful than before. To be honest, it wasn't only his passion but hers too. Her need for him was something she never experienced. She craved her need to belong to him. While she wasn't crazy for the interruption, it was probably for the best. For she needed more time. Not away from him, but time to bring their passion under control. It remained too strong of an emotion for her to handle.

Zane knew she was frightened. Of what, he didn't understand. He didn't believe it was of him. Their kiss was one of mutual desire. He felt it in her touch and moans. Did their passion bring back haunted memories of her time on Shears's ship? If so, then he needed to slow down and not frighten her away.

"Please forgive me, Skye. I have pushed you too far, too fast."

Skye reached out to him, putting her hand on his chest. "No, I am not frightened of you, Zane, but of what you make me feel."

He squeezed her hand. "Is that a dreadful thing?"

She released a nervous laugh. "No, just an overwhelming thing."

"Then I will accept that as a positive sign."

"Zane—" Skye began.

"There you two are, I hope we aren't interrupting?" Raina inquired, smiling innocently at Zane.

Raina knew damn well she'd interrupted. If Zane didn't know any better, he would have thought she was involved with Ivy on keeping them separated. He didn't bring a chaperone for a reason, but it would seem he would have one nonetheless.

"No, I was showing Skye the lake."

Raina walked around in a circle. "From inside the trees?" she quipped.

Charles chuckled. "Let us leave them be, my dear. Will we see you tonight at the Winchester Ball?"

Zane looked across at Skye. "Will you be attending?"

"Yes, I am attending the ball with Thorn and Ivy."

"Then yes, you shall see me there this evening."

"We will leave you to your ride. A small offer of advice, my friend, the crowds are filling out in the park. It would be for the best if you leave with us from this small gathering," Charles suggested to Zane quietly to the side. He didn't want to embarrass the young lady, who discussed this evening's ball and what to wear with Raina.

Zane nodded in understanding. The last thing he wanted to bring upon Skye were false stories. He didn't need the gossip scandal spreading rumors about Skye before they met her. They'd kept her capture aboard Shears's ship a secret. It would already be difficult as it was with her beauty and his attachment to her, especially because there wouldn't be a member of the ton who didn't recognize she was his after tonight. No gent would court her; he would make sure her dance card was filled with names of no threat to him. He couldn't wait to see her tonight. It would be his first time seeing her dressed in a ball gown with her hair done. She needed jewels though. What kind? Emeralds and diamonds, of course. He would send them over after he returned home from their ride.

After they followed Charles and Raina out of the wooded area, they strolled to their horses. He helped Skye onto her horse and chatted a few moments with them, not drawing gossip their way. As Charles and Raina headed in a different direction, Zane guided their horses along the path back to Hillston House. Neither one of them spoke of their embrace from earlier, as each lost in their own thoughts. As they rode, they exchanged glances with one another until Skye fell into a fit of giggles. It was an unknown sound coming from her, and he pulled their horses to a stop as they arrived.

"Now, what is so funny to have you giggling like a schoolgirl?"

"Only how ridiculous we are. We act as if we are a young smitten couple, too afraid to tell the other how we care about each other."

"And how do we care about each other?" he asked her as he drew her from the horse.

"I think our kiss from earlier says it all."

"I think it still leaves much unspoken," Zane replied.

Skye placed her fingers to his lips, silencing him from saying more. "All in time, my love," she whispered as she turned from him and walked to the house.

"Skye?" he called out.

She continued walking toward the townhome. As the door opened, she turned and blew a kiss to him before the door shut behind her.

My love? Did her term of endearment mean what he thought she meant? Did she love him? He would know tonight. He would discover what he meant to her from her own lips. Then the rest of their lives would fall into place.

Chapter Eighteen

WHEN SKYE ENTERED THE Thornhill's residence, Sims informed her she had a visitor awaiting her in the parlor. Thorn and Ivy requested her presence. She informed Sims she would change her clothes and be there shortly. As she entered her room, Mabel waited to help her change. Skye inquired on the visitor, but Mabel didn't know who it was. She changed into a green day dress with white ruffles on the sleeves. As she touched up her hair, Skye glanced at her reflection in the mirror. She didn't need to pinch her cheeks, for they were full of color. Her ride through the park with Zane did her well. Not only the ride, but the kiss itself helped her tremendously.

When she walked downstairs to the parlor, she stood outside the door, wondering who was inside inquiring after her. Maybe they had learned word of her brother. Sims stood to the side. When Skye nodded her head, he opened the door and announced her arrival. After she entered the room, her body became enveloped in a giant hug with the life being squeezed out of her. Her captor picked her up and swung her around the room. Skye panicked when her arms became pinned at her sides. Her breathing turned deep and shallow, making her feel faint. Since she couldn't stop the attack, the ringing began in her ears, and her mind became separated from her body.

"Put her down, MacKinnon, can you not see she is fainting?" Thorn shouted.

Her brother was twirling her around, as he did the countless times when they grew up. Even though Skye heard the mention of her brother's name, her mind refused to tell the difference. She thought she was being attacked again. She threw out her arms and hit him.

The twirling stopped, her arms held in a gentle, secure hold, and her brother whispered quietly for her to stay calm and that she remained safe. He guided her to a chair and lowered her down. Ivy threw a blanket across her legs and Logan kneeled at her side, bringing warmth into her hands. A chill sank into her body. A warm cup of tea settled in her hands, with words of persuasion to drink. Skye drank the calming tea, her body relaxing and coming back to her senses. When she rose her head, she noted the concern on her brother's face.

She folded her hands over his, nodding. "I am fine. You caught me unaware, tis all."

"I am sorry, Skye. Thorn informed me of your ordeal, and I blundered my reaction in seeing you."

"I am well."

"Oh, sis, what you had to endure. I want to kill Shears, if it were possible."

"Shears is dead and can harm no one else."

"The terror you suffered from his hands, you should not have. I lay the blame on myself."

"No, Logan, it is mine. I didn't follow the warning signs and landed myself in a predicament I shouldn't have. I risked the lives of our clansmen."

As they talked, Skye looked around and noticed they were alone. Thorn and Ivy left them to discuss Skye's capture in private. Their kindness meant a lot to her.

"We did not lose many, and the rest are recovering," Logan informed her.

"Yes, Isobel wrote and told me."

"What happened, Skye? What had you so distracted you didn't realize Shears had set a trap for you?"

Skye didn't answer him. He would recognize her feelings as a sign of weakness. Granted, he felt strongly for Isobel, but he would think Skye couldn't focus if she felt the same.

"Did your actions have anything to do with Lord Maxwell?"

Still she did not answer him.

Logan rose and walked over to the fireplace. He picked up his drink he left behind and took a swallow.

"I have failed you as a brother and mentor, Skye."

"No. Logan, it is I who failed you."

"Hear me out Sis. I have failed you in not allowing you to express your emotions. I have kept you isolated and trained you as a warrior instead of letting you become the lady you were meant to be. While I have treated you like a man, I still protected you from harm. Our parents were failures, and when mother died, I let father treat you as a boy instead of letting you be the little girl you needed to be. I tried to protect you the best way I could, but in doing so, I only made you more vulnerable."

Logan took a long drink, sighing as he settled in the chair opposite from her. He was relieved at discovering his sister was well. He had been frantic for her since he found out about her attack. Not only at her attack, but that Lord Maxwell had ruined her during his capture. From what he heard from Gregor, it was more like a stay, for he was not treated as a prisoner but like a guest who made use of the charms of his sister.

"I have intelligence on Maxwell, and from what I gathered from the clan, I understand the path your relationship took. Am I mistaken on this?"

"No."

"Do you care for him?"

"Yes, but it's complicated."

"Because of Shears's attack?"

"Yes."

Logan nodded his understanding. "Do I need to force him to the altar?"

Skye laughed. "He would go gladly. It is I who refused him."

"Why? Are ye crazy? The man has ruined you."

"Maybe it is I who have ruined him."

Logan laughed in return. This was his sister—a strong-willed woman who didn't abide by the standard rules. Only she would turn the tables on reputation.

"So will ye make an honest man out of him or make him suffer through his ruination."

"Mmm, I have not decided yet."

"I think you already have. All joking aside, are you well?"

"Yes, Logan. You caught me by surprise. Shears never succeeded in his attack toward me. Maxwell stopped him in time. My fears are subsiding."

"Shears wreaked havoc everywhere. The world is safer without him."

"I agree. Since you have returned, were you able to complete your mission? Did you find the missing heir?"

"Yes, but sadly it was for naught."

"What do you mean?"

"The heir is dead. The governess killed the child. The old man's story was false, another one of Shears's devious plans."

"Oh no. This will tear Maxwell apart."

"What is Maxwell's connection to the missing heir?"

"She was his sister. His mother gave birth to the child. She gave the child away on command from the Crown and her husband. Zane has searched for this child for ages."

"Zane?"

Skye blushed as she realized she called Zane by his Christian name.

"Are you positive the child is dead?"

"By all accounts from witnesses, the child drowned. The missing jewels were all I found."

"Did they discover a body?"

"None."

"So, there stands a chance the child lives?"

"If so, it is farfetched."

Skye thought of the loss. It would devastate Zane. How would he react to the news? He searched and double-crossed for so long to locate the child, to make a wrong right. Now his path came to another dead end. She wanted to tell him of this news before he found out from anybody else. She couldn't visit him alone though—another rule to obey in this society. Skye would have to find a way to visit him this afternoon and inform him of this latest information.

"It is good to see you, brother. When are you returning home?"

"On the morrow. I must get back to Isobel before she gives birth again or she will never forgive me. Are you returning with me?"

Skye shook her head. "If it is not too much trouble, I will continue my stay with Thorn and Ivy."

"I hear we have a ball to attend tonight. Will Maxwell be there?"

"Yes, he is attending."

"I might call on him this afternoon; I would like a few words with the fellow."

Skye stood. "No, tonight will be sufficient." She tried to dissuade her brother from visiting Maxwell this afternoon.

"Very well, I must attend to some business anyhow. Then I will escort you to the ball."

Skye rose and hugged her brother. She was glad he was finally home safe and could resume leadership of the clan. While she loved her clan very much, it was time for her life to take a different path. She only hoped it would be with Maxwell. If she was not mistaken, she thought he might wish the same.

After her brother left, Skye tried to come up with a plan to visit Maxwell. She only needed a couple of hours to sneak out and return. She didn't want to involve Ivy but realized she was her only way. Ivy would know how to sneak Skye into Maxwell's residence. Also, she needed her help because she had no clue where Maxwell lived. Luck was on her side when Ivy floated into the parlor. You couldn't mistake the smile gracing her lips. She must have been thinking along the same lines and had concocted a plan.

"You wish to visit Maxwell, am I not mistaken?"

"You are correct. Do you know how I can?"

"I have just the plan. I figured you need to tell him the devastating news before he hears it from anybody else. Also, I spoke to Raina, and she told me your ride was interrupted this morning."

"It was probably for the best. It was the wrong place and the wrong time. I need to see him before tonight, and without my brother finding out."

"Yes, we must take you shopping this afternoon to finish your ensemble for tonight. I will have the carriage brought around immediately,"

Ivy spoke loudly for anybody to hear. She winked at Skye to follow her lead.

"That sounds like a marvelous idea. Thank you so much for suggesting this excursion."

"My pleasure."

The ladies set out for what was perceived as a shopping expedition. Ivy told Skye of her plans. They would stop by Maxwell's townhome, where Ivy would deliver a missive from Thorn. While Ivy distracted the butler, Skye could slip upstairs to Maxwell's private rooms. When the butler returned with a reply, Ivy would make her excuses of Skye's whereabouts. Ivy explained how Maxwell carried a skeletal staff, liking his privacy more than being smothered by servants everywhere he turned. Ivy gave Skye the layout of the townhome.

"How will Maxwell know I am there?"

"It will be in this missive I am about to deliver."

"Ivy Thornhill, you are a very sneaky lady."

"All in the game of love, for my friends." She winked.

"I don't know how to thank you for everything you have done for me. I was jealous of your relationship with Zane in the beginning, but it was all for naught. You truly are an amazing friend."

"Oh, posh. You can thank me by loving him."

"I do."

"Good. Now you only have a couple of hours to spare. I will take myself over to Raina's to grab her for some shopping. Then I will return for you."

As the carriage arrived at Maxwell's townhome, his footmen helped the ladies to the front door. Maxwell's butler led them inside to the foyer; Ivy's plan was working like magic. Skye ascended the stairs quickly, slipping inside the first room she came upon. The room was an artist's studio filled with canvases and paints scattered everywhere. Skye wandered around the room, forgetting the reason she was here as she gazed at the drawings spread around her. They were amazing, and in such vivid detail. After seeing his other two pieces, she understood the passion of his work. A huge canvas rested in the corner, covered with a tarp bearing traces of paint. Skye slid the cover aside and saw a painting full of vibrant color. She dragged off the tarp, wanting to see the whole picture. A picture of beauty stood before her, and she admired the attention to the detail. Every stroke of the brush captured the love of the subject. The colors only made the painting bolder.

Skye gazed upon herself. Zane captured his love for her in every detail, straight from his heart. He painted her wearing a long green ball gown, covered in diamonds. She was elegant, but it was the look in her eyes that drew her attention. It was the look of love and desire. An invitation to her soul. A look only meant for him. He painted her hair unbound, falling around her in waves. Long curls winding themselves down her body and settling near her breasts. There were emeralds and diamonds draped from her neck and hanging from her ears. Skye couldn't believe it was her in the picture, but he made her believe in him. In them. She saw his initials at the bottom: ZM, elegantly drawn. She bent and traced her fingers across them.

"This is how I have pictured you in my mind since I met you."

Skye turned around slowly. Zane had propped his body against the doorjamb. His shoulder leaning in with his, feet crossed at his ankles. He looked relaxed, as if he watched her for a while.

"It is exquisite."

"You are exquisite."

Skye blushed at his words. He made her feel that way. Suddenly, she didn't want to discuss why she paid him a visit. Not right now anyhow. They were alone. She wanted to continue what he started at the park. She was no longer frightened of the passion they shared. Skye wanted him.

Skye strolled toward Zane and stopped when she reached him. He came off the door and stood tense before her. She knew he wanted to touch her. She sensed his need coming off him in waves. He stood as still as a statue, not wanting to rush or frighten her. That was when her final shell fell and shattered around her. She laid her palm over his heart, and his heartbeat quickened at her touch. Her hand trailed down his stomach and across to his sides, where both her hands continued to trail up his arms and over his shoulders. He never moved a muscle. When her hands trailed back to his hands, they intertwined with his fingers. She stood on her tiptoes to kiss his chin, her lips trailing along his cheek toward his ear.

"Zane," she whispered.

Still, he did not move. She trailed her lips back, hovering over his lips. She closed her eyes and pressed her lips against his. Her tongue traced his lips, asking them to open so she could taste him. He let her control the kiss—soft, slow, and wanting to drive him beyond desire. He didn't take over the kiss, but kissed her in return, following her lead.

She pulled back, but still he didn't reach for her. So, she did what any lady would do and slipped past him. She continued to the room across the hall and opened the door, noticing his bedchamber. When she turned, she noticed he turned to watch her. She slid her bonnet off, taking the pins from her hair and letting her tresses fall around her shoulders in waves. Next, she took off her gloves and tossed them behind her.

There was still no movement from him, but she saw he wanted to move toward her. His hands gripped the doorframe, turning white. He held himself with such restraint. Skye lowered herself on his bed and took off her shoes. She stood back up and rolled down her stockings, lifting her skirts above her knees.

"Skye," he growled.

As she unbuttoned her gown, he rushed into the room, shutting the door behind him. He gently grabbed her arms to stop.

"You don't have to do this. I can wait until you are ready."

"I am ready."

Zane didn't know how to respond to her. He saw the fear in her eyes earlier this morning and realized he had pushed her too fast. What she did now pushed his level of restraint. He must remove her from his room. She was here because she needed to tell him something that couldn't wait until this evening. He would inquire to her visit, then send her on her way. It would be the best outcome for them. She was distracting him. A distraction that took every ounce of his willpower to ignore.

Somehow, she managed to work her arms free of his hold and untied his cravat. Before he realized it, it laid on the floor and her fingers were working on the buttons of his waistcoat. She had the buttons flying apart as she opened his shirt. When her hands touched his bare skin, Zane lost the last of his control he was holding onto. He pulled her in for an all-consuming kiss. Their lips met passionately as their hands worked to remove each other's clothing.

"Finally," he heard her mutter.

He pulled back from the kiss, laughing at her sarcasm. When he ran his fingers through her hair, he looked into her eyes and saw the woman he fell in love with. He wanted to tell her before they went any farther. He needed her to understand the depth of his emotions.

"I love you, Skye MacKinnon."

"I know you do," she whispered as a tear slid down her cheek. "You hold my love in return."

He bent to kiss the tear trailing across her cheek. When he heard her moan her need, he swept her into his arms and carried her to his bed. As he slid between the sheets with her, he slowly slid down her body, leaving a trail of kisses in his wake.

There was not a place on her body he didn't kiss or touch. His tongue trailed a path to her breasts, where he enfolded them in his hands, lifting them to his mouth. Slowly sliding her nipple in his mouth, he sucked gently as the pebble tightened against his tongue. When he kissed a path to her other nipple, he slowly sucked it into his mouth. Her moans grew louder as he caressed her breasts.

His lips followed the path of his hand as he kissed the trail from her chest to her stomach. He straddled her body as his hands stroked her thighs. She briefly tightened them in reaction to his touch. He pulled back, his fingers lightly stroking across her legs.

The bruises had long since healed, but she would always carry the invisible scars upon her body. They were scars he wished carry as his own. As he bent his head, he placed featherlight kisses along her thighs, hoping to kiss the pain from her soul. She ran her fingers through his hair as she slowly opened her legs to him. His hands were gentle as he spread them wider. His kiss trailed a blaze up her thighs to her womanly core.

Zane's tongue stroked her as he gently slid a finger inside her wetness. Her hips raised to his lips as he stroked her passion higher. As the stroke of his tongue tasted her wetness, she tightened her grip on his hair, holding him to her as he made love to her with his mouth. Wanting and needing to take this slow for her so as not to frighten her was what drove him. Her pleasure. That was all he wanted. He would sacrifice his own for her.

He sensed her body tightening, ready for release. His tongue stroked faster, teasing her clit as he slid another finger inside her. She tightened around his fingers, moaning his name over and over as she exploded under his tongue. Her body became motionless under his hands, her fingers fluttering through his hair. He pulled away and rested his head on her thighs, running his fingers over and over her invisible scars, lightly kissing them.

"Zane?" she whispered.

Still, he wouldn't meet her eyes. He had failed her when she needed him the most. Never again would he not protect her.

As Skye floated from his touch, she sensed his distance. She knew he was holding onto his passion so as not to frighten her. The way he loved her was one of the gentlest experiences for a woman to endure, but still he held himself back from her. This wasn't why she gave herself to him or why she teased him into his bedroom. She wanted him. All of him. She didn't want him holding back from her. While the care he gave to her touched her heart, it wasn't enough. She was not fragile. She wanted everything he could give her, for she would give him the same in return.

When she rose, she tried to get him to look at her, but he only gripped her thighs tighter, placing kisses after kisses on them. She stroked her fingers through his hair and tried to relax him, but still he wouldn't loosen his hold. When his tears graced her legs, she raised his head to her.

"Zane?" she whispered again.

His eyes gazed at her filled with a haunted look. Her fingers trailed over the tears coursing across his cheeks. It was then Skye realized he blamed himself for the attack.

"It was not your fault."

"Because of my arrogance, I failed you."

Skye rose to her knees and reached out to him to do the same. She laid her head against his chest and listened to his heartbeat. He pulled her in close, and they held each other for endless moments. After he relaxed against her, she ran her fingers over his chest, her hand dipping and swaying against his ridges. Her lips placing soft kisses across his chest. She sensed his strength in many ways.

Her kisses traveled lower across his stomach, kissing lightly, softer than a butterfly. The strength of his grip tightened on her. When her lips danced lower, she felt the strength of his body tightening in anticipation. When her tongue slid along the length of his hardness, she felt the strength of his hand tighten in her hair. As her mouth slid down the length of him, she tasted his strength to her soul. His moans vibrated through her body as she slid him in and out of her mouth, her tongue stroking his strength. Licking his strength. Sucking his strength. It was his strength that made her whole again.

He pulled her up against him, rolling her underneath him. He crushed her to him and took her mouth in a soul-searing kiss. His mouth devoured hers, taking everything she had to give him. Where one kiss started and ended, another began. Their tongues clashed in a powerful dance, each drawing and tasting from the other.

"Skye, I don't think I can be …"

She interrupted him. "I don't want you to be, I want you to take me with all your strength. Do not hold back from me. I want all of you. I need all of you, Zane."

Zane couldn't see reason. His need for her was more powerful than anything he had ever experienced. He wanted to take her gently for her first time after Shears attacked her. As soon as her lips kissed him, he lost control. He had none left. He needed her now.

When he slid in between her legs, he entered her swiftly. Her breath caught at the sudden intrusion. Zane stopped and held himself still, calling himself all sorts of names at his rush to be inside her. Now he had hurt her, but he could no more pull out of her than he could let her go.

Skye's breath caught as he entered her. It was heaven. Her need for him was so strong. He held himself still above her, and she saw the indecision in his eyes. She rose her hips and drove him all the way inside her. As she wrapped her legs around his waist, she rotated her hips to give him the encouragement he needed. Still when he didn't move, she bit at his chest.

He growled at her as he released himself inside her. She matched him stroke for stroke, their rhythm in sync with each other. Where he slid in deeper, she opened herself wider for him. When he pulled out, she raised her body, pulling him back inside her. Their touches became stronger, and their kisses even stronger. They became stronger together as one.

Skye's wetness tightened around his cock, her body releasing around him over and over, making his strokes harder and harder. She cried out his name as he sank into her deeper for more of her. From her. When she exploded around him, he came deep inside her. He released his strength into her soul. He caught her as she floated back to him and held her tight to him, afraid to let her go. His heart continued to beat fast; holding her would always make his heart race.

Skye felt the beating of his heart against her cheek. Her hand slowly rubbed against it, trying to calm it. As they lay there, it seemed to beat faster. She rested her chin on her hand and looked at him, raising her eyebrow in question.

"You make my heart race," he responded to her unspoken question. She laughed and placed a kiss over his heart.

"Skye?"

"Mmm."

"I love you."

"I know."

"Do you forgive me?"

"Mmm, I am still thinking about it."

He growled and flipped her over. "Thinking about it? How can I change your mind? Maybe a little of this?" he asked as he took her nipple between his teeth, his tongue sliding back and forth.

Skye moaned. "Some of that might work."

He threw back his head and laughed, sliding up to place a kiss upon her lips.

"I love you too, Zane. I forgave you a long time ago."

"Mmm," he answered her in return as he continued kissing and touching her. Softly. Slowly. He enjoyed the sensation of her in his bed.

"The portrait you painted of me is stunning."

"You're a stunning muse."

She blushed at his compliment. The red was a lovely hue on her body. He decided that would be his next painting. One he could paint from memory unless he could persuade her to pose. He would leave that discussion for another time.

He knew their time was ending. While he didn't want her to ever leave his bed, he understood he had to play by the rules until she was his. After tonight, he would make sure of their union. He already had a plan. In the meantime, he needed to get her dressed before Ivy returned.

"Zane, there is something I must tell you before I leave."

"It sounds dramatic."

"It is news you won't take well, but I wanted you to hear it from me."

"I am not letting you go, Skye. You are mine."

"I am nobody's but my own. We need to discuss my brother's return to London."

"When is he to return?"

"He has this morning, but he didn't bring good news with him."

"What of the heir?"

"That is the dreadful news, and I'm sorry to tell you. Logan said the governess killed the heir as an infant. The old man on our land was sent by Shears to draw Logan away from the clan and to set up my demise. He had figured out my deception with the weapons and wanted to destroy me."

Zane rolled away from Skye and grew pale. She sensed the loss of him in an instant. She knew this news would devastate him.

"So my deception has been for naught?"

Skye didn't understand how to soothe him. He was a proud man whose actions were directed by the King. She knew he didn't take his paths lightly. His ultimate betrayal toward his friends almost cost him their friendships. All for what? For the return of the King's missing jewels. While the King only cared for the jewels, Skye knew Zane cared for the missing child. The child was his last true connection to a family he no longer had. Without the connection, he would feel alone in the world. She didn't know how to answer his question either. All she could do for him was to offer her support.

"I am sorry for your loss."

"You cannot grieve for something you never had," he told her as he climbed from the bed.

He began to collect their clothing from around the room. Skye sat up, bringing the blanket to her chest. She knew he hurt and tried to shut her out. Skye was raised around enough men in her life to understand this was how men dealt with their problems. She wouldn't let Zane get away with this.

"Yes you can. You must mourn for the loss of never experiencing that love."

"Well that would be a worthless emotion," he scoffed.

"Zane Maxwell, stop this."

"Why Skye? What would you have me say?"

"I want you to share your grief with me and express your disappointment in not getting a chance to make right by this child. How you will miss not having a sibling. How sad you won't experience her love."

Zane settled on the bed next to her, his clothing in his hands. He lowered his head in defeat, taking in her words. He'd lost so much. Everything he fought for wasn't meant to be. Where did he go from here? The war was over. The destruction of Shears was over. His search for a sibling was over.

"I am all those things, Skye, but it is pointless to speak of them."

"No feelings are ever pointless Zane, unless you don't feel them."

"I feel them Skye."

He dropped the clothes and pulled her into his arms. Zane gathered her close and gave her what she wanted. He spoke of his loss for all he would never experience. He poured out his emotions to her. Then he spoke of all he would experience. With her. All he wanted for them together. By the end, Skye was crying in his arms from his sweet gentle words of love he spoke. He explained that as long as he held her love, he could survive anything.

Zane leaned against the pillows and cradled her near his heart. They lay there and basked in their love for one another until there was a knock on the door. Zane rose and talked briefly to the servant. He gathered Skye's clothing and helped her dress. While she fixed her hair, he donned his clothes. It was time for her to leave. He pulled her into his arms and kissed her gently. No more words needed to be spoken. They understood their love for one another. They walked downstairs, where he delivered her back to Ivy. He held Skye's hand and placed a kiss upon it.

"Thank you, my dear."

Skye cupped his cheek with her palm and smiled her goodbye.

Chapter Nineteen

SKYE STOOD IN FRONT of the mirror; she didn't recognize herself
again. The woman gazing back at her held stars in her eyes with her body
adorned in silk and jewels. They were waiting for her on her return. It was a
silk creation in green, quite like the one she wore in Zane's painting. Next to
the dress laid a box of diamonds and emeralds. They now hung from her
neck and ears, sparkling in the candlelight. She instructed Mabel to dress her
hair cascading around her shoulders, the way Zane liked. Among the gifts
nestled a note:

> *Just because I can.*
>
> *All my love,*
>
> Z

Skye smiled at his arrogance. She twirled around, and the silken
skirts caressed her legs. In all her life, she never appeared so grand. She
stood a far way from Scotland. Gone from the rolling mountains, riding
bareback on her horse, and fighting with her fellow clansmen. She was out
of her element here in London, but she was neither scared nor nervous.
Maybe she was as arrogant as him. Or perhaps the security of his love made
her comfortable dressed as a queen, giving her the confidence to attend a
ball.

With a quick knock at the door, her brother entered. He appeared as
elegant as her, dressed in a dark suit. He walked around her with a frown,
looking her up and down.

"Where did the jewels come from?" Logan inquired.

"A secret admirer."

"Do not sass me."

"You will find out later."

"Where were you this afternoon?"

"With a friend."

"The same friend who gifted you with this dress and jewels?" Logan asked.

Skye smiled at him with a look of innocence. He would find out soon enough. She wanted him to meet Zane first and approve of him before he discovered the depths of their relationship. It would make things smoother. If Logan found out they took up their romantic involvement again this afternoon, she couldn't guarantee the outcome of his reaction.

She slid her arms through his and guided him out the door, telling him how handsome he looked this evening. He indulged her secrets for the time being, but he knew she had something planned. And she was definitely involved with somebody. Now to figure out her secrets. He had an idea, as a few hints were thrown his way. While he was angry she was taken advantage of, he knew his sister well enough. If she hadn't wanted to be taken advantage of, it would never have happened. And if this person made her smile and turned her into the beauty he always believed her to be, then he supposed he might like the fellow. If Maxwell didn't measure up to the gentleman she deserved, then he would step in for her own good.

When they entered the ball, it was as he expected: grand décor with overdressed young ladies competing for the attention of the season's most sought after bachelor while the married couples flirted with anybody but their own spouses. Money and wealth flashed from everyone attending, unaware of the dangers that lurked in their society. While Skye never had a season, he had been to London a few times from his university years, and from when the King demanded him for missions. Being stuck in London was not his cup of tea, as he preferred his quiet life in Scotland. How he missed home. As soon as this ball ended, he would return home to Isobel. But first he needed to make sure Skye was settled. She remained his first duty.

As he stood around and made small talk with the Thornhills, he waited impatiently for Maxwell to make his arrival. As the evening drew on, Maxwell never made an appearance. He snarled as his sister declined dance after dance, watching as her smile slipped more and more as the evening continued. His anger at the man grew. If this was how he treated his sister then he wasn't good enough for her, and he refused to allow the man to court her, let alone wed her. Where was the coward? Oh, he listened to the rumors about Maxwell's double-crossing and his alignment with Shears. Did he have these people fooled? Did he have Skye fooled? Logan caught her searching the crowded ballroom but saw in her eyes that there remained no sign of him. Maxwell was here though. He overheard the ladies whispering how they wished to coax him into their beds later this evening. He hoped to hell Skye didn't hear the gossip. It would break her heart.

He noticed the change in her at once. Logan turned his head, searching in the direction she gazed upon but came up empty. When she excused herself to use the powder room, Logan followed at a discreet distance. He tried not to lose sight of her, but one of the King's advisors waylaid him. His eyes followed even though he couldn't. He lost her as she rounded the corner.

Skye knew her brother followed behind her. Right before she slipped into the quiet alcove, she glanced behind her and saw that he'd become detained. A hand reached out to grab her, pulling her into the dark space. When his lips met hers, she smiled into his kiss.

"You look exquisite, my dear. You don't know how much I want to peel you out of your dress and have my way with you."

Skye blushed at his words. Her imagination grew wild at the thought. It would be so scandalous. But with what his hands were doing to her at the moment, she didn't care. His fingers floated across the top of her breasts as his kiss slid down her neck to them.

"I want to slide my fingers inside your dress and bring these out for my mouth to love," he whispered as his fingers brushed across her nipples, making them harden.

Skye leaned into his kisses, wanting the same thing. His hand slid her dress up her legs, caressing her soft skin. His fingers drew her desire for him into a passionate need. She needed him to touch her; her body ached for him again.

"Your body is as smooth as your dress. How does the soft silk feel, Skye? Does it make you feel desirable when it caresses your skin?" his dark husky voice whispered against her skin.

"Yes," she breathed as she arched her body to his touch.

He slid his hand up higher, sliding it over her wetness. She moaned louder, and he captured her moans in a kiss. The vision of her standing out among the other ladies in the ballroom was like viewing a butterfly leaving her cocoon. He realized he was a fool for not joining her earlier. He saw her wings began to sag the longer he stayed away. His nerves kept him from joining her. He knew it to be a weak excuse, but it was his excuse nonetheless.

He removed his hand from under her dress and turned the passionate kiss into a gentle one. One filled with promise. When she returned his kiss in full, he understood what he needed to do. She would be hurt, but it was the only way. Zane pulled back and gazed into her eyes.

"Promise me that no matter what happens tonight, you are mine as I am yours."

"I promise." She gave him her trust as he had given his to her.

He placed a quick kiss upon her lips. "Now you must return to your brother. Do not leave his side the rest of the evening. Promise me," he demanded.

"I promise. What is wrong, Zane?"

"Do not believe everything you hear or witness tonight."

"As in what?"

Zane didn't give her time for an answer. He gently nudged her out of the alcove. When she turned around to speak with him, he disappeared. She slowly twirled around to see he was nowhere in sight. Suddenly, she was thrust into the crowd, her body pushed and jostled around the packed ballroom. She stood at the top of her toes, scanning the ballroom for any sign of Zane. His words made no sense.

An arm came around her middle, and she panicked. She caught sight of her brother ushering her over to the side. He continued walking them out to the balcony. Fresh air brushed across her skin.

"Where did you go? I looked everywhere for you," Logan demanded.

"I went to the powder room, but it was full. I was on my way back to you when I got lost in the crowd." She hated lying to him, but until he met Zane, it was the only way.

"Skye, I can tell when you are lying."

"How?"

"Your face expresses every emotion you have."

What he spoke was true. She wore her feelings plainly for anyone who knew her to see. Through the years, she had perfected hiding her emotions while being a spy. She'd had to, for her very life and the lives of others depended on her skill. But she never could when in the presence of her brother or her clan. She could always be herself around them. She growled, arching her eyebrow to defy him. Logan's reaction to her was to lean against the balcony rail, crossing his feet in front of him and his arms across his chest.

"I have the entire evening, my dear, to wait you out. The crowd in there bores me to death, so we can remain here on this balcony until you are honest with me."

Skye crossed next to him, leaning her elbows across the railing, and stared beyond into the well-lit garden. She watched as couples strolled through the paths. She even spotted couples sneaking away for a quick kiss. They thought they hid from prying eyes, only to be visible from the balcony. She smiled as she felt a kinship with them, for she escaped with Zane only a few moments before. As she watched, a cloud crossed over the moon, making the garden darker and the figures harder to gaze upon.

She saw the hostess of the party emerge from the garden with a well-dressed gentleman on her arm. Skye stared as the widow became handsy with her companion. She pressed herself up tight and stopped every few paces, trying to kiss him. Skye would normally not regard a private couple, but the gentleman drew her eye. There was something familiar about him. The way he carried himself, the dark mane of his hair, but it was the sound of his voice she heard on the wind. It was the same voice who whispered his love to her this afternoon. The couple moved closer underneath the balcony. Skye's smile disappeared from her face, and she stood frozen in time. She didn't want to draw attention to their presence above the couple, but she needed to listen to what they discussed.

"Maxwell, darling, meet me upstairs in my boudoir. You remember the way."

"What will your guests say to that, my dear?"

She laughed. "They will gossip about how lucky I am to draw you into my web."

He threw back his head and laughed. However, it wasn't a laugh Skye recognized. It was a harsh, bitter laugh filled with darkness. She leaned over the baluster, trying to glimpse them, only to be pulled back by Logan. Skye forgot her brother stood next to her. She struggled with him, needing to see Zane. In doing so, she knocked over the plant, watching as it hovered in the air before falling to the ground, crashing near the couple's feet.

"See, my dear, we are already being envied." Lady Cassandra's laughter grated over Skye's nerves.

Not wanting the couple to catch them, she pulled Logan inside the nearest door. She found Ivy and Raina with their husbands nearby, so she joined their party. Ivy sent her a questioning look. Skye shook her head to silence her from asking questions. She sensed her brother's anger. He overheard Maxwell's name and knew he was the man below them.

Skye tried to distract the group by discussing the ball with Ivy and Raina. She couldn't draw Ivy into the discussion. When she tried to get Ivy's attention, her friend looked behind her with her mouth open in shock. When Skye tried to turn around to see what grabbed her attention, Ivy tried to distract her and put herself in Skye's line of sight. She was too late; she realized what Ivy noticed. It was the same view that had distracted her on the balcony. It was Zane with the hostess draped across his arm, his cravat mussed and an expression of lazy indulgence on his face. That wasn't the only thing out of place on him. His hair appeared in disarray from where the lady raked her fingers through it, from a passionate embrace.

As they walked toward them, her brother drew himself up and blocked her from their sight, but it didn't deter the couple. They stopped at their party, where Logan and Skye were introduced. The lady didn't loosen her hold from Zane the whole time. He leaned and whispered into Lady Cassandra's ear every now and then, and the lady would swat him on the arm and tell him to behave.

Skye felt heartbroken as she stared at them. She didn't understand his actions, or even how they affected her emotions. No more could she turn and walk away then she could not watch them. When Zane sensed her hurt gaze upon them, he cocked his head to the side and raised his eyebrow at her in his arrogant way. She tried remembering his words and the promise she made to him, but she couldn't think past the hurt and pain of him holding another woman.

"My pleasure to make your acquaintance, Lady MacKinnon," he slurred as he bowed before her.

It was the slurred words and aroma of alcohol coming from his person that made Skye aware he played a game. There was no way he was drunk, for not a half hour had passed since he held her in his arms. The flavor of his kiss held no hint of whiskey. He acted a ruse. Why? What game was he playing?

She curtsied before him. "The pleasure is all mine, Lord Maxwell."

He sauntered off with the hostess, leaving their party with questions about his behavior. When they turned to her, she held no answers for them. Skye begged their leave, running off into the crowd. Her brother yelled out after her to stop, but she needed to find out why Maxwell was behaving as he was. She kept the couple in her line of vision, hoping her party would follow her. Maxwell was in trouble, and he needed their help. Her promise to him to stay with her brother was forgotten. She followed them along a dark corridor, where they slipped into a room. The room held a sliver of light peeking underneath the door. When she pressed her ear to the panel, she could only make out muffled voices. As she turned the knob beneath her hand, she tried to open the door, but something pressed into her back, halting her action.

Chapter Twenty

"WELCOME TO THE PARTY, my dear," a voice whispered in her ear. Not any voice, but the voice from her nightmares. He was alive. Not only alive, but he held a pistol pressed to her back.

"Let us join the merry couple. Open the door slowly. We don't want to frighten them."

Skye turned the knob, pushing open the door. He nudged the pistol in her back again, urging her into the room. Skye took small steps, her body numb as she followed his directions. When she entered the room, she discovered Zane embracing Lady Cassandra in a passionate kiss.

Shears chuckled behind her at the scene, but she sensed his anger on what he viewed, for the pistol dug deeper into her back, and his hand clutched the back of her neck to keep her still. His grasp tightened as his fingers gripped her skin. Skye sensed the bruises forming from his hold. She tried taking deep breaths to fight her way through her panic.

"Honey, I am back," he snarled into the silent room.

Skye watched as the couple stilled at his words. The woman gasped and removed herself from Maxwell's arms, backing away from him. Maxwell's reaction confused Skye. He nonchalantly strolled across the room to lean against the fireplace. He wasn't surprised by Shears's appearance, but Skye did catch his shock at her presence and watched as he tried to control his fear for her.

"You! You are dead," the lady stuttered.

"As you can see, my dear, I am very much alive. It didn't take you long to find another to spread your thighs for."

The woman paled. She understood what his tone of voice meant. He was a man who didn't want to share his property. And she was his property, for she had sold her soul to him years ago. She knew this act of betrayal would cost her dearly.

"Welcome back from the dead, Shears," Zane said, drawing Shears's attention toward him.

"Was never dead to begin with."

"You will be soon."

Shears laughed. "I don't know if you are aware or not, but I seem to have the upper hand." He held up his gun, then pointed it at Skye's back.

Maxwell looked at his fingertips, pretending boredom. "Mmm, so you say."

Shears growled at Maxwell's indifference. "I see that your favors have turned once again."

"How so?" Maxwell inquired.

"Let's see, first your heart desired Lady Ivy. Then when her charms found the attention of another, you bedded this bitch here. Then, after I had a bit of fun with your lady, you decided to bed mine."

Skye saw Maxwell tense at Shears's words. She sent him a warning sign with her eyes not to let Shears bait him. Maxwell appeared to relax under Skye's signal.

"Let us discuss why you are really here, Shears. Release the lady. She is of no use to you or me."

"That is what you lead me to believe, but I know better. She spent the afternoon in your bed, and let us not forget the little meeting you two shared earlier this evening."

"You rogue! You laid your hands on me tonight, but you are bedding this Scottish heathen?"

"Shut up, woman. You are no longer of any use. I will take care of you later," Shears growled. "As I was saying, Maxwell, I think I will hold on to Lady MacKinnon a while longer."

"Well, let it be known that I warned you Shears."

"I will bed her and allow you to watch this time, Maxwell. But before I do, there is the matter of the missing jewels. I've heard MacKinnon's brother has returned them to the King. You two will get me those jewels, and in return, you can have the missing heir."

"The heir is dead," Skye interrupted.

Shears laughed. "No, my dear, the heir lives. She is hidden upstairs as we speak. After I have the jewels, I will let Maxwell have the child."

"Then you can release Skye now."

Shears's evil laugh filled the room. "No, you will choose, Maxwell. The girl or MacKinnon. You cannot have both. Either way, I will be the winner, for I will take either one. They both will serve their purpose, and that purpose is to serve me."

Maxwell advanced on Shears but stopped when he heard the pistol cock. He played this scene himself only a few months past. He had only wanted to cause fear. Shear's only wanted death. He stared as Skye's face paled and eyes grew large.

"Now, now, Romeo. Back away. I would hate to kill your latest love," Shears said as he dragged the pistol across Skye's cheek.

"Tell me what you want, Shears." Zane gritted the words between his teeth.

"I want you to visit your friends in the ballroom. Make nice with Logan MacKinnon and get me those jewels."

"I will need Skye to return with me."

"Nice try, but she will join the heir upstairs. After the two are secure, I will follow you as you get those jewels for me. When they are in my possession, I will take you to the two ladies, where you will choose which one you want to keep."

Shears turned to the hostess. "Now you are of use, my dear. Take us to the girl."

The hostess led them up the back staircase, where they climbed three flights of stairs. Skye counted the stairs and the number of steps they took to the locked room. The light was kept to a minimum in the hallways and stairways. She paid attention to the detail. She knew that for her to get them to safety, she would need to know the layout of their path. When they stopped before a locked door, Lady Cassandra took out a chain hidden in her pocket and unlocked the entryway. Shears shoved Skye inside and locked the door behind her before she had a chance to send Maxwell a signal.

When she looked around the small room, she spotted a figure huddled on the bed. A small light cast the bedroom in shadows. As she strode to the bed, she saw a young girl lying upon it, fast asleep. Skye hoped she was sleeping, for the young girl's breathing was shallow. She sat down on the bed, touching her warm forehead, and realized she had the start of a fever. The girl might be too weak to escape. If Skye could move her to a different room to hide her, then the girl stood a chance at being rescued. She nudged the girl on the shoulder to rouse her from her nap. When the girl opened her heavy lids, she appeared frightened. Skye realized she was too afraid to speak.

"Hello. I mean you no harm. I am a friend. My name is Skye. What is yours?"

"I am Elizabeth. My friends call me Lizzy."

"Well I consider you my friend, Lizzy. I will find a way to safety. Do you think you can walk?"

Elizabeth nodded her head weakly. Skye could tell the girl had spirit; a trait they would need during their escape.

"You rest. I will search for a way to escape this room."

"It is useless. I have been trying for weeks. There is no way out."

"Let me see what I can do."

Skye moved to the door and examined the lock. She pulled the decorative hair pin from her head and bent the pin into one long piece. Lowering herself to her knees, she picked the lock. She listened to the young girl fighting a cough behind her. She waited for the click and heard when the lock opened. Skye returned to Lizzy and urged her to drink a glass of water. When she glanced around the room for Lizzy's slippers, Skye realized the room was bare. The only items left were the bed and a blanket. She helped the girl to her feet and guided her to the door. Skye didn't want to open the door until she saw to their safety, as she didn't want to draw any unwanted attention their way. She opened the door a crack and peered into the dark hallway. There was nobody standing guard. Shears must have trusted that they couldn't leave the room. Only opening the door enough for them to slide through, Skye pulled the door shut behind them.

She aided Lizzy along the hallway, sticking close to the walls. Skye tried the doors as they went, but the rooms remained locked. After they made it to the stairway, she decided they must work their way downstairs.

"Can you continue, Lizzy?" she whispered.

At the young girl's nod, Skye led them down the stairs. After two flights, Lizzy's steps lagged. Skye realized she needed to find a room for the girl to hide in, then go for help. As they searched another hallway, luck came their way. When she tried another door, it opened into a linen closet.

She helped Lizzy to the back of the room and rested her in the corner on a stack of sheets. Skye pulled a sheet over the girl to hide her, promising her she would return. The girl drifted off to sleep, exhausted from their short excursion. Skye watched the vulnerable girl sleep, not wanting to abandon her. She held a sweet disposition; Skye noticed the similarities to Zane. Lizzy shared his dark black hair, and her eyes were the same smoky gray. She ran her hand along the girl's hair in affection, whispering her promises to return. She knew the girl slept, but it made her feel better to speak the words.

As she continued along the last flight of stairs, Skye heard the musicians playing a waltz. She hoped to dance one with Zane tonight. She dreamed romantic thoughts for tonight to play out, but instead it turned into her worst nightmare. Skye stood on the edge of the ballroom floor, her gaze scouring the room for any sign of Maxwell and Shears. She spotted her brother dancing with Raina. When she saw Charles standing along the outer wall, she made her way to his side.

"I don't have time to explain. Please sweep me into this dance toward my brother."

Charles didn't hesitate at the urgency of her tone. As they tried to dance toward the couple, Skye filled him in on the details of Shears's return and his demands. Mallory didn't appear shocked by her words.

"How long have you known?"

"Since this afternoon. Thorn received word, and we concocted a plan. We were hoping your brother would keep you occupied while we took care of Shears."

"Does my brother hold knowledge of your plan?"

"No, we thought the fewer people involved, the better our plan would succeed. We underestimated your determination to steer clear of Maxwell."

"No, I think the man underestimated my love for him. Fool. All of you are fools."

By then they waltzed next to the couple. After a twirl, they switched partners, and Logan danced Skye away from the Charles and Raina.

"Where have you been this time?"

"There is no time to explain. Shears is alive and holds Maxwell hostage. They are looking for you, he wants the jewels. Shears locked me in a room, and I escaped."

"I need to get you to a secure location."

"No, we have to rescue Maxwell."

"From what I can tell, Maxwell can rescue himself."

"No, that is not him. He is undercover and playing a part. We must help him."

"Give me one good reason to help that double agent."

"The heir is alive."

"Impossible."

"No, tis true. Shears locked me away with her. I helped her escape and have her hidden. I must return to her before they discover where I hid her."

"Take me to her, and I will get you both to safety."

"I need you to help me lead Shears into a trap."

Logan waltzed her over to the doors that led to the balcony, he needed to keep her hidden from Shears. If Shears discovered that she'd escaped, there would be no telling what the mad captain would do. He was stuck. His sister wouldn't budge. He must save Maxwell, or she would never forgive him. As he moved her to the dark edge of the balcony, Charles and Raina joined them.

Skye directed Charles and Raina where they could locate the young girl. They were to rescue her and take her to Hillston House. She felt relieved knowing the girl would be safe from Shears's revenge. Soon, Thorn and Ivy joined them, and they filled them in on Shears's plan. Thorn, not wanting Ivy anywhere near Shears's, had her father escort her home to await them. Logan and Thorn devised a plan to draw Shears away from the ball. Logan wanted Skye to return with Ivy, but Skye wouldn't leave. As they discussed their plan, Skye saw Shears and Maxwell enter the ballroom. She pressed herself deeper in the shadows. Hiding in the dark, she kept herself as still as she could. She noticed when Shears spotted her brother on the balcony. He motioned for Maxwell to continue outside.

Skye also saw Lady Cassandra following at a discreet distance. She glanced nervously around her, hoping nobody noticed Shears pressing a gun to Maxwell's back as they strolled across the dance floor. She was mistaken, for the gasps and screams as the crowd parted for the men weren't going unnoticed. Lady Cassandra tried to calm her guests, but they would have no part of the drama unfolding before their eyes. In anger, Shears fired his gun at the ceiling. The guests backed away frightened, but that didn't stop him. He continued with his prey. Skye held her breath as Shears pointed a gun at the man she loved, but Zane didn't allow the threat to faze him. He stood relaxed under Shears's control.

Maxwell relaxed as Shears dug the butt of the gun into his back. He wouldn't show this man fear. The man thrived on and grew stronger with fear. Maxwell was concerned though; he feared for Skye's life. No way in hell would he choose. He would have them both, for this time he would kill the man and take pleasure from it. Shears was a fool if he thought he would leave this ball alive. The place was swarming with undercover agents. They were ready for him this time. While it seemed Shears survived his injuries, Maxwell perceived his recovery to be false. He walked with a limp and favored his right side. The only mistake Maxwell made tonight was not confiding in Skye and her brother. Maybe if he had, then she wouldn't have followed him. He foolishly thought she would buy into his scheme. He was all kinds of a fool.

"Just the man I was searching for, Logan MacKinnon," Shears snarled.

"What do you want, Shears?" MacKinnon replied.

"I want my jewels you stole from me. In return, I will give you back your sister."

MacKinnon came at Shears. "You bastard, if you touch her, I will kill you."

"Did you not hear? I already touched her," Shears boasted.

MacKinnon reached Shears and wrapped his hands around his throat. He started to choke him, but Shears moved the pistol to MacKinnon's gut. He pressed the pistol deeper until MacKinnon let him go. Logan backed away, glaring at the captain. Shears pulled another pistol out of his waistband and motioned for the men to stand in front of him.

"Now then, I want the jewels in my possession within the hour, or your sweet sister will be mine. Now you gents are probably wondering which sister I am referring to. Well, I shall make it easy for you. Whoever brings me the rubies gets to keep their sister. The other will be mine to enjoy."

"Never," both men spoke at once.

Skye stepped from the dark shadows. She walked behind Shears quietly as he spoke his vulgar comments to the men of his plans for her and

Lizzy, as she stood at his back. As she listened to his words, they gave her the power to confront him. She was going to steal his power away. He would never hurt another soul again.

Maxwell watched her come out of the shadows. He was able to keep the shock hidden from his face. He didn't want to give Shears any reason to turn around. Skye's life was held in the balance. He knew if Shears realized she had escaped, he would kill her to prove the extent of his power.

She looked amazing, like a warrior goddess. His warrior goddess. She stood tall and powerful behind the evil man, her long red hair blowing in the wind. She slid her skirts above her knees and reached her hand to her thigh. She pulled out a dirk. Only his Scottish beauty would come to a ball ready for battle.

Before he realized what she planned, she stuck the dirk into Shears's right side and twisted the small knife in and up. However, Skye wasn't finished with him yet. She pulled the knife out and held the weapon to his throat. She did it all so quick, Maxwell could tell Shears knew none of it was coming.

"Your destruction has finally come to an end. You will harm no one ever again," she whispered behind him as she slid the knife across his throat, slicing open his skin.

But her attack wouldn't dissuade the captain. He turned swiftly, catching Skye off balance. With her heavy skirts she stumbled backward and fell. When she braced for her fall, her dirk slipped from her fingers, scattering across the floor. He advanced at her in a rage. She tried to rise, but her dress held her legs in a tangle, so she tried to scoot across the floor. It was his cabin all over again. She braced herself for his fists to connect to her face like before, but instead she stared down the barrel of his gun. She raised her chin in defiance, daring him to pull the trigger.

"You bitch. You evade me at every turn. But not this time." He aimed the pistol at her.

The shot rang in the air. Ringing into emptiness. The bullet hit the air above her into the silent night as the three gentlemen rushed at him. In a rage, each man punched Shears from all angles, their frustrations from the terror he put them through over the last year fueled their attack. He was pummeled left and right. As he backed away from their punches, he lost his footing and fell over the balcony. The men watched as their nemesis crashed into the dirt below them. He stayed dead this time. There was no mistake about it. Shears lay twisted, and blood flowed from his body like a river. Thorn ran below to confirm his death. He sent a signal above, covering Shears's body with his coat jacket. Maxwell didn't wait for the confirmation, for he had already gathered Skye in his arms. He cradled her close as he spoke of his love for her, rocking her back and forth as the drama faded away. Logan regarded Maxwell comforting his sister. Thorn guided the agents to remove Shears's body and arrest Lady Cassandra for harboring the fugitive.

As they made their return to Hillston House, Zane continued holding Skye. She had not spoken since she stabbed Shears. Maxwell thought her reaction was shock. Her hands were ice cold as he held them. He looked up and caught the threat in her brother's eyes, but he didn't back away from her. He understood he had much to redeem himself for, and he would in time. The only thing that mattered now was Skye's peace of mind.

As they alighted from the carriage, Zane had no option but to pass Skye into her brother's arms. When his feet hit the ground, he reached for her, but her brother already entered the house and carried Skye to her bedroom. He moved to follow, only to have Thorn hold him back. Once they entered the townhome, they joined the rest of the family in the library.

Thorn informed them of Shears's death, and everybody sighed with relief. Shears had put everybody in this room through some sort of torture this past year, and now his reign of evil was finally over. They could finally live in peace.

Ivy joined Maxwell near the fireplace. Her friend gazed into the firelight, lost in his thoughts. She placed a comforting hand on his arm, where he squeezed his gratitude in return.

"Your sister is well. The doctor visited her and gave her a sedative to help her sleep. She has a slight chill but will recover. She seems to be unharmed by Shears and is not frightened in the least. The doctor thinks it would be best for her to stay here overnight."

Maxwell agreed. While he knew he had a huge undertaking with a new sister, his thoughts would not stray from the woman he loved. He was deeply concerned for her. Her silence since Shears's death terrified him. He only wanted to hold her in his arms. Hold her until her nightmares disappeared. For after tonight, there would be no more.

"I will check on Skye for you."

"Thank you," he choked out.

The ladies retired from the room as Logan entered. Maxwell stood up straight and waited for the man's attack. He couldn't blame him. He risked Skye's life tonight by not warning her of Shears's return from the grave. While he thought he protected her, he only harmed her instead. When her brother stood face-to-face with him, neither of them wavered.

"I can't decide whether to punch you or shake your hand."

"You are welcome to do both."

"Do you love her?"

"With all of my soul."

Logan nodded his understanding. He left Skye in her bedroom and her only desire was to see this man. While he felt the loss of not being the man his sister depended on, he was grateful she found the love she deserved. He recalled his conversation with Skye as he measured the gentleman before him.

"How long have you known I loved him?" Skye asked Logan.

"Gregor dropped a few hints, Aggie cackled her glee, and Isobel filled in the rest."

"Why did you not say anything?"

"I was waiting for you to confide in me like you always have before."

"I couldn't tell you when I had not told him first."

Logan wrapped her in his arms and gave her his blessing.

"May I see her?" Zane asked for permission.

"I think the morning will be sufficient. Then only with me present."

Zane nodded. He brother acted fairly, and he didn't want to cause discord with the man who would be his brother-in-law before long. Zane thought there was no harm in letting him believe he would wait for tomorrow morning to see Skye. When Logan retired for the night, he glanced around the library to notice his two friends waiting to speak with him. He had a lot he needed to tell them. As he slid in a chair, he took the cigar and the glass of whiskey Thorn offered him.

He closed his eyes, taking a long drag on the cigar. He puffed out a cloud of smoke, inhaling as he breathed in the rich aroma. Then taking a long drink from the whiskey, he relaxed as he had not in ages. For the first time in a long time, he felt content. As soon as he held Skye tonight, he would be whole. But for now, content felt good.

Opening his eyes to the silence, he addressed his two lifelong friends.

"I once again owe you both my deepest apologies for my actions this past year. Thank you for your help bringing Shears to justice and for helping me with Skye. I will be forever in your debt. I hope we can mend our friendships."

"We forgave you a long time ago. Next time trust in us a little more," Mallory told him.

He nodded and looked over at Thorn, knowing he failed him more. Thorn stared back at him, making him wait. Maxwell deserved to wait for as long as he could. He betrayed Thorn in the worst possible way. He made advances toward Ivy that were uncalled for.

"I suppose if Mallory forgives you then I will too. But if you so much as ever kiss my wife again …" He left the threat hanging in the air. Maxwell understood him completely without him finishing his thought. For he had no desire to kiss Ivy. The only woman he wanted to kiss was Skye.

"I suppose you want me to tell you how you can sneak into her room," Thorn added as he rolled his eyes.

"Well, that is what friends are for, right? To help one when they are in need?" Maxwell laughed.

Chapter Twenty-One

When Zane snuck into Skye's room, he found her sleeping on the divan. She held the ruby he gifted her in her hand, and his letters were scattered around her. He closed the door and leaned against it, taking in the sight of her. She was safe. When he strolled to her, he gathered the letters and stacked them on the floor. He kneeled before her, brushing the hair from her face. Her eyelids fluttered open.

"Hello," he whispered.

"Hello," she whispered back.

"Why are you reading my letters?"

"I missed you."

This warmed his heart. He pressed a gentle kiss to her lips.

"I love you, Skye."

"I love you, Zane."

He reached into his pocket to pull out his mother's ring and slid it onto her finger. The emerald and diamonds winked at them in the firelight.

"Will you do me the honor of becoming my wife?"

Skye began to cry. Tears trailed along her cheeks. She wanted to answer him, but no sound came forth. He was such a romantic. The proof lay scattered around her. His letters, his gifts, and his kneeling on the floor to propose. How she desired to tell him yes, but her emotions were on a ride of a lifetime. Every emotion she held poured out of her in tears.

Even though she didn't answer yes, Zane felt her love. He gathered her close as she cried. She deserved to shed these tears. He gently kissed them from her cheeks. His lips found hers, and he kissed the tears that wetted her lips. As he kissed her, he drank in her emotions kissing her more deeply. The kiss was soft and gentle and full of love. It was a kiss of longing, of loving, of belonging. They belonged together, and their kiss fused them as one.

He stood, picking her up into his arms and carried her to the bed. He slid under the covers with her and held her as she cried, gently kissing her in between her tears. As her tears subsided, she drifted asleep in his arms. He embraced her through the night, near his heart. While she didn't respond, he knew her answer to be yes. When she was ready to answer him, he would be there for her. Waiting.

When dawn rose, he slid himself out of the bed, being careful not to wake her. He gazed at her with her hair mussed and her gown wrinkled, smiling at the image of her. Before her brother caught him in her room, he needed to slip out. He didn't want to marry her out of necessity. He wanted her to come to him with an open heart. Sighing, he made himself leave her side. With one last glance across the room at her, he left her room smiling. He sneaked down the servant's staircase and out the door as he made his way home.

~~~~~

When Skye awoke the room stood empty. She wondered if she dreamed that Zane came to her room. As she read his letters by the fire, she fell asleep. She ached from the loss of his embrace and knew he held her in his arms through the night. Skye stretched her arms out in front of her, her body aching from the previous evening. As she lowered her arms, she had to stretch them out again, for she caught sight of the ring that adorned her finger. As she brought her hand in closer, she saw the emerald and diamond jewels resting on her hand.

Then it returned to her in a rush of memories. Zane kneeling before her asking her to marry him. Her crying like a baby at his question. She never answered him. All she did was cry in his arms. He held her through the night as she cried, gently kissing her, never once asking for an answer. She remembered falling asleep in his arms, feeling loved and secure. As she watched the sun rise, she felt the heat of him from her bed and knew he had not been gone long.

She didn't answer him, and now he had left. Skye scrambled from the bed, ringing the bell. She needed to change and find him. She needed to give him her answer. Not waiting for a servant, she ran toward her wardrobe and dug through her clothes until she found the outfit she wanted. She dressed swiftly and pulled her hair back, securing it with a hair clip. She sat on the bench and pulled on her boots. Skye went over to the desk to write a quick note. She slipped from her room, running down the back staircase and out to the mews. She talked the groomsman into lending her a horse. Skye saddled the mare herself and set off for Zane's house. She remembered Ivy telling her that Zane didn't have many servants. She figured she could sneak inside his home.

Once she arrived at his townhome, she noticed the cook directing a delivery from the butcher. While the cook was distracted, Skye sneaked inside Zane's home. As she stood outside his bedroom, she overheard him inside. She silently walked into his room and listened to him in the bathroom, taking a bath. While she wouldn't mind joining him, she wanted to surprise him. She laid the note on his bed and curled up in a chair hidden in the corner. As she sat in the chair, it let out a squeak as she settled to wait.

"Is that you, Smith?"

Skye stilled, she hoped she hadn't given herself away. So, she stayed silent, hoping he would forget the noise. She heard him splashing around in the water before getting out of the bath. His footsteps grew closer to the room. She gazed as he came into the bedchamber wrapped in a robe, rubbing his hair dry with a towel. She smiled as she watched him, feeling like a wife admiring her husband. As he bent to grab the letter, she saw the confusion on his face. She waited for his reaction as he read the simple one-word letter, smiling to herself.

He stopped rubbing his hair and threw the towel across the floor when he saw the note lying on his bed. Maxwell could have sworn he heard somebody in his room, but with a quick glance around while he rubbed his hair dry, he didn't see anybody. When he spotted the letter on his bed, he knew he hadn't been mistaken. When he reached for the letter, he glanced around again. It was then he noticed her sitting in the chair in the corner. He allowed his gaze to continue to roam around the room, pretending he hadn't spotted her. Did she really think he wouldn't realize she was in his bedchamber? He sensed her whenever she was near. He turned his back on her to read the letter, even though the presence in his bedchamber was answer enough.

He opened the letter and read the simplicity of it.

Yes.

Zane spun as he advanced on her, trapping her as he rested his hands on the arms of the chair. He leaned over, gazing into her love-filled eyes. Her eyes captured his, reading his soul. This time he didn't shut her out but opened himself to her for eternity.

"Did you think you could hide from me?"

"I wanted to see your reaction."

"Yes?"

"Yes."

Zane picked her up and swung her around, loving the sound of her laughter. He settled back on the chair, holding her in his lap. He rested his forehead against hers.

"How did you get here?"

"I stole a horse from Thornhill."

"Your brother is going to kill me."

"Nonsense."

He threw back his head and laughed. "I need to get you back to him before he sends out a search party for you."

"I think we have a little bit of time," she murmured as she slid her hand inside his robe. Tenderly stroking his chest, she kissed his neck. When she lowered her hand to his lap, her touch made him grow hard. She heard him growl deeply. Her hand began to stroke him faster.

"Skye," he moaned.

She gazed at him with a look of innocence. He lowered his head and devoured her lips, kissing her hungrily. "Do you realize how wild you make me dressed like this?" he asked as his hands ripped her shirt open. Her buttons flew across the room. "The first time I ever saw you, you made me hard."

He worked her trousers down over her long legs and swung her on his lap. She guided him inside her, slowly embracing his cock. He moaned. She was amazing. She slowly rode him, sliding up and down. He grabbed her hips and helped guide her, their passion growing out of control. His need for her was overwhelming. She cried out as he drove his hips into hers. He had no control left. He needed to possess her. He pulled her head to his for a kiss as he drove them over the edge. She collapsed against his chest, placing soft kisses on him. He held her to him tight while he tried to slow the beating of his heart. This was not how he wanted to celebrate their engagement. He'd wanted to take it slow. He laughed. He should have known better with Skye. Everything with her was a whirlwind. There would be time later for slow. They had a lifetime of slow.

"What is so funny?" she asked.

"We are, my dear."

"Mmm, I think you may be correct on that."

She rose from him and continued to his closet. When she wandered inside, she found a shirt to her liking. As she returned to him, she was sliding the buttons through their holes.

"Are you raiding my closet?"

She arched her eyebrow at him. "Did you not just ruin my shirt?"

"I suppose I did, but do you have to take my best one?"

She winked at him. "Of course. It shall be returned to you in time."

Together they dressed and headed to Hillston House. When they arrived, it was to find her brother pacing the parlor floor, threatening to murder him. Skye laughed at him and urged the two men to talk. She left them to change her clothes. On her way back to the parlor, she stopped by Lizzy's bedroom to look in on her. When she walked in, she found Zane talking to her. While he explained to Lizzy the nature of their relationship, Skye stood by his side with her hand on his shoulder.

"Where are you sending me to live?"

"You will live with me," Zane replied.

"With us," Skye emphasized.

"With us," Zane seconded, squeezing Skye's hand.

"Like a family?"

"Exactly like a family," Zane confirmed.

They stayed and talked with the young girl awhile longer, assuring Lizzy of her place in their lives. When they noticed her tire, they left her to rest. As they walked downstairs, they decided to take a stroll around the garden. Zane didn't want to leave either one of them. The sooner he could get them to his home, the happier he would be.

"Do you want one of those big fancy weddings, Skye?"

"Who, me?"

"Yes, you. Because if you do, I can wait."

"And if I do not?"

"Then I will pull out the special license I am carrying and ask you to marry me tomorrow."

"Well?"

"Well what, my dear?"

"Ask me to marry you tomorrow.

"Skye, love of my life, will you marry me tomorrow?"

"Yes."

Zane couldn't wipe the smile from his face even if he tried. She made him the happiest man on earth. His existence was complete in this moment.

"Zane?"

"Yes, my dear."

"I love you."

"And I love you."

And so they became man and wife the next afternoon. Skye's brother offered his consent and gave the bride away in front of their family and friends. He had family now. Skye and Lizzy. Now his family would grow. He couldn't wait to have children with Skye. Thorn and Ivy agreed to keep Lizzy while he whisked Skye away on a small honeymoon. They deserved to have a few days to themselves. He knew he was asking a lot of Skye to take on a ready-made family. They were taking in a girl who neither of them knew. But together they would prosper. They were stronger as a couple. The girl was a quiet, mild-mannered young lady. Skye had a lot of love to give her. They had already bonded. The two were always together with their heads close whispering. Skye would be a wonderful mother and wife.

After the wedding, he took Skye away to his townhome, where he surprised her with the trip. She was excited to travel for their honeymoon and showed him her appreciation under the covers. When he made love to her on their wedding night, the image for his next picture he painted of her entered his mind. It would hang in their bedchamber.

Epilogue

SKYE WANDERED TO THE creek. She'd just come from spending time with Isobel and the babe. Skye enjoyed holding a new baby in her arms. She wished to hold her own. Lizzy played with Lachlan in the courtyard. Lizzy blossomed during the time they spent in Scotland. She loved to run and play in the wild, just as Skye used to do when she was her age. Maybe they could continue their stay here awhile longer. The girl appeared shyer in London, but Skye also felt out of place in the crowded city. While she had Ivy and Raina, it wasn't the same as being at home with her clan. After they left, they would move on to visit Maxwell's estate. He promised her they would love it there too. As long as she lived under the open country sky and had her mare to ride, then Skye would be content anywhere. In truth, she would only be happy wherever Maxwell lived.

She stopped by the big oak tree and watched as Zane painted. His paintings developed a new edge in the open wilderness—more defined. Skye convinced him to hold a showing when they returned to London; his work deserved recognition. His landscapes made one imagine they were wandering the countryside with him. He agreed only if she would share some of her drawings with him. He explained how he admired her sketches while he was held captive in her office. While she didn't have the same level of talent as her husband, she did enjoy the time they spent together doing what they both loved. Her favorite portrait was still the one he painted of her in the green dress. It made her smile secretly to herself every time she gazed upon it.

Maxwell turned, sensing her nearby. She watched him from afar. She still thought she could sneak up on him and catch him unaware. But he sensed her every time she was near. Even when she wasn't, he craved her and searched her out. He never desired them to be apart, and he knew she held the same need. When he arched his eyebrow at her, she smiled and sauntered over to him. He waited for her opinion of the painting. He started it this morning, hoping he was correct.

Skye examined the drawing. She wondered how he had known. She could keep no secrets from him.

"How did you know?"

"I know everything about you, Skye. You are my other half. There is nothing that can be hidden between us."

"Are you happy?"

"What do you think?" he nodded to the picture.

Her tears slid along her face as she stared at his painting. It was beautiful and touched her soul. They were tears of joy. So much had happened to them these past few months. So much had kept them apart, mostly due to their own faults. But they worked through the doubts and mistrust to become one as a couple.

Standing on the easel was a picture of her rocking a baby as the sun set behind her. He painted her as he saw her, as a mother cherishing her child with all the love in her soul. Shears had set out to destroy her. To destroy them. But because of Shears, their love only grew. What started out as a crisis developed into a love stronger than anybody could tear apart.

"I think you are thrilled."

"I am, my dear." He gently kissed her on the lips.

He wanted to pamper and cherish her these next few months. She deserved a little of that. Maxwell wrapped her in his arms and carried her over to the tree. He lowered himself to the ground and sat with her on his lap. There they relaxed and gazed at the sun setting against her Scottish mountains. As they watched the mountains turn different shades, they talked of the child she carried. Their child who would be loved and cherished by both.

She fell asleep as they talked, and Maxwell continued to hold her. Throughout the danger and deception, he discovered her love, which had made him whole. He had set out in his life with no intention of ever being loved. She rescued him from himself and taught him how to love another. Leaning his head back, he rested with his Scottish bride; he would take her inside soon. But for now, he wanted to enjoy their time alone, even if she was quietly snoring. His life couldn't get any better than holding his beloved in his arms.

~~~~~

Check out the first book:

Whom Shall I Kiss... An Earl, A Marquess, or A Duke?

in my new series:

Tricking the Scoundrels

~~~

Visit my website www.lauraabarnes.com to join my mailing list.

~~~

"Thank you for reading Rescued By the Scot. Gaining exposure as an independent author relies mostly on word-of-mouth, so if you have the time and inclination, please consider leaving a short review wherever you can."

Desire other books to read by Laura A. Barnes

Enjoy these other historical romances:

Fate of the Worthingtons Series
The Tempting Minx

The Seductive Temptress

The Fiery Vixen

The Siren's Gentleman

~~~~~

Matchmaking Madness Series:
How the Lady Charmed the Marquess

How the Earl Fell for His Countess

How the Rake Tempted the Lady

How the Scot Stole the Bride

How the Lady Seduced the Viscount

How the Lord Married His Lady

~~~~~

Tricking the Scoundrels Series:
Whom Shall I Kiss... An Earl, A Marquess, or A Duke?

Whom Shall I Marry... An Earl or A Duke?

I Shall Love the Earl

The Scoundrel's Wager

The Forgiven Scoundrel

~~~~~

Author Laura A. Barnes

International selling author Laura A. Barnes fell in love with writing in the second grade. After her first creative writing assignment, she knew what she wanted to become. Many years went by with Laura filling her head full of story ideas and some funny fish songs she wrote while fishing with her family. Thirty-seven years later, she made her dreams a reality. With her debut novel *Rescued By the Captain*, she has set out on the path she always dreamed about.

When not writing, Laura can be found devouring her favorite romance books. Laura is married to her own Prince Charming (who for some reason or another thinks the heroes in her books are about him) and they have three wonderful children and two sweet grandbabies. Besides her love of reading and writing, Laura loves to travel. With her passport stamped in England, Scotland, and Ireland; she hopes to add more countries to her list soon.

While Laura isn't very good on the social media front, she loves to hear from her readers. You can find her on the following platforms:

You can visit her at *www.lauraabarnes.com* to join her mailing list.

Website: **http://www.lauraabarnes.com**

Amazon: **https://amazon.com/author/lauraabarnes**

Goodreads: **https://www.goodreads.com/author/show/16332844.Laura_A_Barnes**

Facebook: **https://www.facebook.com/AuthorLauraA.Barnes/**

Instagram: **https://www.instagram.com/labarnesauthor/**

Twitter: **https://twitter.com/labarnesauthor**

TikTok: **https://www.tiktok.com/@labarnesauthor**

BookBub: **https://www.bookbub.com/profile/laura-a-barnes**

Made in United States
North Haven, CT
18 February 2023

32795625R00159